"I have a plan to fl___
you that card and ___
the one who killed ___ _____ ____ __
your house."

"They must be," Trent said. "I have no idea why else anyone would have been shot and killed in my home."

Heather shrugged. "Who knows? It might have nothing to do with you."

"I hope that's true," he said. "But I think we both doubt that."

"The card, the murder, the fire..." She shook her head. "I don't believe in that many coincidences."

"So what's your plan to find out the truth?" he asked, and all that tension was back in his body again.

"You're going to have to start dating again."

"You read that card. You know that'll put that person in danger," he said.

She smiled. "That's what I'm counting on, to flush out whoever sent that card when they make an attempt on your date's life."

He narrowed his eyes as suspicion gripped him. "Who is my date going to be?"

"Me."

Dear Reader,

Happy holidays! I am so happy to bring you *Hotshot Hero for the Holidays*! Trent Miles has been patiently waiting for years for me to tell his story, and it's been worth the wait. Throughout the Hotshot Heroes series, he's been such a fun character in all his interactions with his Huron Hotshot team members. But Trent's holidays aren't very much fun for him. He's under attack, and the person determined to protect him might also wind up destroying him. Detective Heather Bolton is my favorite kind of heroine—so strong and smart and independent that she doesn't need anyone. But she knows what she wants—a *hotshot hero for the holidays*!

I hope you've all been enjoying this Hotshot Heroes series as much as I've been enjoying writing it. The camaraderie between the hotshot team members has been such fun to write. They all feel like family to each other and to me. I especially enjoyed writing this story with the holidays in it, and I actually wrote it over the holidays, too. So with snow falling and lights twinkling and a fire crackling, I was able to really get the feel of the season!

Happy holidays to all of you and happy reading, too!

Lisa Childs

HOTSHOT HERO
FOR THE HOLIDAYS

Lisa Childs

HARLEQUIN
ROMANTIC
SUSPENSE

HARLEQUIN®
ROMANTIC SUSPENSE™

Recycling programs
for this product may
not exist in your area.

ISBN-13: 978-1-335-59384-9

Hotshot Hero for the Holidays

Copyright © 2023 by Lisa Childs

For questions and comments about the quality of this book, please contact us at CustomerService@Harlequin.com.

Harlequin Enterprises ULC
22 Adelaide St. West, 41st Floor
Toronto, Ontario M5H 4E3, Canada
www.Harlequin.com

Printed in U.S.A.

New York Times and *USA TODAY* bestselling, award-winning author **Lisa Childs** has written more than eighty-five novels. Published in twenty countries, she's also appeared on the *Publishers Weekly*, Barnes & Noble and Nielsen Top 100 bestseller lists. Lisa writes contemporary romance, romantic suspense, paranormal and women's fiction. She's a wife, mom, bonus mom, avid reader and less avid runner. Readers can reach her through Facebook or her website, lisachilds.com.

Books by Lisa Childs

Harlequin Romantic Suspense

Hotshot Heroes

Hotshot Hero Under Fire
Hotshot Hero on the Edge
Hotshot Heroes Under Threat
Hotshot Hero in Disguise
Hotshot Hero for the Holidays

The Coltons of New York

Protecting Colton's Secret Daughters

Bachelor Bodyguards

Bodyguard's Baby Surprise
Beauty and the Bodyguard
Nanny Bodyguard
Single Mom's Bodyguard

Visit the Author Profile page at
Harlequin.com for more titles.

For my hero for the holidays and every day,
Andrew Ahearne. Love you so much!

Chapter 1

The big box in the corner of the firehouse was filling up, wrapped and unwrapped toys overflowing from it, and the box was nearly as tall as Trent Miles's six-foot-four-inch height and twice as wide around as he was. Trent tossed a toy fire truck onto the top of the pile and grinned. Black Friday wasn't even over yet, and they'd already filled one box. They would definitely beat the local police precinct in their usual competition to see who could collect more for Toys for Tots. Not that it was all about the competition.

Just mostly.

"You're back," the captain said as he stepped out of his office off the main area of the firehouse.

Trent nodded.

"Hell of a thing to have to fight a wildfire over Thanksgiving," the captain remarked. "Sure you're not ready to give up being a hotshot?" Captain Rodriguez was in charge of this firehouse here in Detroit; Trent's US Forest Service hotshot team was comprised of firefighters from all over and operated out of a small town in northern Michigan with a superintendent in charge.

Trent chuckled, as the captain probably expected, and shook his head. But the truth was that he didn't love being a hotshot firefighter as much as he once had. He still loved flying off to wherever he was needed to fight wildfires, but he hated what had been happening with his team over the past year. He hated how his team wasn't the team he'd known and loved like family.

He'd always thought he was so close to those guys, closer than even with his crew here at the firehouse in Detroit where he worked full-time. The hotshot gig, with the US Forest Service Department, was on an as-needed basis. But with the number of wildfires over the past five years that Trent had been a member, he'd worked with the Huron Hotshots almost as much as he had out of his local firehouse in Detroit.

"But do you have the fan club in Northern Lakes that you have here?" the captain asked, his dark eyes sparkling with amusement. Manny Rodriguez had served in the US Marine Corps with Trent's dad, who had died during a deployment when Trent was young. Manny had known Trent his whole life and would have taken him in after his mom died, too, if someone else hadn't stepped up. Someone who hadn't had to welcome a traumatized, almost-teenage boy into their home but had chosen to anyway.

"What fan club?" Trent asked, wondering what the joke was. Manny didn't usually tease him like Trent's fellow hotshots did.

The captain opened his office door and stepped back

inside for a moment. When he came out, he had a small stack of envelopes in his hand. "Christmas cards from your fan club."

"Christmas cards?"

Manny shrugged. "Guess my wife isn't the only one who still sends them out in November."

"I thought she was the only one who still sends them out at all." Trent counted out five of them, not quite enough for the fan club his boss claimed he had.

"Open them up," Manny said. "Maybe they're all from my wife."

Trent chuckled. "Maybe so…" He held up one of the envelopes. "'To the hot firefighter'? How do you know this is for me?"

"This motley crew isn't your hotshot team," Manny said. "Nobody's knocking on our doors to put out a calendar." He patted his belly that protruded over his belt.

Because of how dangerous fighting wildfires was, hotshots were required to be in peak physical condition. Their lives literally depended on it. But Trent respected every fire he fought. He knew all too well how an innocuous one in an abandoned warehouse could suddenly consume a city block and claim multiple lives. Or how what looked to be a run-down, empty apartment building could still have residents. He knew that too damn well. And because of the nightmares he had over it, he would never forget.

"My hotshot team has never done a calendar," Trent said. He'd just recently found out that they'd been asked, but other hotshots had pressured the superintendent to turn down the offer. Now he knew why. One of his team members wasn't really who he'd claimed he was for the past five years.

And that was just one of the secrets that had recently been revealed. That was why his hotshot team didn't feel like the family he'd once thought they were—because of all the damn secrets and lies. Hell, even his *family* didn't feel like his family anymore, not after his sister put his team at risk just to further her own damn career.

"You okay?" Manny asked.

Trent nodded. "Yeah, just tired."

"You've been out West for two weeks. You don't need to be here after just getting back," Manny said. "Forget about the cards for now. Go home. Get some sleep. You know things will also be getting crazy around here given the time of year. Holidays mean home fires."

Trent groaned. More candles burning, dried-out Christmas trees and hot lights, if they were still using the old, non-LED ones, never made a good combination. But he didn't want to go home either. Knowing how much he was gone during the wildfire season, he'd opened his place up to other people living with him. Or just using it while he was gone.

He doubted he would go home to the empty house he wanted it to be right now so he could actually unwind. "No, I'm still pretty keyed up," Trent said. More at the people who'd used him and kept secrets from him than from the wildfire. "I better open up these cards and make sure they're not really for you, Manny." Only a couple had "to the hot firefighter" on them; the rest were addressed directly to Trent Miles, care of the firehouse.

Manny chuckled. "I can only hope this old man would get fan mail like you do."

The two cards to the hot fireman contained flattering and flirty personal messages with cell numbers scribbled under the names of the senders. A couple of other cards expressed gratitude for him saving them in the past. That was why he did what he did. For the people he could save.

If only he could save them all…

But he couldn't. Despite his best efforts, they lost people in fires. They weren't able to get them out in time. Weren't able to save them.

The last card he opened was also addressed to him by name. But it wasn't thanking him. Not at all. Dread twisted his stomach when he read the message written inside. Maybe it was from a family member of someone who hadn't survived.

Or maybe it was about that other thing, the thing he'd just learned was going on with his hotshot crew. The sabotage. The attempts on their lives and the notes his boss and some of his teammates had been receiving. The threats.

This note, scrawled inside a card with a gold Christmas tree on the outside, was definitely as threatening as some of those had been. *You're going to find out what it feels like to lose someone close to you. Soon.*

"What the hell…" he muttered, the dread in his gut growing even heavier.

"What is it?" Manny asked with concern.

Trent shook his head. "Nothing." He didn't want to worry his boss. Not like Trent had been worrying even before receiving this card. He had already lost more than one *someone* close to him. A few of them before he had even become a firefighter. And more recently, he'd lost a hotshot buddy, and a few other teammates, really close ones, had nearly died as well. He didn't want anyone else getting hurt or worse, and especially not because of him.

"Trent, I know you've had a lot going on with the

Huron Hotshots," Manny said. "But I hope you know that I'm always here for you."

Trent bear-hugged his boss and chuckled. "I swear, none of these cards are from your wife."

Manny laughed and slapped his back. "I don't know if that is a relief or a disappointment. I might like a break from her nagging. Speaking of which, I better get home before another call—"

An alarm pealed, echoing off the concrete and metal of the firehouse walls and floor.

Manny cursed.

"You can leave, man. I'm sure the crew's got this," Trent assured the captain.

The firehouse erupted with movement: firefighters coming down from the floor above while others rushed in through the open doors, getting their gear, starting the engines.

"What's the address?" Manny asked the lieutenant in charge of the crew. "What kind of fire?"

"Sounds like arson. Fire started after a report of shots fired at the same address," Lieutenant Ken Stokes replied.

Manny gripped Ken's broad shoulder and advised him, "Be careful. Make sure police have secured the scene and that there is no active shooter before you guys get anywhere close to it."

"Where is it?" Trent asked since Ken hadn't answered that part of the boss's question yet.

Ken glanced down at his tablet that held the information from Dispatch and read off the street number and name.

Panic gripped Trent, pressing so hard on his lungs

that he had to cough to clear his throat. "I'm going with you," he told the lieutenant.

"What? Why?" Manny asked. "You just got back from a hotshot run."

"That's my address," Trent replied.

The lieutenant sucked in a breath. "There's already a possible fatality, Trent."

Just moments ago, Trent had read that ominous note that warned he would find out how it felt to lose someone close to him. Soon. Had that warning already come to pass? Had he just lost someone close to him?

Who?

Shots fired. Something had definitely happened here tonight before the fire. But would Detective Heather Bolton be able to figure it out?

She leaned against the side of her vehicle, studying the scene playing out across the street in the faint glow of the streetlamps. The firefighters rushed around the house, spraying water onto the flames. If the fire hadn't already destroyed whatever evidence might have been left at the scene, the water was probably washing away anything that might have survived the fire.

The victim hadn't. The body had come out first. In a body bag. But the smoke or the flames hadn't killed the victim. The bullet hole in her skull had. The coroner had confirmed that before even loading the body into his van and driving away.

Heather could leave now, too. She'd already talked to the neighbor who'd called 9-1-1 about the gunshots she'd heard. The woman hadn't seen anything; she'd only heard the shots. And while she'd called the police, she'd been too afraid to look out the window.

"People are always coming and going at that house," she'd told Heather in a conspiratorial whisper. "I heard the owner is or was a member of a gang."

Heather had widened her eyes with surprise over that speculation. The burning house in question was located in an upper-middle-class neighborhood. But she knew from her year and a half working with the vice unit that drugs could be dealt and manufactured anywhere and a lot of the time gangs were involved.

That was why Heather had decided to stick around; to wait for the owner to show up. The owner wasn't the person who had left zipped inside that body bag in the coroner's van. As well as determining cause of death at the scene, the coroner had also been able to determine sex. Female. Heather had already accessed the property records and had found out that the name of the owner was Trent Miles.

The name had a ring of familiarity to Heather. Either she'd heard it before or their paths had previously crossed. Had she investigated him? No charges or convictions had come up in the quick criminal check she'd done on him.

Not even prior arrests or warrants. So if he was a gang member, he hadn't gotten caught doing anything criminal. Yet.

But Heather was working toward the highest case clearance rate in the department right now. She was so close that she could taste the victory. So close that Detective Bob Bernard could probably just about taste the crow he was going to have to eat over his remarks about girl detectives not earning their jobs. He claimed that females were only promoted to detective so that the police department could avoid getting sued for sex discrimination.

Heather couldn't wait to tell the misogynistic jerk to suck it when she surpassed his record. She needed to close this case and at least one more before Christmas in order to secure bragging rights before the office holiday party. Because who knew—maybe Bob was actually working on improving his own closing rate. Though she doubted it.

She also doubted that this fire was an accident; it had obviously been set in order to destroy evidence of the murder. The flames were out now. Only smoke rose from the blackened structure. She crossed the street and stepped closer to the crime scene tape that she'd given to the uniformed officers to cordon off the area.

One of the firefighters stood just inside that tape, staring very intently at the damaged house. His square jaw was clenched so tightly that a muscle twitched in his lean cheek.

"Did all of the firefighters make it out?" she asked with concern.

She wasn't a fan of firefighters, not after having dated a couple of them back when she'd been a uniformed officer. Most of them were like Bob Bernard, chauvinists who didn't respect women and just wanted to brag about the dangers of their careers. How they were such he-men for fighting fires. While she didn't want to date any of them again, she didn't deny that their jobs were dangerous. She also appreciated what they did and didn't want any of them to get hurt doing it.

"All of the crew made it out," the man confirmed, and he turned back to tip up his hat and stare at her.

His face was streaked with soot; he'd definitely been

in the fire. The dirt on his face made his eyes glow even more; they were an eerie light brown, topaz, like the eyes of the cat that had shown up at her house a year ago.

"Are you a reporter?" he asked.

She reached for the badge that dangled from the chain she wore around her neck; one of the links of the chain snagged the red scarf partially tucked inside her long puffer coat. Winter had come early to Michigan this year; even now snowflakes drifted down around them. "I'm a detective with Detroit PD. Detective Bolton," she said. "This is my case."

"Do you know what happened?" he asked. "There was a report of shots being fired and the first fire crew on the scene said that a body was found inside. Was it identified yet?"

She narrowed her eyes and studied his face. He was damn good-looking. And curious, so curious that he stayed with her instead of helping his crew with the hoses and equipment. No. He was more than curious. His eyes glistened a bit, and she didn't think it was from the smoke because his big, broad body was nearly shaking. "What's your interest in my case?" she asked.

"This is my house," the firefighter replied, and his voice cracked. "I need to know who was inside."

"So do I," she said. "You must know who would have been here, who was living with you or visiting you."

He shook his head. "I've been out of town for two weeks. I just got back to Michigan earlier today."

"Who can confirm that for you?" she asked.

"My hotshot crew. My superintendent is in Northern Lakes. My captain, at the firehouse here, can confirm it, too. Manny Rodriguez," he replied, and he glanced around as if looking for the man.

So Trent Miles was a hotshot.

She nearly groaned. He wasn't just a firefighter. He was an elite firefighter. And probably an even bigger daredevil than those couple of jerks she'd gone out with.

"How long ago did you get back to Michigan?" she asked.

"Just a few hours."

"A few hours is a long time," she pointed out. Especially when the 9-1-1 call had come in just a little over an hour ago. "And you didn't come by your own house? Not even to drop off your bags?"

He shook his head. "My one bag is still in my truck at the firehouse."

"Where have you been since you got back?" she asked.

He shrugged. "I stopped at the outlet mall on my drive down from Northern Lakes and did some shopping and got something to eat. Gassed up my truck, too."

"Got any receipts to back that up?" she asked.

"I—I don't know," he said. "Are you saying I need an alibi?"

She shrugged now. "It's your house."

"But I don't even know who was here, who was in the fire," he said, staring as intently at her as he'd been staring at the house. His strange eyes were hard with indignation and frustration. "Why won't you tell me who was inside?"

"The body hasn't been identified yet," she said.

"The coroner had already taken it away when I got here. So let me see it," he said, his deep voice gruff with emotion or maybe the smoke he'd inhaled in the fire.

When had he inhaled it? When he'd been fighting the fire just now? Or when he'd set the fire?

"I need to know who it is that…" His throat moved as if he was struggling to swallow. Then he finished, "…that I lost…"

Heather had a pretty good bullshit meter. She could usually tell when someone was lying or trying to manipulate her. That was why she went on a lot of first dates but very few second dates. While low-key and trying to maintain control, Trent Miles seemed genuinely upset. He attempted to control his emotions instead of what Heather considered putting on a performance. She never trusted the people who were overly dramatic when the cameras were rolling and then showed no emotion when nobody was watching.

A couple of news crews had arrived at the scene and were setting up behind the police barricade. But instead of turning toward the cameras, Trent Miles turned away and ducked his head down inside the raised collar of his coat as if he didn't want to be caught on film.

He could have another reason for that, though. He didn't want there to be evidence of him at the scene. But if that was the case, he would have walked away from her instead of asking her questions, instead of asking about the body.

Unless he was lying about who he really was. Or maybe he just wasn't taking her seriously, like so many other people failed to do. With her long blond hair pulled back in a ponytail and minimal makeup, she looked younger than her thirty years, which often had people underestimating her. Like Bob Bernard.

The old man was going to realize soon how wrong he was when she closed this case. But to close it, she needed to find out who the victim was, just as Trent Miles claimed he needed to know. "You really have no idea who was staying in your house?" she asked skeptically. "What? Do you Airbnb it?"

He shook his head. "No. I just… A lot of people know the code to the digital locks and may have shared it with other people."

She swallowed a groan of frustration. That was going to make it a lot harder to identify the body and the killer. Unless…the killer was standing right in front of her.

"Your neighbor said something about people coming and going all the time…" she said, watching his face carefully as she trailed off, giving him the chance to add more.

"Did they see who was here tonight?" he asked, and again that intensity was back on his face, that fear, as the muscle twitched along his square jaw again. "I need to know!"

He wasn't the only one.

She nodded. "Okay. Let's take a trip to the coroner's office. See what we can find out. My car's just over here." She gestured to the other side of the street where her unmarked cruiser was parked in front of the house of the neighbor who'd reported hearing the shots. She waited, expecting an argument. A stall. Something.

"Let me tell my crew," he said. And he headed toward one of the fire engines.

A few of the guys hugged him. And an older man, who was in a DFD uniform but not his gear, handed Trent something and then glanced in her direction. Envelopes. Trent Miles wrapped his gloved hand around them like he was holding a snake. Just what the hell had the older guy given him?

Trent shoved the envelopes into one of the deep pockets of his coat and headed back toward her. He had to duck low and hold up the crime scene tape to maneuver underneath it and join her in the street.

"Over here! Over here!" a male reporter shouted. "We have questions for you about the fire!"

Trent turned away again and focused on her. "Let's go."

"You don't want to talk to the reporters?" she asked.

He shook his head. "Not that one," he murmured.

"Why not?" she asked. "Bad blood between you?"

He shook his head again. "I don't know him."

"Over here! Over here!" another reporter yelled out. "Detective!"

Either that reporter or one of the crew must have noticed the badge dangling around her neck. Heather ignored the media and clicked the fob for her vehicle.

"You don't want to talk to them either," Trent observed as he walked beside her as they crossed the street. With his long legs, he probably had to slow his stride to match hers.

"Nope. I don't want to talk to any reporters." She didn't have enough information yet. About the fire, the victim or the possible suspect.

Trent stopped on the passenger's side of the unmarked vehicle. "Want me to ride in the back?"

Her questioning him about his alibi had probably clued him in to the fact that he was a suspect. But just a suspect...

"You can ride in the front." She doubted he would try anything. And if he did, she was armed.

He opened the front passenger door while she went around to the driver's side. When they'd both closed their doors and she started the ignition, she asked, "Have you ever ridden in the back of a police car?"

He released a ragged-sounding sigh and nodded. "I have...a long time ago..."

Heather was intrigued, more than she should be about the man when she had a murder to solve. But in order to find out who the killer was, she first had to find out who the victim was.

Or had she already met the killer? And was he sitting right next to her?

Chapter 2

Trent was surprised the detective hadn't had him ride in the back behind the shield that would have protected her if he tried anything while she was driving. She clearly suspected he knew more than he was telling her about whoever had died in the fire at his home.

He wished like hell that he did. But the calls he'd made on the way to the fire, to his sister's cell, had gone unanswered. And Brittney hadn't shown up at the scene like he'd expected she would, if she could. And if she couldn't...

Tears stung his eyes, and they weren't from the smoke. He blinked and glanced across the console at the detective. She had just one gloved hand wrapped around the steering wheel as she drove away from the scene of his burned home. Her other hand was close to her side. Or maybe her weapon?

She really did have suspicions about him. He probably hadn't helped his case when he'd admitted to having ridden in the back of a police car before. He was kind of surprised she hadn't frisked him before letting him get into the front with her.

"So what was the reason you were picked up in the past?" she asked.

"Traffic accident," he replied.

She glanced across at him. "You were at fault?"

He shook his head. "I wasn't the driver. My mom was. She didn't make it. The police officer drove me to social services."

She sucked in a breath. "I'm sorry. How old were you?"

"Twelve."

"Why didn't they have your dad come pick you up?"

"He was already dead," Trent said. "Died the year before during a deployment with his Marine unit."

She glanced at him again, sympathy in her green eyes. A deep, vibrant green. "Tough childhood you've had, Mr. Miles."

"Trent."

"Trent," she said. "Is that when you got into a gang?"

He snorted derisively. "Why do people assume a young half Black man growing up in Detroit must have been a gang member at some point?"

"I wasn't the one who made the assumption," she said. "Your neighbor, the one who called in about the gunshots, told me that."

"Then she probably told you my name, and you checked my record. I don't have one."

"Just because you never got convicted doesn't mean you never did anything illegal."

"Doesn't mean that I did." He couldn't deny that he'd done some stupid things in his life, though. And getting into this car with Detective Bolton was probably another one. Even though he had nothing to hide, he would have been smarter to talk to her with a lawyer present. Just like Moe had taught him growing up because of all those times the police had picked him up for something he hadn't done. Thank God Moe was a lawyer, or his record probably wouldn't be as clean as it was. She would lecture the hell out of him over talking to Detective Bolton without her present, but he couldn't call her until he knew whose body that was.

Who had been shot in his house? He didn't want to devastate her until he knew for sure that it was Brittney. It couldn't be Brittney.

"What else did my neighbor tell you?" he asked. "Did she say who she saw going in there tonight?" People tended to recognize his sister, especially after the big story she'd done at the expense of his hotshot team.

"She just heard the shots. She didn't see anything tonight," the detective replied. "But she said that a lot of people come and go at your place."

He snorted again. "So what? You think I'm dealing drugs out of my home?"

"I think someone got shot in the head and killed in your house before it was set on fire in order to destroy evidence, and I'd like to find out who that was and why they were killed," she replied.

Feeling like she'd just punched him in the gut, he lost his breath for a second and had to gulp in another before speaking. "I want to find that out, too. Since you know the person was shot in the head, you must know more about whoever it was. What else did the coroner tell you?"

She peered straight ahead as if focused on the road.

But this late at night, there wasn't much traffic, despite it being Black Friday. Maybe all the shoppers were back home, exhausted from getting up so early and standing in lines for deals. They were probably eating Thanksgiving leftovers while sacked out on their sofas.

His sofa was gone. Most of his house, too. What else had he lost? And more importantly, who else? He'd already lost too damn many people, and his pulse quickened with the fear that someone else he cared about might have died. Brittney?

He had to know.

"Detective Bolton," he prodded her, his heart beating heavy with dread. He could tell that she knew more than she'd revealed.

"The body is female," she said.

Panic pressed on his chest so heavily that he jerked open his jacket, trying to breathe. But he couldn't draw in any air as that pressure intensified, squeezing his chest. His heart...

She pulled over to the curb and parked. "Are you okay? You know who it is? Your wife?"

He shook his head. "Not married..." was all he could rasp out.

"Girlfriend?"

He shook his head again. "No..."

"You obviously have some idea," she said. "Who are you afraid that it is?"

He pressed his hand harder against his aching chest. "My sister..."

"She lives with you?"

"Sometimes," he said. "She knows the key code and lets herself in and out when she needs a place to stay in the city." Otherwise, she lived in the suburbs with her mom, Moe, and her stepdad. Moe had been his dad's second wife, after Trent's mom, but due to his frequent deployments, their marriage hadn't lasted either.

"Have you tried calling her?"

"Yes," he said, choking out the word through the lump of fear in his throat.

"And she hasn't answered?"

He shook his head.

"When did you talk to her last?" she asked.

"Uh…it's been a while," he admitted, that pressure even heavier on his heart now.

"You didn't have time to talk to her when you were gone with your hotshot team?" she asked.

He swallowed the emotion rushing up on him. "No. And I didn't talk to her for a couple weeks before I left with my team."

"Was she staying with you then?" the detective asked, her brow furrowing beneath her wispy blond bangs.

He shrugged. "I don't know if she was here. I was mostly staying at the firehouse. I've been avoiding her," he admitted. But maybe not well enough that whoever had sent that card didn't think it would hurt him to lose her. That wasn't why he'd been avoiding her, though. He'd had no idea someone had it out for him.

"Sibling squabble?" she asked. "I can relate. I have sisters, too. We fight over the stupidest things."

"It wasn't like that," he said. "It wasn't over something stupid." Not when it had nearly cost Ethan his life.

"Then what was it like? Just how pissed off are you at your sister, Trent?"

He groaned. "God, you are determined to think I'm the one who shot that person…" It couldn't be Brittney. It just couldn't be. He would never forgive himself for not forgiving her or at least speaking to her again. Guilt and regret rushed up to choke him, but he cleared his throat and finished, "…and set fire to my own house."

"Well, doesn't sound like *you* actually spend a lot of time there," she remarked dryly. "So whoever was in there shooting probably wasn't after you. Is there a reason someone would be after your sister?"

He shuddered with the heaviness of the sigh he expelled. "A lot of reasons. She's a reporter. Brittney Townsend."

"Townsend? Is she married?"

"No," he said. "She's my half sister." He hated saying that, though. She was wholly his sister in his heart even when he was pissed at her. She had to be okay. But why hadn't she called him back? He'd left her voice mails. He reached into his pocket for his cell and pulled out the envelopes with it. The screen was black; it had died on him. He couldn't remember when he'd charged it last.

"So different dads?" the detective asked.

He glanced at her with irritation, wondering if she was making assumptions about him again. "Same dad. She took her stepfather's last name. She was so little when our dad died that she didn't remember him."

"Brittney Townsend," the detective repeated, and her eyes widened with recognition. "She's that reporter. Used to do fluff pieces but has stepped it up lately."

At his expense and the expense of his hotshot team.

The detective's eyes narrowed again and she nodded. "Oh, now I know why you haven't been talking to her. She blew up the lives of your hotshot team."

And his best friend had nearly been blown up because of that, because Brittney had exposed his true identity and his whereabouts to a man who wanted him dead.

"I'm pissed at my sister, but I would never hurt her."
He was in pain just worrying that something might have
happened to her. If she was truly gone…

He definitely wasn't acting. The pain on Trent Miles's
handsome face was real, so real that Heather felt a
twinge of it striking her heart. Which was weird.

She'd never experienced anything like that. In fact,
her two sisters often accused Heather of having no em-
pathy. What they probably meant was sympathy, because
she refused to give them any when they complained
about their lazy husbands and their screaming, spoiled
kids. They'd married the immature idiots whose moms
had waited on them hand and foot growing up, and they'd
somehow expected them to not expect their wives to continue to coddle them?

She sighed and focused again on the man in her passenger seat. While she struggled to hang on to any suspicion about his guilt, she still suspected he knew more
than he had admitted to her. He was holding something back.

She glanced at those envelopes on his lap, lying beneath his cell. His finger was pressed against the power
button, but the screen remained black.

"Your phone dead?" she asked. She flipped open
the console and pulled out a cord. "Here's a charger. I
think we have the same cell." Probably the model that
the city ordered for all their employees. She plugged the
end into that charging portal on the console and held
the other end out over his lap, her hand coming dan-
gerously close to his thighs that were so muscular they
strained even the thick material of his uniform pants.

The man was built like a…hotshot firefighter, like

the ones from every calendar she'd ever seen. The ones her sisters had bought for her when she'd dated the couple of firemen.

Neither of her dates had looked like those calendar pages, though. Not like Trent Miles did.

His fingers brushed hers as he took the end of the cord from her. And she experienced a curious little jolt, like she was getting charged. He plugged in his phone, but the screen stayed black.

"How long was it dead?" she asked.

"I called Brittney on the way to the fire," he said. "She didn't pick up, so I left her a message, and I sent a…" His voice trailed off, gruff with emotion. With fear for his sister.

She could empathize with that. Even as crazy as her sisters drove her, she loved them and wouldn't want anything to happen to them. Ever.

"She might have been busy when you called, and then when she tried to call you back, your phone was already dead," she pointed out.

He released a shaky breath and nodded. "Yeah, yeah, that could be why."

She reached across the console again and squeezed his arm. Through the heavy material of his firefighter jacket and her gloves, she shouldn't have felt another jolt, but she did. *What the hell…*

He jumped, too, and grabbed his vibrating phone.

The cell.

That was it; she'd felt the vibration. But still, it was good that they were parked or she might have jerked the wheel when she'd jumped.

His breath shuddered out in a ragged sigh. "It's a text from her."

Heather read it off the screen. "'So you're talking to me again?'" The time the text had come through was also on the screen. "She sent that after the report of gunshots being fired at this address and also after the body had been removed from the house."

Relief surged through her. She wasn't sure why; it wasn't as if she knew Brittney Townsend. She'd only watched a few of her reports over the years because Heather didn't really care where the hot spots in town were and what the upcoming fashion trends were going to be. But she cared about people, more than she would ever admit to her sisters. Even more than she cared about her case clearance rate.

"You can call her back," Heather told him. "She might know whose body was found in your house."

He nodded, but he didn't make any move to return his sister's text or calls. There were missed calls from her, too. "I don't know if I should."

"Just don't reveal anything specific about the investigation," she said. After what his sister had done to his hotshot team, he probably didn't trust her, and neither should Heather.

"It's not that…" He pulled the envelopes out from under his cell and flipped through them.

She smiled as she noticed some addressed "to the hot firefighter." But a few had his name on them. He handed one of those across the console to her. "What is this?" she asked.

"A Christmas card."

"A Christmas card?" A body had been found in his house and he was showing her his holiday mail?

But the tension was still in his body even after finding out his sister was not the person who'd been killed in his house. Maybe he had some idea, despite denying it, who that person was.

She pulled the card out of the envelope and stared down at the gold Christmas tree on the red background. "Pretty..." she murmured. Then she flipped it open. On one side the printed message from the card company told him to enjoy the holiday season with those he loved. On the other...

"'You're going to find out how it feels to lose someone close to you. Soon,'" she read aloud. Then she turned back toward him. "When did you get this?"

"It came to the firehouse here in Detroit while I was out West with my hotshot team. I don't know when it arrived."

She focused on the envelope. The postmark was smudged. "I can't read that...the date or the place from where it had been mailed." It was already pretty light and then must have gotten damp and the ink bled into the paper. "And of course they didn't include a return address."

"It was mailed, though? Not dropped off?" He flipped through the other envelopes on his lap. "These were dropped off."

She reached across and took those envelopes from his hand to look through them herself. Once again, despite the thickness of her gloves, her fingertips tingled from touching him. *Must be a lot of static electricity in the car.*

"It probably would have been kind of hard to mail out something addressed 'to the hot firefighter,'" she said, amusement tugging her lips into a smile. "But if they'd had the address for the firehouse..." They'd probably wanted to see him, though, which was why they'd personally dropped off the cards.

She didn't blame his fans for being fans. Trent Miles was one of the best-looking guys she'd ever seen in person and not on a movie screen. Hell, he was probably even better looking than those Hollywood superstars because he wasn't wearing makeup, just that fine sheen of soot from the fire.

She pulled her gaze from him to focus on the smeared postmark. "I'll see if the techs can figure out where it was mailed from," she said. She had a favorite in the unit who managed to pull off magic for her all the time.

"Have them check if it was mailed from Northern Lakes," he suggested.

"Northern Lakes? Where that Canterbury heir was found hiding out while letting everyone believe that he was dead for the past five years?" She knew, though, that had been his sister's big break, the scoop that had taken her off the restaurant and fashion beat.

"*Ethan* was actually hiding out in a national forest," Trent said, "but he is part of my hotshot team and one of my best friends."

"That's why you don't want to talk to your sister. Because she let the world know he faked his death and was living under an assumed identity?"

"There's more to the story than that. He didn't fake anything. He was in a plane crash five years ago. He just…" Trent sighed. "The details don't matter now. That is why I haven't been talking to her. When she exposed Ethan's secret, she put his life in danger. Now I'm worried that, if I start talking to her again, I'll put her life in danger. That message in the card is threatening to take away someone close to me, and Brittney is the closest family member I have."

"Oh…" Heather murmured over the clarification. He wasn't hanging on to his righteous anger with his sister, like she probably would have; he was trying to protect her. "That makes sense." And was probably safer for Heather, too, so she didn't have to worry about the reporter revealing too much about the case before she'd had the chance to really start her investigation. "Do you think that whoever died in that fire might have been mistaken for her?"

He shrugged. "I don't know."

"You really have no idea who else it could have been?"

He shook his head. "No. I'm just relieved it's not my sister. But I hope that someone else didn't die because of me."

"We don't know anything for sure yet," she reminded him and herself. She didn't really know that he'd had nothing to do with those gunshots and that fire. She had to verify his alibi first. Had to make sure that he wasn't a suspect.

But…

Wouldn't it be easier for her if he was? If he was, she could close this case quicker and move on to the next. If he had no alibi, then he had the most means and opportunity to have committed this murder.

She glanced down at that strange Christmas card someone had mailed him. It made more sense that whoever had sent this threat was behind the murder. They'd thought the person in his house was the "someone close to him" they'd wanted him to feel the pain over losing.

But he had no idea whose body that even was.

Heather had some idea, not about the identity of the

dead victim, but about how to flush out the person who'd sent that card. It was a dangerous plan, though.

Probably the most dangerous for her.

Trent Miles had to suffer. Really suffer.

He had to be forced to feel the pain that his actions— no, his inactions—had caused others. From the image playing across the television screen in the dark room, it was hard to see if Miles was suffering or feeling anything at all. As the reporters called out to him from the scene of the fire, he ducked his face into his coat, hiding it from the cameras like he'd been hiding these past two weeks.

The reporters didn't know who Miles was, but the person watching the television knew. Then Miles maneuvered around the crime scene tape and joined someone else in the street. The watcher sat forward, leaning close to the television.

Was it…?

The detective. Bolton with her blond hair and her pretty face and her bitchy ways.

She deserved to suffer, too.

Chapter 3

The body was burned beyond recognition. But even if it hadn't been, if *she* hadn't been, Trent doubted he would have recognized the victim. And she was a victim. The hole in her head proved that she'd been dead even before the fire. This had been no accident. Someone had wanted her dead.

But why? Was it about him or was there some other reason someone had wanted this woman dead?

Even if he hadn't talked to Brittney, he would have known it wasn't her. His sister was taller than this woman. Hank was also taller than the body. Henrietta "Hank" Rowlins and Michaela were the female members of the hotshot team, and they were like family to him, too. Fortunately, they were both in Northern Lakes or maybe just north of it in the little town of St. Paul, where they worked out of a small firehouse.

"You really have no idea who she is?" the detective asked.

He glanced up to find her staring at him as intently as he'd been staring at the body. He shook his head.

"No girlfriend? No female friend that might have been crashing at your place?"

"I already told you no. The only female I know who would have been in my house is Brittney." And that pressure in his chest eased again knowing she was alive. This wasn't her lying on the cold metal table in the morgue.

"She's wearing a wedding band," the detective said, pointing to one of the victim's hands where a ring was fused in with the charred flesh.

He'd seen bodies before, victims of fires, but knowing this person had been in his home and might have died because of him made it even more horrifying and sickening. And he felt some of the pain that note had promised he'd feel, but he didn't know this person. Or...

"What is it?" Detective Bolton asked. "Did you think of someone?"

"The body is so badly damaged." Maybe he'd been wrong to dismiss everyone he knew. "Moe, but I don't think it would be her..." There was a reason, but at the moment, exhausted and emotional, he struggled to remember why it couldn't be her.

"Who's Moe?" the detective asked.

"Brittney's mom." He'd been worried about having to call her about Brittney. But could she have come by his house? She had the key code.

"What's her full name?"

"It's Maureen Townsend." Relief rushed over him as he remembered why it couldn't be her lying in front of him, burned beyond recognition. "No. No. She's gone. She always goes away over Thanksgiving. She and her husband take a cruise over this week because the courts are shut down."

"She's a lawyer?"

"Used to be," he said. "She's a judge now."

"Of course. Judge Townsend. Impressive family. A lot to live up to."

Maybe that was why Brittney was so ambitious. She was trying to live up to her mother's success. Despite the realization, Trent couldn't cut his sister any slack. Not right now. Not without the risk of putting her in danger like she'd put Ethan.

And him. Trent had nearly died in one of those attempts on Ethan's life. He would rather be at risk himself, though, than put his younger sister in danger.

"If your sister is the only person you can think who might have been staying at your place—"

"She's not the only one," he said. "Coworkers crash at my place a lot because it's close to the firehouse. Brittney is just the only female."

She narrowed her startling deep green eyes and stared at him with obvious skepticism. "Really? You never date? Never have anyone who might have been waiting at your house to greet you when you returned from that wildfire?"

Heat crawled into his face, despite the cool temperature in the morgue. He usually dated. A lot. And women had tried to surprise him at his place. "That's happened in the past," he admitted. "But I've been taking a break from dating."

He'd recently lost a fellow hotshot because his cheating wife had murdered him, brutally, gruesomely, and another hotshot had been stalked and nearly killed by some woman who had been obsessed with him for years. After that tragedy and near-tragedy, Trent had decided it was smarter, with so much going on right now with his professional life, to forego a personal one and focus instead on being safe rather than having sex.

Maybe going without for a while explained why he was so damn aware of the detective. Every time she'd touched him, while they'd been parked at the curb in her car, tension had gripped him, tightening his muscles. At first he'd thought it was just because she clearly suspected him of murder and he was feeling fear.

He'd been concerned that he'd broken Moe's rule, the advice she'd given him in his youth to never speak to police without legal representation. But he had nothing to hide, then or now, except this attraction for the detective.

Even in the weird fluorescent glow of the morgue lights, she was beautiful. Her eyes were so heavily lashed and vibrant, skin so silky-looking and features so delicate. And when she'd unzipped that puffy jacket, she'd revealed two things: the holster holding her weapon and a curvy, athletic body that had brought all that tension back.

"You might be taking a break, but maybe somebody isn't happy about that," she said.

He flinched. There had been a few snippy texts. A few voice mails from disgruntled female friends with benefits, but that had been months ago. "It doesn't matter. I changed my locks to digital ones, and I only gave the code out to my coworkers, my sister and Moe, but I have no idea who they might have shared it with," he said. He stared down at the body again, that horror gripping him. "This isn't anybody that I personally know."

Or so he hoped.

"I'm going to need a list of everybody who has that code," she said. "And I'm going to need to speak to them and find out who else they might have shared the code with. Maybe this is a spouse or girlfriend of one of them. Maybe this has nothing to do with you."

"I want to believe that," he said. But that card, and all the sabotage and other things that had happened in Northern Lakes, made him think otherwise.

"But you don't," she said.

"Do you?"

"I'm not going to make any assumptions until I've done more investigating."

The coroner had left them alone in the morgue. Maybe that was why, despite the chill, the detective had unzipped her jacket. Not because she was warm but to show Trent her gun, to warn him that she was armed.

And dangerous?

The way she affected him, this weird attraction despite the circumstances, made her very dangerous to Trent. But he couldn't stop himself from moving a little closer to her, from staring at her with some of that heat starting to burn inside him, starting to dispel the cold. "So you haven't made a decision about me yet?" he asked. "About my guilt or innocence?"

She shook her head, and that blond ponytail bobbed around her shoulders. "No."

"What will it take to prove to you that I could never hurt anyone?"

She snorted. "Everyone is capable of hurting someone else. Maybe not purposely but…it happens. We hurt people without trying. That note in the card makes it sound like you hurt someone."

He tensed as he realized now what the note meant. "You think someone blames me for losing someone they loved?"

She glanced at the body on the table. "Like a husband who lost a wife…"

"Even when I was dating, I never dated a married woman," he said. "I would never mess with someone else's marriage." That was how his hotshot friend had died, because someone had messed with his, and Dirk Brown had suffered a horrible fate because of it. Fortunately, the lover was in jail now as an accomplice. And the wife who'd killed him…

She was dead.

Trent glanced at the table. This person had suffered a horrible fate, too. Why? Because of him?

"We need to figure out who this is," he said.

"The coroner is going to see what DNA he can get from the remains, and he's also going to check dental records, but it'll be easier for him if he can have something to compare that DNA and dental records to, if we can come up with some possible identities of the victim."

He nodded. "Right. I'll get you the names of everyone who had the code."

"I'll have to talk to your sister, too," she said, as if warning him.

Ever since his phone had charged, it had been vibrating with more incoming texts and voice mails from Brittney. "I'm pretty sure she knows my house burned down. She's going to want to interview you about it."

"You're the one she wants to talk to now," the detective

said. Obviously she hadn't missed what had been going on with his phone.

He shook his head. "I can't. I can't risk whoever sent that damn card realizing just how close she is to me." Or how much he would miss her if he lost her, despite the way she infuriated him.

"There is nobody else that close to you?" she asked with skepticism.

"My mom and dad are both gone," he said. "Brittney is it for my blood relatives, but then there's my hotshot family." And they were family, but since the sabotage had started on their equipment and there had been real attempts on their lives and losses, everything had been different. Tense. Distrustful. But maybe that was like real family, too.

"Seems like a lot is going on with them, according to that report your sister ran," the detective remarked. "I should talk to them, also."

He sighed. "They're all over the place now since we just got back from that wildfire." But he knew when they would all be together.

She seemed to know it, because she arched a dark blond brow over one of those vibrant green eyes. "But they will be getting together again sometime?"

He sighed again. "For the hotshot holiday party," he admitted. "But that's over a week away."

"If I don't talk to them sooner, we'll make it a date," she said.

"You're going to go with me to my Christmas party?"

"If I haven't closed the case by then, I will," she replied matter-of-factly. "I have a plan to flush out whoever sent you that card and determine if they're the one who killed the person found in your house."

"They must be," he said. "I have no idea why else anyone would have been shot and killed in my home."

She shrugged. "Who knows? It might have nothing to do with you."

"I hope that's true. But I think we both doubt that."

"The card, the murder, the fire…" She shook her head. "I don't believe in that many coincidences."

"So what's your plan to find out the truth?" he asked, and all that tension returned to his body.

"You're going to have to start dating again."

"You read that card. You know that'll put that person in danger," he said.

She smiled. "That's what I'm counting on, to flush out whoever sent that card when they make an attempt on the life of your date."

He narrowed his eyes as suspicion gripped him. "Who is my date going to be?"

"Me."

"You want me to start dating you?" he asked, and despite the coldness of the morgue, heat surged through him again. For her, he would be tempted to think about having a personal life again. If it wouldn't put her life in danger…

Trent Miles probably thought she was as sex-crazed as those fans who'd addressed their Christmas cards "to the hot firefighter." They'd also written notes inside, but they had offered to get close to him. *Very close.* Not threaten to take away someone close to him.

The coroner returned before she'd had the chance to explain what she had really meant. And she hadn't wanted to lay out her plan in front of someone else in case it was as impulsive and reckless as she suspected.

So they'd left the morgue to head over to the police department. She had Trent sitting in an empty interrogation room to make the list of people with the key code for his digital locks while she checked out his alibi.

With his permission, she accessed the GPS on his truck, which proved he hadn't been anywhere near his house since returning from Northern Lakes. He couldn't have fired the shot that killed the woman or set the fire to cover up the murder. His stops at the outlet mall and burger place checked out, too, and quite easily. People tended to remember someone who looked like Trent Miles. They also had security footage they emailed to back up his alibi.

He'd had nothing to do with the murder. But did he really have no idea who the victim was? He'd changed the locks on his house for a reason; there must have been someone he'd wanted to keep out.

An obsessed former girlfriend?

Heather jumped up from her desk in the detective bullpen of cubicles and headed down the hall to the interview room. This close to midnight there weren't many people in this area. Most of them were down on the lower floors. The holding cells, the front desk. This floor was quiet, so Trent had probably heard her coming, her boots pounding on the worn linoleum floor. But he didn't look up when she opened the door to the interrogation room. He was focused instead on the pad of paper she'd given him, staring down at his writing on the top sheet as he clutched the pen in his hand.

"Is that your confession?" she asked but was only teasing. She had proof now of his innocence, which made her strangely happy. Strange because it would have been easier for her to close the case if he'd been guilty. She wouldn't have had to look for other suspects.

He looked up then, but he didn't seem surprised to see her standing in the doorway. He must have been aware that she'd opened the door. "I confess that I have no idea who could have been in my house tonight. I keep looking over these names that I wrote down for you, and Brittney was the only one who could have…" His gruff voice trailed off and his throat moved as if he was struggling to swallow.

No matter how betrayed and used he felt from his sister exposing his friend, he obviously still loved her. Somebody else might have betrayed him, too, and given out that key code to someone Trent wouldn't have wanted to have it.

She stepped inside the room and let the door close behind her. "We'll figure it out," she vowed.

"Yes, you have a plan." He leaned back in his chair and stared at her with those intriguing topaz-colored eyes. He'd taken off his jacket; it hung over the back of the chair. His shirt was thin enough that it molded to the sculpted muscles of his chest. It wasn't just his face that was good-looking. "You're going to date me."

Her pulse quickened until she reminded herself about the cover. "To flush out whoever wants to hurt someone close to you," she said. "That's the only reason why."

"That puts you in danger," he said. "You might get hurt, and maybe it won't be by whoever's after me."

"So who do you think is going to hurt me, then?" she asked.

He arched a dark brow. "Your husband? Your lover?"

She snorted. "If I had either of those, they would probably hurt you instead."

"Someone could still hurt you." The tension was back in his handsome face, making him clench his jaw so tightly that muscle twitched again.

"Who?" she asked. "The killer or you? Don't worry. I can take care of myself. I have a gun and a hard heart. I won't forget that we're just faking and fall for you."

His mouth curved into a slight grin. "What if I forget and fall for you?"

She laughed at the thought. "Yeah, I doubt that you're looking for a relationship any more than I am. Or you wouldn't have changed your locks. Any particular reason why you did that? Any former girlfriend so obsessed that she would have let herself in like that woman probably did tonight?" Unless someone had lured her there, someone who had his key code, which would have been someone he considered a friend. Or a relative, like his sister and stepmom.

She definitely needed to speak to his sister.

His face flushed a little. "There were a couple of women I was seeing who wanted more serious relationships than I wanted," he admitted.

She nodded in appreciation of his honesty. "Write down their names, too."

"But they don't have the key code," he said. "And I think one of them even got married…" His eyes widened with surprise as he probably realized what Heather had already been considering, that the dead woman could be someone he had been involved with before her marriage.

"Married," she said, "like the woman found in your burned house."

He shook his head. "No, she wouldn't have been there. She moved on. She got marri—"

"How do you know that?" she asked. "Was she communicating with you even after she got involved with someone else?"

His face flushed slightly beneath the soot, and he rubbed his hand along his jaw. "Uh…"

"Maybe she thought you would pull a Dustin Hoffman in *The Graduate* and barge in to stop her wedding, and when you didn't…"

"She what?" Trent asked. "She showed up at my place? She didn't have the key code."

"And she didn't know any of your coworkers? Anyone that might give it to her?"

He sighed. "Maybe she could have gotten it from someone who had it."

She stepped closer to the table and grabbed the pad. There were a lot of names on it. A lot of people she would have to call. But first she would call the married woman to find out if she was alive or if hers was the body found in the fire. "This might not be what you think. Maybe she got the code, got in your house, started the fire and then shot herself. The fire might not have had a chance to get going for the smoke or flames to show when your neighbor called 9-1-1 about the shots she heard. That was why she didn't mention the fire during her call to Dispatch."

"You think what happened could have been a suicide?" he asked, clearly horrified. "But that card…"

"Maybe she was the one who sent it. She figured she was closer to you than you did."

He didn't reach for the pad. Instead, he pulled out his phone and scrolled through his contacts. "Her number is in here, but I still don't get it. We didn't even go out that long."

"*You* weren't that close to her," she said. "But she obviously felt more than you did." If that was the effect Trent Miles had on women, maybe Heather should have concerns about going undercover as his girlfriend. But she might not have to; if her suicide theory was right, she could close this case tonight.

She pulled out her cell and dialed the number he showed on his screen for Caitlin. It rang a few times. But it was late. Maybe her phone was off. Or maybe, because the woman didn't recognize the number, she was just going to let it go to voice mail.

"Hello?" The woman's voice, husky with sleep, emanated from the speaker of Heather's cell.

"Caitlin?"

"Yes. Who is this?"

"Detective Bolton with Detroit PD," she replied.

The woman gasped. "Oh, my God. What's happened? Has someone been in an accident?"

"Probably no one you know," Heather said. "But your name did come up in the course of an investigation into a fire at Trent Miles's house."

"Oh, my God!" she exclaimed again, her voice cracking with sobs. "Is Trent okay?"

A male voice grumbled in the background of the call. Heather couldn't make out his words, but he sounded irritated. Maybe his irritation was over the late-night call or maybe over the subject of the call. He obviously wasn't as concerned about Caitlin's ex-boyfriend as she was.

"Trent is fine," Heather assured her. Actually, he was *damn* fine. She wasn't going to have to stretch her acting abilities to pretend to be his girlfriend.

The woman released a shaky sigh. "That's good. I—
Is there anything I can do?"

"No. You answered the question I had just by answering the phone," Heather assured her.

"I don't understand."

"Thank you," she said and disconnected the call.

Trent released a shaky sigh of his own. "That's good.
It wasn't her." His cell vibrated, and the same number
Heather had just dialed showed up on his screen. He
ignored the call.

"You really aren't much of a phone talker, huh?" she
asked. "You don't take many of your calls."

"You know why," he said. "I don't want to put anyone
in danger. That's the reason I'm not sure your plan is a
good idea."

"I told you. I can take care of myself. I have a lot of
training and a gun."

His lips curved into that slight grin again. "And a
hard heart," he added.

She smiled. "Very hard," she assured him with pride.
"I've never even been close to falling in love, let alone
getting obsessed with anyone." That was mostly because she'd dated idiots, though, and hadn't wanted to
wind up as unhappy as her older sisters. "I'm not going
to get hurt."

"Then maybe I should be worried about me."

"Remember, I'm armed," she said. "I can protect you."

"But who's going to protect me from you, Detective?"
he asked with a slight, sexy grin.

She could keep him safe, and she wasn't worried about
him falling for her. Nobody else had yet. Probably because she was too independent and focused on her job
to give anyone the time or attention necessary to sustain

a relationship. But despite her gun, and her resolve to never get involved, she was a little worried about herself.

Because he was so damn good-looking.

Brittney was frustrated. One, because her brother would not return her calls and texts. And two, because she was trapped at the station, editing some fluff piece that she'd shot a while ago.

They'd promised her that she would cover more important stories after she'd gotten such a scoop. But then they'd changed their minds, using the holidays as an excuse and that people needed feel-good stories right now.

Brittney didn't feel good. She felt sick over upsetting Trent, sick that he wasn't even talking to her. And sick that something had happened to him, because she'd heard about the fire.

What the hell was going on?

Chapter 4

Trent hadn't been entirely joking when he'd said he was worried about himself. He had no home. No possessions but for the duffel bag of clothes in his truck at the firehouse, and they needed to be washed. But that was the least of his concerns because the house and possessions were just things. He was worried about people, about feeling the pain of loss like the Christmas card note threatened. He didn't want to lose anyone, especially not Detective Bolton, which was strange since he'd just met her.

And under the worst of circumstances. Somebody had been murdered in his home. Who?

He glanced across the console at the detective. He didn't want her to wind up like that woman had: dead. Sure, she had a gun and training and could take care of herself. But if she got hurt because of him…

"You didn't need to do this," he said.

"Do what?" she asked.

"Drive me back to my truck." It was already after midnight.

"I couldn't let you walk."

"I could have taken an Uber or a cab or called a friend," he said. She wasn't a friend. He wasn't even sure that she still didn't consider him a suspect. Maybe that was why she'd proposed the plan of pretending to be his girlfriend, so she could get close enough to him to get evidence against him.

"You weren't going to call a friend. You don't want anyone that you consider a friend near you right now."

"No, I don't," he agreed. "So I would have called a cab."

"The least I can do is give you a ride back to your vehicle," she said. "You're a victim, Trent."

He cringed at the word and shook his head. "No. That woman lying in the morgue is the victim."

"You lost your house, and you've been threatened," she said. "That makes you a victim, too."

He groaned. "I hate that word. But I guess I should be happy you're calling me that instead of a suspect. Or do you still have your doubts about me?"

She shook her head, and that long ponytail bobbed around her shoulders. "Not anymore. Your alibi checked out."

He expelled a ragged sigh. "Good."

"Did you have doubts?"

"Not me. I know I'm innocent."

"Somebody doesn't think so," she replied. "Or why else would they want you to know what it feels like to lose someone close to you, unless they held you responsible for them losing someone close to them?"

He sucked in a breath, pain jabbing him. "I have never purposely hurt anyone."

"But inadvertently…?"

He shrugged. "I don't know. But I must have or why would someone have sent that card?" Why had someone been killed in his house?

She sighed. "We'll figure it out. We need to find out who that woman was."

"I gave you that list."

However, she hadn't called anyone but Caitlin. Instead, she'd offered to drive him back to his vehicle. Actually, she hadn't offered; she'd insisted. She probably hadn't wanted to make those calls in front of him or leave him too long in the interrogation room after clearing him as a suspect. He'd almost rather have stayed there than return to the firehouse.

He didn't want the pity of his crew. Didn't want them offering him sympathy over a house or over that body found inside when he didn't even know who she was and what she'd been doing there. She was the one who deserved all the sympathy.

"Who's going to be around the firehouse when we get there?" she asked.

He glanced at the clock on the dash of the unmarked vehicle. They'd been at the morgue and the police station for a couple of hours. "The guys who were on call and responded to the fire at my house are probably gone now, unless there was another fire. And the night crew is probably asleep, unless there was another fire."

"So you're telling me if I want to find any of them at your station, I better hope there was another fire after yours?" she asked.

Tension gripped him at the thought. "I hope there wasn't another one."

"Because you missed it?" she asked.

"Because I don't want anyone else getting hurt."

She braked at a traffic light and glanced over at him. "You're not like the firefighters I've met in the past," she said. "They were adrenaline junkies who couldn't wait for the next fire. Maybe just because it gave them the chance to talk about that fire, how dangerous it was, how close they came to dying in it."

"Sounds like the firefighters you met were idiots," he said.

"You haven't worked with any like that?" she asked with another pointed glance. Then she focused on the road, driving through the green light.

They were nearly at his firehouse, where probably a few of the guys were up talking about the fire, about the body they'd found. There were some who thrived on the adrenaline of the job. He sighed.

She chuckled. "Thought so."

"But most of us do this job because we want to help people," he insisted. That was the motive for every single member of his hotshot team, except maybe one. The one who was sabotaging the equipment, getting people hurt.

Was a member of the team really responsible for those accidents? For the faulty equipment? The superintendent of the team, Braden Zimmer, had received an ominous note of his own a while back claiming that one of them wasn't who he thought he was.

Braden had assumed the person was referring either to the arsonist who'd terrorized Northern Lakes several months ago or to whoever had been sabotaging the equipment. The arsonist hadn't been a member of the team, so the note must have been referring to the saboteur.

Or Ethan Sommerly. He wasn't who everyone had thought he was, as Trent's own sister had revealed. His cell vibrated again, probably with another text from Brittney. He'd have to talk to her eventually, but he hoped he could put it off until Detective Bolton figured out who had sent him that card, who wanted him to suffer. He was already suffering at the thought that someone might have died because of him.

What had he done or failed to do that made this person want revenge on him? His head throbbed, and he raised one of his hands to rub his temples.

"That's why I'm driving you back here," the detective remarked. "You're clearly exhausted."

She didn't even know the half of it, of everything that had been going on with his hotshot team. And he needed to tell her just in case that murder and that fire had something to do with all that.

With the saboteur...

Trent had fallen strangely silent on the last few miles to the firehouse, as if he dreaded going back there. Or maybe he dreaded her being there with him, interrogating his coworkers. Heather had no choice. She had to do her job. She had to find out the identity of the woman who'd died in his house, as well as the person responsible for her death.

Or maybe he was just, as she'd mentioned moments ago, exhausted. He'd just recently returned from a wildfire out West and then had helped out fighting the fire at his own house. Despite their efforts, the house was probably another casualty, like the woman found inside it.

Where was he going to stay? She knew he wouldn't put one of his friends and certainly not his sister in danger and stay with them. What about the firehouse?

Or a hotel?

Would he be safe at either of those places?

But this person, the one who'd written that ominous note, didn't sound as if he or she wanted Trent dead. They just wanted him to suffer.

For what?

"You really have no idea who would have sent you that note?" she asked as she turned onto the street where his firehouse was located. All the buildings around it were dark but for security lighting. It was late. That was why she hadn't made any more calls tonight. Chances were the family of that woman would report her missing if they hadn't already. She'd asked Dispatch to contact her immediately if anyone called about a missing woman.

Unfortunately, Heather knew where the woman was: the morgue. DNA or dental records would be necessary to determine her identity. Even family members wouldn't recognize her in that condition, and Heather wouldn't want to put them through that.

But she'd put Trent Miles through it. A twinge of guilt struck her, and she grimaced. She'd still considered him a suspect at the time, so she'd wanted to shake him. And she had, but not into a confession. He hadn't done anything wrong, at least not that she knew about. But he'd curiously remained silent in response to her question.

"Did you think of someone?" she asked. Or maybe of something he'd done to someone?

Maybe he wasn't as perfect as he looked.

But then who could be?

She certainly wasn't. She was probably handling this whole case incorrectly, and not just because she wanted to close it so quickly, but because of him.

He was distracting. Unsettling. So unsettling and distracting that she drove past the firehouse. But a parking lot, with an assortment of trucks in it, was on the other side. She slowed and steered into the lot and breathed a soft sigh of relief that he probably hadn't noticed how he got to her.

She found an open parking space near the street. "Looks like a lot of people are still here," she remarked.

Trent didn't look around the lot but looked at her with his brow furrowed slightly and an intensity in his light brown eyes. But still he remained silent.

"What is it?" she asked. "Who did you think of?"

He shook his head. "It's not... I don't have a name. I don't have any idea..."

"Then what is it?" she asked. Because he was holding something back, something weighing on him that he hadn't shared with her, that he almost seemed to want to share. "What's wrong?"

He released a shaky sigh. "When we go in there, what are we going to say to the crew? What's your *plan* for this?"

A smile twitched her lips. "Ah, you're worried about my plan to play your girlfriend."

"Yes. I'm worried you're going to get hurt."

"I told you not to worry about me. I thought you were worried now about yourself, about you getting hurt," she said, reminding him of what he'd said back in the interrogation room. "I figured then that you were refer-

ring to your life or your heart, but you must have really
been talking about your image. Don't I measure up to
your dating standards?"

He was probably only attracted to women who made
an effort with their appearance, who wore makeup and
curled or flat-ironed their hair into submission. Heather
just dragged hers back into a hair tie and swiped a little
mascara onto her lashes if she remembered. And she
certainly didn't dress to attract male attention, usually
the opposite. On duty and off, she wore black pants, a
sweater and long coat in the winter. And in the summer,
black pants and a tank top with an oversize blouse, so
she could hide her holster.

He laughed. "Fishing for compliments, Detective?
You've got to know you're gorgeous."

Her pulse sped up so much it seemed to skip a beat.
His tone was too matter-of-fact for him to be just trying
to charm her. Or maybe he was that good of a charmer,
and if he was, she might have to work a little harder to
protect her heart than she'd thought.

"You're already the best boyfriend I've had in a
while," she said with a smile.

"But I don't even know your first name," he said.
"So I'm not sure any of my coworkers are really going
to buy this relationship, especially when they all know
I haven't been dating for a while. And a detective? Are
you sure we should tell them what you do?"

She wasn't charmed anymore. She glared at him.
"What's wrong with *me* being a detective?" Too many
men had a problem with her career. The ones she'd dated
and the ones she worked with; even her dad thought it
was too dangerous for her, that she should have a nice
safe career or be a stay-at-home mom like her older sis-

ters and her own mother had been. While her mom had been happy with that choice, Heather would be even more miserable than her older sisters were.

He held up his hands as if she was pointing a gun at him and looked about to shoot. "Nothing's wrong with detectives. But you know there's always been a rivalry between the fire department and the police department."

She shrugged. "So? I've dated firemen before, and they obviously dated me."

He sucked in a breath as if she had shot him. "You have?" Then he nodded. "Guess that explains why you think we're all daredevils who want fires to happen just so we can brag about them. You dated the wrong firemen."

She nodded now. "You'll get no argument from me on that. But even though I dated duds, I know of a lot of relationships between cops and firefighters, as well as between cops and paramedics and cops and nurses—"

"Okay, okay," he said. "You don't have to convince me."

Heat rushed to her face. Had she sounded like she was begging him to date her? "This is just for pretend, you know," she reminded him. "Just a ruse to flush out whoever the hell is out to hurt someone close to you."

"I know," he said. "But if we don't want everyone else to know that this is just a pretend relationship, I really think I should know your first name. Calling you Detective Bolton in front of my friends isn't going to fool them into thinking we're really romantically involved."

A smile twitched up her lips again. "Maybe that's my kink," she said. "I prefer you call me Detective, and if you don't, I use my handcuffs and my nightstick on you."

He closed his eyes and groaned. "You have a wicked sense of humor, Detective."

"Who says I'm kidding?" she asked, but she was only joking.

"I think you're wrong about nobody falling for you. I think plenty of men have."

"I was just messing with you. I'm not really kinky," she admitted.

"You're funny, and that's even sexier than kinky." He opened his eyes, which were suddenly dark, the pupils dilated.

Was he actually attracted to her? Or was he just getting into the role she'd talked him into playing? Her boyfriend. She nearly snorted at the possibility of that ever becoming a reality. A guy like him, this good-looking, was probably used to women throwing themselves at him and lavishing him with time and attention.

Heather was too busy to dote on anyone, which reminded her that she should be busy trying to clear this case. Trying to find out who that poor woman was.

"We better go inside," she said. "Find out if anyone knows who might have been in your house tonight."

He nodded. "Okay, so you're just going to ask…"

"What are you nervous about?"

"How do I act like we're a couple?" he asked. "I've never gone undercover before."

Maybe not this way, but Trent Miles had definitely spent some time under the covers playing the part of boyfriend. Since he'd admitted that he hadn't had any lasting relationships, maybe all he'd ever done was play.

She smiled and assured him, "I think you'll be just fine. And my name is Heather."

"Heather…" he repeated in that deep, sexy voice.

And she had to resist the urge to shiver as her skin tingled a bit, like he'd touched her, when all he'd done was say her name. She would have to keep reminding herself that this was just a ploy, a way to find out who a victim was and how she'd become one, and to close a case. She couldn't get distracted again. Next time she might miss more than a firehouse.

She drew in a breath and reached for the door handle. "Okay, when we get inside, you need to let me know which of your coworkers are on that list you gave me of who had the key code to your place."

"So we're just going to be straight that you're investigating, even though we're involved? Wouldn't that be a conflict of interest?" he asked.

Damn him and his logic.

"It would be if we were really dating," she agreed. "But since we're only pretending, it's fine for me to investigate. Do you think any of your coworkers are really going to be concerned about police protocol anyway?"

He shrugged. "I don't know. If you're right, and one of them might be involved in what happened at my house, that person could be very concerned."

"Agreed," she said. "That's the reason for the pretend relationship. And we can just say we've been keeping it quiet because of our careers, being so busy, you being gone so much, we didn't know if it would last, yada yada…"

He chuckled. "So my real reasons for not having a relationship."

"Mine, too," she said. "And then we say that, now with this happening at your house and the fire, we need to continue to keep it quiet at least for my job. We bring them in on the secret with us and hope that inspires them to share some secrets of their own."

"I'm not sure that'll work," he said.

She sighed. "It might not. But if the person who sent you the card is behind what happened at your house, then they'll want to try to take me out if we can convince them we're together."

"That's what worries me," he said and then uttered a sigh of his own. A heavy one that sounded resigned; by now he had to know he wasn't going to win this argument with her.

"Okay," she said. "Go time." She opened the door and stepped out into the parking lot. The temperature had dropped, the cold in such sharp contrast to the heat they'd generated in the car that she sucked in a breath and a few of the snowflakes that drifted down.

"Okay?" Trent asked as he came around the vehicle to join her on the driver's side.

She nodded. "Just colder than I thought."

"'Tis the season," he said but shivered a little as well. "The entrance I have the key to is over here." He moved his hand to her back, planting it just above the curve of her hips as he turned her toward the building.

Heat streaked through Heather, chasing away the chill. As they walked across the parking lot, an engine started and revved. Then lights flashed on high beams, bright and blinding as the vehicle turned toward them.

Heather squinted against the light, trying to see the driver as she unzipped and reached inside her coat for her weapon.

Tires squealed and the engine roared as the vehicle bore down on them. And they stood, frozen, in that bright light.

* * *

Were the firefighter and the detective dead? A glance in the rearview mirror as the driver sped away confirmed they were lying on the pavement. It had all happened so fast. The driver wasn't even sure if they'd struck them. The vehicle was so big and had been moving so fast. And their bodies were lying there, unmoving. Had they just jumped out of the way? Or had the vehicle struck them but the driver was so high on adrenaline they hadn't noticed?

Hopefully they were dead.

Both of them. So Trent Miles hadn't just lost someone close to him. He'd lost his own life as well.

Chapter 5

Had the vehicle struck her? Trent wasn't even sure if it had struck him. Everything had happened so fast. One second they were standing in the bright beams of those headlights and the next they were somersaulting through the air, trying to leap out of the way of the bumper of the speeding vehicle.

He'd struck the pavement so hard it had knocked the breath from his lungs. She'd grunted then, too, but now she was frighteningly quiet as she lay beside him on the pavement in the shadow of the firehouse. He couldn't see her face, couldn't see if she was conscious or even hear if she was breathing.

"Detect—Heather," he said, his voice gruff with the fear he hadn't had time to feel when that vehicle had tried to run them down. Tried…?

Maybe it had succeeded. While it hadn't hit him, maybe it had struck the detective.

"Heather!" he called louder, his heart pounding fast and furiously.

Still lying on her back, she turned only her head toward him, and her eyes gleamed in the shadows. "Are you okay?" she asked.

His heart skipped a beat now that her first concern was for him. But she was an officer of the law and had vowed to serve and protect. So this was just her professional reaction, not a personal one. He nodded. "Yeah, I'm fine. What about you?"

She rolled to her side and pushed herself up from the pavement. A grimace gripped her beautiful face for a moment before she sighed and nodded. "Yeah, I'm fine. I didn't get hit. Just hit the ground hard."

Trent shoved himself up and to his feet, ignoring the slight shakiness of his legs. He had bumps and bruises, too; he could feel the ache in his muscles already. And he grimaced, too.

"Are you sure?" she asked. "Nothing broken? Do we need to call an ambulance or make a trip to the ER?"

He shook his head. "I'm fine. Are you sure you are? You said you hit the ground hard, and I know I did."

She took a few steps and nodded. "Yeah. Nothing broken on me."

"That was too damn close!" Hopefully it had just been an accident, someone who hadn't seen them starting across the parking lot.

"It was perfect!" she exclaimed, excitement quivering in her voice. "The plan is already working!"

Metal creaked as the back door of the firehouse opened.

Heather reached for her weapon, but Trent caught her arm as he turned toward one of his bosses.

"What the hell happened?" the lieutenant asked. "Did that vehicle just run you down? Are you two all right?"

"Yes, we're fine," Trent said.

"Did you get a good look at it?" Heather asked. "Do you know who was driving it?"

The man stared at her for a moment. "I don't know who you are."

"Detective Bolton," Trent said. "And, Heather, this is Lieutenant Ken Stokes. He was in charge of the crew that responded to the fire at my house."

The lieutenant extended his hand to her. "I'm not sure I'll be able to help you. Our fire investigator is who you'll want to coordinate your investigation with…"

"I will follow up with him, too," Heather said. "This is a possible murder investigation."

Trent almost hoped the woman had killed herself in the scenario Heather had suggested in the morgue. Then he wouldn't have to worry about anyone else getting hurt. But still a life had been lost, a life that wouldn't have been lost if not for him. A pang of guilt struck him, and he grimaced again.

"Are you really okay?" the lieutenant asked.

Trent nodded.

"You must have seen something, to come out here like you did," Heather prodded the man.

"Oh, yeah, I was on the second floor, in the kitchen." He gestured toward a window that overlooked the parking lot. "I heard the revving engine and squeal of tires, but all I saw was the roof of the vehicle. I couldn't see what it even was or who was driving it."

"What color was it?" Heather asked. "Was it long, like an SUV, or shorter like a truck?"

The man shrugged and shook his head. "I don't

know. It all happened so fast. Didn't you two see what it was? Who it was?"

Heather cursed. "No. The lights blinded me." She glanced at Trent, as if asking him.

And he shook his head. "Just the lights. That's all I saw." Then he focused on the lieutenant again. "What are you doing here still?"

"I stuck around, figuring you'd need to come back for your truck. And that you'd probably wind up staying here since your house is uninhabitable now."

"He's going to stay with me," Heather said. "We just came by to pick up his truck."

The lieutenant's brow furrowed as he stared at them with confusion. "I thought you were just investigating…"

"My interest in the fire at Trent's is personal as well as professional," Heather said. "But that's not something a lot of people need to know."

But it was too late for that. The door behind the lieutenant had remained open, and a few of the crew slipped out from behind it. From the looks of shock and speculation on their faces, it was clear they'd heard what she'd said.

While Trent's stomach muscles tightened with apprehension, she smiled slightly. This was all part of her plan. To do what? Find out the identity of the woman in his house? Find who'd sent Trent that card? Or to get herself killed?

He shuddered over how close they'd just come to that happening. But except for that initial silence from her, when the wind had probably been knocked out of her like from him, she was unfazed. He couldn't say the same. Even after everything that had happened recently with the hotshots, he wasn't used to this, wasn't used to being the target of someone's rage and violence.

He didn't like it. Not one bit. Especially if whoever was after him was someone close to him. Someone he worked with.

Heather stepped closer to him, and he didn't know if it was part of the act until she nudged her elbow into his ribs. And he remembered what she'd wanted him to do. So he introduced her to the guys.

"You met my lieutenant. These guys are Gordy Stutz, Harold Wyzocky and Tom Johnson. You all stranded here since my place burned down?"

Gordy, an older guy with thinning hair, shook his head. "Your beds are more comfortable than the bunks, but I've been staying here during my shifts. It's been quieter at the firehouse than your place the past couple of weeks."

"What's been going on while I was out of town?" Trent asked.

Tom, a young Black man, snorted. "Ask Barry. He's been the one using it the most since your sister hasn't been around." The guy grinned. "Speaking of your sister…"

Trent glared at the younger man. "My sister's off-limits." He'd had to tell his crew that a few times. Unlike his hotshot team, who hadn't known about his relationship to Brittney Townsend until a week or so after she'd shown up in Northern Lakes, the local crew had always known about their relationship. She tended to drop by the firehouse a lot, much to Tom's delight.

She hadn't been doing that lately, though, not since her betrayal and his refusal to talk to her. If she had been the one found in his house…

He swallowed down the guilt threatening to gag him. He couldn't make up with her now, especially not after what had just happened. Heather had nearly been run down just for walking next to him.

"Where is Barry?" Heather asked the question.

The guys glanced around the lot. "He was here a little while ago. He must have just left."

Heather glanced up at Trent, and he read the question in her eyes. Could it have been Barry who'd tried to run them down? He shook his head.

"Where's he going?" she asked. "Since Trent's house burned down? Why wouldn't he stay here?"

"His shift was over," Tom replied. "He was going home to his place in the burbs and his wife and kids." He grimaced as if the thought of a family disgusted him.

"Were his wife and kids staying at my place, too?" he asked Gordy. "Is that why it was too loud?"

Gordy smirked, then glanced at Heather and shook his head. "I don't know what was going on."

Trent didn't have to be a trained investigator to realize Gordy was lying. They must have heard the part about her being a detective, and it was clear they weren't going to reveal any more information.

Heather was determined, though. "You all had the key code to Trent's place," she said. "You know that a body was found inside. Do you have any idea who she was?"

Tom's mouth dropped open, and his eyes went wide. "She? Was it your sis—"

Trent shook his head. "No. Brittney is fine." From the number of texts and voice mails she'd left for him, she was probably frustrated as hell that he wasn't talking to her. But that was for the best right now, or hers might have been that body found inside his place.

"That's why we need to know if any of you gave the code out to anyone else," Heather said. "We need to know if you have any idea who that might have been."

"You're not able to identify her with DNA or dental records?" the lieutenant asked.

"We need some DNA or dental records to use for comparison, so we can determine a match," Heather explained.

"I really don't know," Harold said with a glance at the others, as if he suspected one of them might.

But they crossed their arms and shook their heads. And Trent knew that none of them was going to talk, at least not to the detective. Remembering they had another role to play, Trent slid his arm around her.

She tensed at his touch. Maybe she'd forgotten their game. Then she slid her arm around him and smiled up at him.

His body tensed also, muscles tightening as desire gripped him. Or maybe it was just the adrenaline from their near miss moments ago. "Hon, my truck is over here," he said. "I'll grab it and follow you back to your place." Because he had absolutely no idea where she lived. He wasn't even sure he was really going to follow her. He just wanted to get the hell out of that parking lot where they could have died. He wanted to get away from the crew that he couldn't trust.

"The captain told me to tell you to take as long as you need off," Lieutenant Stokes told him.

"Of course he did," Gordy murmured with a trace of the resentment Trent had detected in him before.

Some of the crew at this firehouse thought he got

special treatment because the captain had been friends with his dad, because the two men had served together. And because Trent had been a Marine as well. Maybe they weren't wrong. Manny had never made him choose between Trent's full-time position at the local firehouse and his gig as a hotshot. Other team members hadn't been as fortunate with the flexibility as Trent had.

But none of them had lost their house to a fire and maybe someone they knew along with it, or at least someone who'd been killed because of being in their house. Someone else could have just been killed as well. He tightened his arm around Heather for a moment before releasing her. Even though he walked toward his truck and she toward her vehicle, he wasn't sure he should really follow her home or just keep driving. It would probably be best for her. And maybe for him as well…if he kept going, getting as far as he could away from her.

Usually, Heather monitored her rearview mirror to make sure nobody was following her. With all the cases she'd cleared, and the criminals she'd sent to prison, she'd gotten a few warnings like Trent had. But hers didn't come in Christmas cards, and the postmarks were easy enough to read because they generally came from prison. So she didn't worry much about a vengeful criminal following her home, but she was cautious.

Now she kept glancing into her rearview mirror to make sure she was being followed, that Trent was sticking with the plan. It was working. After nearly getting hit in the parking lot, he must have realized that.

Too bad they hadn't gotten a good look at the vehicle that had nearly run them down, and would have had they not leaped out of the way. Tomorrow she would pull all the security footage in the area, but for tonight...

She wanted to get Trent back to her place. He had to be exhausted. Physically and probably emotionally as well. He'd been so worried that the body found in his house was his sister's. Despite being angry with her, he obviously still loved Brittney Townsend very much, so much that he wanted her to stay away from him.

He didn't love Heather. Hell, after she'd treated him like a suspect, he probably didn't even like her, but he clearly wanted to keep her safe, too. So she kept watching, making sure that the lights of his truck stayed behind her, that he was following her home. Because she was so focused on him, she would probably miss anyone else who might be following them. Was that vehicle that had nearly run them down behind Trent, following him? Waiting for another opportunity to try to kill them?

Because it wasn't just Heather who'd nearly been struck. Trent could have been hurt as well. Probably was hurt and just too proud to admit it. Was he too proud to stay with her? Or too stubborn?

His lights remained behind her, but there was more than just his back there. Light shone through the cab of his truck, illuminating the dark shadow of his tall body behind the wheel. He was a big man, but he could have been hurt just as badly as she if that vehicle had struck them.

Maybe the killer had decided that, after killing whoever had been in Trent's house, it was time to kill him now. Heather was definitely not the only one in danger. He was, too. And he needed her help and her protection; she wasn't sure if he would actually accept it, though.

If he didn't, the next time he might not be so lucky.

Instead of surviving with probably just the same bumps and bruises, he could wind up dead…like the woman in his house.

Brittney grasped her cell phone in one hand as she stepped out of her small SUV. Maybe Trent would call her back or at least text her. But she doubted it.

Was he that mad at her? Or was it this…?

Crime scene tape, cordoning off the area around his house, fluttered in the slight evening breeze. Beyond the tape, faint plumes of smoke rose from the burned-out structure. The acrid odor hung in the air, burning her nose and lungs with each breath she took.

"What the hell…" She rasped the words out of her scratchy throat.

When the call had come into the TV station about a fire, she'd been trying to edit that damn fluff piece so that when it aired she didn't undo all the strides she'd made to become a serious journalist. She'd wanted to take that call about the fire, especially when she learned there had also been a report of shots fired at the same address, but the producer had assigned it to one of the male reporters like he usually did with anything that might be a crime or at all interesting.

She really needed to find another job, one where they would take her seriously. But right now she needed to find her brother. He'd left her the voice mail and texts after the call had come into the station about the fire, so he had to be okay. He wasn't the body that had been found inside the house.

That person was still unidentified, or so the coroner's office had claimed. Did Trent know who it was? Had he thought it was her? Was that why he'd finally contacted her again after weeks of the silent treatment? Probably. Because he clearly hadn't forgiven her, or he would have returned her calls or texts. Unless he was busy dealing with this, with the fire, with the investigation.

There was a detective on the case already: Heather Bolton. From what Brittney had learned about her from her contacts in the police department, Bolton was a badass with the best case clearance rate in the precinct.

The right person was on the case for Trent as long as he had nothing to do with this. And he couldn't...

Brittney had spent so much of her life idolizing her big brother that she worried she wasn't always objective when it came to him. She'd recently learned how many secrets people were capable of keeping, even from those closest to them.

Trent had certainly been keeping secrets from her about what had been going on with his hotshot team. After that arsonist had been caught all those months ago, Brittney had thought the only danger he faced were the fires he'd fought. But there had been so much more going on, with sabotage, with one hotshot's death, with the attempts on the lives of so many other hotshots.

Was this fire and that body related to his hotshot team and what had been happening in Northern Lakes?

Was Trent the next target of whoever had been targeting his team? She turned her attention to her cell again. Still no response from Trent.

So she called. Predictably it went right to voice mail. Was it just her calls that he wasn't taking, though? Or was he unable to take anyone's calls right now?

She held up her cell and snapped a picture of his smoking house. Then she sent it to him with the caption: What the hell is going on, big brother?

Chapter 6

What the hell was he thinking? Trent had no business following Heather home like some stray dog. She was a detective working a case, not a bodyguard. Not that he needed one. She probably needed one more, if whoever had nearly run them down believed that they were together. That they were close.

But was Trent following her home going to protect her or put her in more danger? He wasn't sure, but he suspected that someone might be following him. The same set of lights had stayed pretty steady behind him. With few other vehicles on the road this late, it was easy to track them. A big vehicle, like the one that had nearly run them down.

He shuddered as he considered how close it had come to striking them. How badly they could have been hurt, or worse, if it had struck them. He eased his foot off the accelerator, leaving more space between his truck and the back of Detective Bolton's unmarked police vehicle. He shouldn't go home with her, shouldn't put her in any more danger than she already was. But...

The vehicle behind him slowed as well, then stopped, and a signal light blinked just before it turned left onto another street. Ahead of him, Heather's right signal light blinked, and she slowed before turning onto a residential street. But she didn't continue driving. She braked just around that turn, as if waiting for him.

He had no doubt she would probably follow him if he drove past. She might even turn on the siren and flash the light all but hidden on the dash of her vehicle. He wasn't going to escape her, but he didn't necessarily want to.

He really didn't have any place else to go but a hotel or motel. And it wasn't as if Heather Bolton couldn't take care of herself and him.

He braked and turned onto the street she had, and her vehicle started forward again. He followed her down a couple of blocks until she turned again, this time into a driveway. She parked outside a closed garage door. The driveway wasn't long enough to accommodate his truck, so he parked at the curb in front of the bungalow that outside lights illuminated. Unlike the bungalows on either side of it that had aluminum siding and dark shutters, this one had been updated with cedar shake siding and some stone.

He'd always wanted to make his place look like this, but with as much as he'd worked, he hadn't had the time. Maybe one of his neighbors had torched the place because it had been the ugliest house on the block with its faded beige aluminum siding and sagging black shutters. Or maybe they'd torched it because they thought he was a drug-dealing gangbanger like the neighbor had led Heather to believe.

She didn't believe that anymore or she wouldn't have invited him to stay with her. Had she invited or ordered him? He didn't know for certain.

A fist tapped the passenger's window, and he jumped, startled. Then her face appeared, her eyes intent as she stared through the glass at him. He pressed the power locks, unlocking the door, and she opened it. "You going to sit out here what's left of the night?"

"I've slept in my truck before," he said.

"What? After your parents died?" she asked.

"No, I wasn't homeless. Brittney's mother and step-father took me in then," he said. Probably because Brittney had begged them to and they'd refused her nothing. A pang of guilt struck his heart that he kept refusing to even talk to her. Inside his pocket, his cell kept vibrating with texts and reminders that he had unread texts. Probably several of them by now. He didn't want her in the middle of this, though, didn't want her in danger because of him. "But I was twelve then," he reminded her. "I don't need anyone to take me in now."

"I'm not taking you in out of pity or anything else," she said. "This is just a ploy to flush out a killer, and it's working."

"Too well," he said. "Shouldn't I park someplace else in case I was followed?"

"I hope you were followed. That's the whole point of this. They need to see your vehicle here, at my house, to believe that we're together. This is getting personal for me, too, now. I want to catch whoever tried to run us down." Her green eyes glinted with the determination in her voice.

"Do you always get your man, Detective Bolton?"

She snorted. "I don't want a man. It's criminals I want and only to put them behind bars. They are my fires to put out."

He drew in a breath and nodded. "Okay…" For some reason he trusted her, trusted that she would catch whoever was behind that fire and the incident in the firehouse parking lot.

He wasn't sure he should trust himself right now, though. Maybe his instincts were wrong. Obviously, he'd already trusted someone he shouldn't have. A couple of someones, actually. His sister and whoever had burned down his house, which was probably someone who had the key code. Someone with whom he worked.

Heather had come up to his truck for two reasons. One, because she wasn't sure he was going to get out of it and come up to the house. The other, so she could check the street, see if any other vehicle besides theirs had turned onto it. She didn't notice any other headlights, but a strange foreboding gripped her. And despite the thickness of her puffy jacket, goose bumps lifted her skin beneath it. Was someone out there, in the shadows, watching them?

Or was her sense of foreboding because of the hotshot firefighter she'd invited into her home? This was the plan, though, she had to remind herself. To fool whoever was after him.

Trent grabbed a duffel bag off the passenger's seat and stepped out of his truck. After clicking the fob to lock it, he came around the box of the truck to where she stood on the sidewalk. "Nice place," he remarked as he stared over her head at the house.

She smiled. "Yes, it has become my dad's retirement project." She chuckled. "Probably a way for him to get some time away from my mother and eat and drink what he wants." She often found an empty can or two of beer in her recycling and greasy wrappers from take-out in her trash.

Trent tensed. "If he comes and goes, is this a good idea for me to stay here?"

"Afraid he might threaten you to make an honest woman out of me?" she asked.

"Afraid he might get hurt, just like I'm afraid that you might, especially after that vehicle nearly ran us down." He shuddered as if cold. And maybe he was since he must have taken off his firefighter jacket in his truck and wore just his shirt and the firefighter pants. But she had a feeling that what chilled him was how close they'd come to getting hurt.

"Don't worry about my dad," she said as she started walking toward the side door of her house. "Mom has him working on some projects at their house, getting it ready for the holidays. He won't be allowed over here until he finishes up there, and knowing how they can never agree, that won't be until after the holidays."

She pulled open the screen door and punched in her key code for the lock on her cedar-stained wood door. "These are easier than handing out keys," she said as the light on the lock blinked green and clicked. "Especially since my dad tends to lose them and my sisters tend to overuse them. That's why I put in separate codes for each person. You didn't do that with yours?"

He shook his head. "No. I just bought the lock that has the one code in it. I travel so much, I didn't want to have to remember more than one. I just wish now that I hadn't let so many people use my place."

"I'll work on that list tomorrow," she said. "It's late now." She pushed open her door and stepped inside the dark house.

Trent hesitated, standing outside under the small gabled roof over the side door. The wind kicked up, swirling snowflakes around the house with a blast of cold air.

She sucked in a breath as the cold swept through the open door and hit her even inside the house. He had to be freezing. "You don't have to be scared," she teased him. "I didn't lure you here to take advantage of you."

Finally he stepped across the threshold, and in the limited space between the stairs leading down to the basement and the ones leading up to the kitchen, he stood close to her. So close that his body brushed against hers, and heat shot through her. "That's too bad..." he murmured as he stared down at her.

Ignoring the heat and the mad pounding of her heart, she laughed. "I shouldn't be surprised that you would play with fire. It's your job, after all."

"That's not playing," he said with a heavy sigh.

This close to him, she could smell the smoke on his clothes, probably in his hair and on his skin. "And neither is this," she reminded him. "We're trying to catch whoever is after you."

"They're after you now, too," he said.

"Yes, the plan is working," she reminded him. And feeling that sudden chill, that sense of being watched, she peered around him through the open door. But even with her yard lights on, she couldn't see anyone. If they were out there, they were standing deep in the shadows. Hiding...

Waiting…

Like that person must have waited for them at the firehouse. They must have assumed Trent would have to return for his truck or to stay in the bunk room since his home was a total loss. That threat in the Christmas card wasn't just against whoever was close to him. It was against Trent, too.

He must have felt the chill, because he pulled the door shut and turned the dead bolt.

She climbed up the couple of steps into the kitchen. But when she reached out to flip on the lights, Trent caught her wrist in his big hand.

"Wait," he whispered, his mouth close to her ear.

She tried not to shiver at the heat of his breath against her skin. "What?" she whispered back.

"There's someone in here…" he whispered. "I hear something…"

She tensed and reached for her weapon. But as she listened, she recognized the stealthy noise. The creeping footfalls and then the whoosh of air as the cat jumped onto the counter and stared at them with his eyes gleaming in the dark. Eyes nearly the same color as Trent's.

He gasped and stepped around her, as if to protect her. And Heather flipped on the lights then. The cat hissed at the stranger in their home, the black fur rising on his neck and his suddenly arched back. Then he jumped down from the counter and ran off, footfalls louder now than when he'd sneaked out from wherever he'd probably been sleeping. "Some watchdog you have there," Trent said with a deep chuckle.

"Oh, Sammy would tear you to pieces if he thought I was in danger," Heather assured him. "You should see what he's done to my reading chair in my bedroom. It must look awful threatening in the middle of the night."

"Are you inviting me into your bedroom?" he asked.

She snorted. "You get the guest room, buddy. This relationship is only pretend. Remember that." That last warning wasn't just for him but for herself as well. "But feel free to raid the fridge."

She pulled open the door of the stainless-steel appliance and glanced inside at the mostly empty shelves and groaned. "But you better like pickles." A jar of baby dills and some bottles of condiments were about all that were inside, as well as a few cans of beer her father must have left behind and her green teas. She couldn't have one of those now or she would be awake all night.

She would probably be awake all night anyway, though. And it wouldn't be just because she had to stay vigilant in case they had been followed back to her place.

"I'm not hungry. I'd just really like to take a shower." He held up his duffel bag. "And use your washer and dryer if you have them. I haven't had a chance to wash my stuff from out West yet."

An acrid smoke smell emanated from that bag just as it did from his hair and the clothes he was wearing. "That must have been some wildfire," she mused. And he'd returned from that to battle a blaze at his own home. "The washer and dryer are downstairs." She pointed back down the steps they'd walked up. "And there's a hall bathroom with a great shower my dad recently remodeled."

"Do you want to use it first?" he asked.

She shook her head. "I have an en suite. Dad took out a tiny third bedroom to make a big primary suite."

"With your reading chair," he said.

"Yes." She wouldn't be reading tonight, though. She would be listening for any sign of an intruder. After pointing out the guest room and bath to him, she headed into her suite. She took a quick shower and then pulled out her laptop and cell to check messages and send messages, following up with the crime scene techs and the fire investigator.

It was late, though, so she didn't expect responses. It was so late that she should get some rest. She'd also requested extra patrols in her area overnight; they would be vigilant and close in case she needed backup. She was a light sleeper and would notice if someone tried to get inside. She was such a light sleeper that the sound of Trent showering kept her awake, imagining how he must look standing under the spray, the water rushing over his muscles and sleek skin. Not only was there the possibility of an intruder coming into her house but also into her mind: Trent.

Heat rushed over her, so hot that beads of sweat formed on her forehead and above her lip and trickled between her breasts. Needing some ice water, she tossed back her covers and headed to the kitchen. Her suite was at the end of the hall, so she had to walk past the bathroom where the water continued to run and steam slipped out from beneath the door. Steam with the scent of soap and man.

She hadn't had the smell of man in her house in a long while. Too long. That probably explained why the thought of him naked had her so hot and bothered. No. The thought of Trent naked would bother her no matter what; the man was gorgeous. But he was also in danger, and now, thanks to her plan, so was she. So she had to stay focused.

Had to stay alert. She opened a cabinet and pulled out a large insulated glass, then pushed it against the automatic ice maker. The machine rumbled, then chucked shards of crushed ice into her glass. Maybe instead of water, she should pour one of her green teas over the ice. That way she would stay awake and aware of every noise.

But this late at night, the caffeine would make her jittery, and she wanted to be alert, not trigger-happy. So she switched the ice maker to water. Once her glass was filled, she turned to head back to her bedroom and nearly collided with a big, bare, muscular chest. So much for being alert.

The noise of the ice maker had drowned out the sounds of his approach. She sucked in a breath that smelled like the steam that had escaped from the bathroom, of soap and man. But this close to him, the scent was even more intense.

Her reaction was, too. Her nipples tightened beneath the thin material of the oversize T-shirt she wore as a nightgown. His gaze, those topaz eyes gleaming in the faint glow of the under-cabinet lighting, dropped to her shirt, and he sucked in a breath.

Heather lowered her gaze, too, following the rippling ridges of abdomen muscles to the towel knotted low around his lean hips. The man was the next level of fitness, like there wasn't an ounce of fat on him. Anywhere.

She only saw those sculpted muscles and some red patches that were maybe bruises from when they'd hit the asphalt in the firehouse parking lot, possibly burns from that wildfire or the fire at his house. "Are you okay?" she asked.

He groaned a little. "Just going down to get my clothes out of the dryer." And to do that he had to pass through the kitchen, past her.

She should have stayed in her room, because seeing him like this, standing so close to him, had her even hotter and more restless than before. Maybe she needed to pour that ice water over her head. "I'll…" Her voice was just a husky rasp. "…get out of your way, then." She moved to step around him, but he was so big and the space in her galley kitchen so narrow that she touched him. Her hip bumped against his thigh, and one of her breasts brushed his muscled arm. She nearly moaned as desire shot from her tightened nipple to her core.

He reached out, clasping her hips in his big hands. "You're not in my way," he said, but his voice was so low, so gruff, and the look on his face, the heat in his eyes…

She had no doubt that he felt this, too. This intense attraction, desire.

Need.

We're just supposed to be playing. Pretending…

This wasn't real. The relationship or the attraction. But it felt more intense than anything Heather had experienced before. Maybe because he was so unreal. So handsome, so fit that he couldn't be human. She reached out with her free hand and touched his chest. His heart leaped beneath her palm, then pounded hard and fast.

He drew in a long, ragged breath, as if bracing himself to step away. But instead of releasing her, he clutched her hips tighter and pulled her just a little closer. "I know this isn't what you intended when you told me to stay here…with you…" He closed his eyes and grimaced, as if struggling.

She was struggling, too, and her usual reaction in tense situations like this was to ease the tension with humor. "How do you know?" she asked. "Maybe this was exactly what I intended." And she slid her palm across his chest.

"You're killing me," he said, his jaw clenched as he opened his eyes and stared so intently at her. "I'm trying to resist temptation right now."

"I'm tempting?"

"You're gorgeous. So damn sexy with your hair down and that shirt…" He groaned and closed his eyes again, definitely trying to shut her out.

If only he could turn her off…

Maybe if she closed her eyes…

If she shut him out…

But she could still see him in her mind, all those sculpted muscles and sleek naked skin. Now she could smell him even more intensely and hear him breathe. She was so aware and so damn attracted to him.

His breaths were coming faster and shallower, but his chest moved beneath her hand as if those breaths were hard to come by. She could also feel the heat of his body, the smoothness of his skin.

She opened her eyes just as his thick lashes fluttered open. And he stared down at her with the same raw desire that coursed through her.

And suddenly it was hard for her to breathe.

To not get caught following, a turn had been taken a while ago. A turn that had let Trent Miles and the female detective slip away. For a moment.

Driving up and down the side streets they might

have taken eventually led to the discovery of the hot-shot firefighter's truck parked outside a small house with cedar siding and stone. The detective's unmarked police vehicle was parked in the driveway. Like being unmarked fooled anyone…

Like everybody didn't know what and who she was. And now where she lived for however long she remained living.

She should have already been dead. Her and Trent Miles. They'd avoided getting hurt in the parking lot of the firehouse. But their luck wouldn't last.

And now that they had so easily been found, neither would their lives…

Chapter 7

Trent awoke slowly...due to a strange niggling sensation that someone was watching him. Staring at him...

Through him...

He hadn't slept alone last night like he'd expected to, like he'd been spending his nights unless he was in the bunk room at one of the firehouses. He opened his eyes and returned the unblinking stare focused on his face. A stare probably eerily similar to his in color.

Small paws kneaded his chest, claws nipping slightly into his skin, as the black cat stood on him. It had been somewhere in the bed all night, sneaking in with him when he'd carried in his armload of laundry.

The alarm on the dryer had sounded at the worst time last night, right when he and Heather had been standing so close in the kitchen. Her hand on his chest, both of his clenching the curves of her hips. And the way she'd been looking at him...

At his lips…

She might have even been rising up on her toes to reach for him, to slide her hands around his head and pull it down for her kiss. Or at least that was what he wanted to think…

That she would have kissed him. Instead, when that dryer signal had sounded, she'd jumped back and sloshed the contents of her glass onto that thin T-shirt she apparently wore as a nightgown. Or to drive him out of his mind.

To him that soft heathered cotton was sexier than silk and lace, especially when the water seeped into the fabric, making it transparent over her ample breasts. Over the nipples he'd already been able to see pressing against the shirt. His body hardened just thinking about last night, about her…about how damn badly he'd wanted her.

But the dryer signal and the ice water had apparently brought her to her senses. She'd let out a long, shaky breath and laughed. "I never knew how good firefighters were at starting fires. Good thing I had this water handy to put it out." Then she'd slipped around him and disappeared down the hall.

He'd wanted to follow her. So damn badly…

But she'd obviously changed her mind about acting on the attraction between them. And he couldn't blame her. His life was a mess right now, and she didn't even know the half of it. He hadn't told her about everything that had been happening with the hotshots. And he hadn't put any of their names on the list he'd given her, even though a few of them did have the key code. With everything they'd been through, he wanted to talk to them before she did.

He could hear her talking now, not the words, just the sound of her voice drifting beneath the closed door of the guest room. The cat heard her, too, because he cocked his head and froze, one claw nipping into Trent's skin again. "Hey," he protested.

The cat leaped off him, hitting the hardwood floor with a noise that was surprisingly loud for his slight weight. Before Sammy could get to the door, it swung open.

"Everything okay in here?" Heather asked. She was dressed in faded jeans and an oversize red sweater, probably oversize to hide her weapon. She hadn't been wearing it last night, though. She hadn't been wearing anything but that thin cotton T-shirt.

Just thinking of how she'd looked in the dim lighting had his body reacting, tension and attraction gripping him. He groaned and shifted beneath the quilt, trying to hide that reaction.

She stepped farther into the room. "Are you okay? Did you get hurt worse than you admitted when we hit the asphalt last night?"

He did have some new aches and bruises to go with some of the ones he'd already had from working that wildfire. "I'll live," he said.

"You might not if whoever was driving that vehicle last night has their way. I don't think that's the last time they're going to try for you."

"It's whoever is close to me that's in danger, not me," Trent said.

"We could have both been killed last night."

He shifted against the bed and flinched, the aches and pains proving how true her words were. Hitting the asphalt wasn't the only reason his body was aching, though. Getting so close to her, wanting her so badly and not even kissing her had him aching, too. With longing.

With desire.

He groaned again.

"Don't worry," she said. "I'll do my best to keep you safe and find out who the hell tried to run us down."

"But how are you going to solve this case if you're babysitting me instead?"

"Shh," she said. "Never talk about me babysitting. My sisters will get the idea to try to drop their kids on my doorstep again." She shuddered.

He laughed.

She was so funny and smart and beautiful and sexy. He wasn't sure how he would handle being so close to her and not being able to kiss her, touch her or make love with her.

"I don't have to protect you," she said. "Looks like Sammy stood guard all night in here with you." The cat wound around her legs, purring loudly as if marking her as his and making sure that Trent knew he didn't have a chance of claiming her.

He probably didn't, but for a little while last night she had seemed to want him as badly as he'd wanted her. She was barely even looking at him this morning, though, and certainly not with that look of desire gleaming in her eyes like last night. Maybe he'd just imagined it all. Had he imagined hearing her voice earlier?

"Was someone here or were you on the phone?" he asked.

"Phone," she said. "I was making calls to everyone on that list."

"Who did you talk to?" he asked, uneasily. Hopefully not Brittney, because the more she knew, the more involved she would get, and the more in danger. He didn't want that; he would do anything to protect her, even freeze her out. Last night he had relented and returned her latest text with a text of his own: I'm okay. Back off.

"Not many," she said. "I mostly left messages." Her cell, clutched in her hand, rang now. "Somebody must be calling back..."

Before he could ask her, she ducked out of the guest room, closing the door behind her, as if she didn't want him to hear. These were people he knew, people he'd trusted, but to her, they must be suspects. Could one of them, his friends or coworkers or family, be responsible for that woman's death? For the fire? For the threat against him?

Technology seemed to be conspiring to bring Heather to her senses. Last night, the signal on the dryer had brought her out of that sensual spell she'd been so deeply under that she'd nearly kissed Trent Miles. She was pretty damn sure if she'd given in to that temptation, then she would have given in to all her desires.

So it was good that the dryer signal had startled her into spilling the water on her shirt. The cold had jolted her out of that spell and to her senses. Just as the ringing cell had now. Or she might have given in to the temptation to crawl into bed with Trent like Sammy had.

"Traitor," she hissed at the cat in a soft whisper.

The cat hissed back.

"What?" the voice rumbled out of the cell speaker, bringing Heather's attention back to the caller.

It wasn't one of the firefighters. This call was from a crime scene investigator.

"Did you find anything on the traffic cam footage

from near the area where the house burned and the woman died?" she asked.

"There are no cams close enough to that address to confirm that any of the vehicles came off that street," the tech replied.

"Damn…" she murmured. She had some uniforms canvassing the immediate area to request neighbors' home security and doorbell footage. Hopefully something useful would turn up to help identify the woman and her killer or at least who actually used Trent's house, since the other guys last night had denied that they had. Nobody else she'd talked to so far seemed willing to admit they used it, if they'd even talked to her at all. She'd left a message for the elusive Barry Coats, but he had yet to return her call.

Had they just missed him last night at the firehouse? Or had he just missed them? Why would he have tried to run them down unless he'd had something to hide? Like his guilt…

Just what had he been using Trent's house for that caused his other coworkers to stop using it? She needed more information about the guy.

"Is there anything else you want me to check?" the tech asked.

"Yes," she said. "Traffic cam and security footage near the firehouse on Front Street."

There was another hiss of breath, and she glanced down to see if Sammy had made the sound. But she saw only denim and long, bare feet. Trent had stepped out of the guest room. He'd pulled on a pair of jeans but hadn't done up the top button yet. While he'd pulled on a button-down flannel shirt, he hadn't done up those buttons either, leaving it open over his bare, muscular chest.

Damn him.

She closed her eyes for a moment and drew in a deep breath.

"Detective?" the tech asked. "Any particular time you want me to check the video?"

"Uh…" What time had that vehicle nearly struck them? She'd been so distracted then that she was lucky it hadn't hit them.

"One a.m.," Trent answered for her.

"One a.m.," she repeated. At least he'd been more aware than she'd been. She wasn't sure if he'd shoved her out of the way, or they'd simultaneously jumped out of the way. "A firefighter, Trent Miles, and I were nearly run down in the parking lot," she explained. She should have filed the report last night, after she'd questioned the lieutenant, but she would file it soon.

She needed to get it together or she wasn't going to close any of these cases, and they were starting to pile up. The shooting, the death, the fire and the attempted vehicular manslaughter, or murder, if it had been pre-meditated.

Had the person been waiting for them, knowing that, with Trent's house burned down, he might return to the firehouse to sleep?

Or had it been a crime of opportunity?

She had no idea, but she had to get her act together and figure things out. Or she wouldn't have just her case clearance rate to worry about but her life as well.

"Detective Bolton?" The tech called her name a little louder, as if he'd called it before and she hadn't heard him.

"Yes, I'm here."

"Are you all right? Was anyone hurt?" he asked with concern.

Craig. That was his name. She knew it because she always asked for him. He was young. Bob Bernard complained about his hiring, saying he couldn't even grow a beard, how could he handle his job?

Bob was such an idiot. But that was fine. Craig was smart and strove to be the best at his job, just like Heather did. She liked him. "I'm fine, Craig. Thanks so much for checking into all of this for me. You're the best."

"Thanks, Detective," he said, his voice full of pride. "I'll let you know what I find for that time frame and location."

"Thank you!" she said and then clicked off her cell.

"Not one of my crew," Trent said.

"No, one of mine," Heather said.

"Sounds like an admirer."

"A really good tech," she said. If anything turned up, Craig would find it. "Not a lot of your crew have accepted my calls and even fewer have called me back."

"They worked late last night," he said in their defense.

She didn't think that was why they hadn't called her back, especially Barry Coats.

"But you talked to or left messages for everyone on that list?" he asked, his long body suddenly tense as if he was uneasy.

Was he worried about her talking to his coworkers or his family?

"I haven't contacted your stepmom and your sister yet," she said, thinking that might be who he was concerned about. "I figured you might want to call them and tell them about the fire before handing the phone to me." She still had to question them. "That way they can hear your voice and know for sure that you're fine."

"I guarantee Brittney already knows about the fire," he said and held up his cell, showing her a dark photo on the screen.

She had to step closer to him, to his bare chest, to try to decipher what the image was. But she forced herself to focus just on the phone, not him. Only streetlamps illuminated the scene in the picture, the crime scene, the tape marking off the area around his still-smoking house. The caption on the photo read: What the hell is going on, big brother?

Heather smiled. "I think I'm going to like your sister."

Trent groaned. "That's what worries me."

She laughed now. "So let's give Brittney a call."

He shook his head. "Not until I've had some coffee and figure out how to talk to her and get her to stay the hell out of it so she doesn't get killed."

As well as the text his sister had sent him, she'd seen the one he'd sent to her. Clearly he didn't think she was going to heed his warning to back off.

"I have every strength of coffee pod in the kitchen, and the water in the machine is heated up," she said. "Once you have your coffee, we need to contact the rest of the names on your list and maybe follow up with some in-person visits if I don't get calls back from the others I've left messages for, like that firefighter we just missed last night." Or had he just missed them with his vehicle?

"There might not be enough caffeine for me..." Trent murmured, then passed her in the hall to head toward the kitchen. He passed her so closely that his bare chest brushed across the front of her sweater.

And heat shot through her body, making her jump

back like she'd been burned. She had probably just had too many cups of coffee since waking up. Hell, she hadn't really woken up because she hadn't really slept at all.

She'd lain in her bed wishing that Trent was in it with her. That was definitely a temptation she had to fight. She'd already crossed so many lines by having him come home with her. She'd done it for his protection, but she couldn't protect him or herself while being so distracted.

She had to stay focused for both their sakes. For both their lives.

"Where the hell is he?" Brittney asked, frustration gripping her. She'd checked everywhere for Trent last night. At her mom's. At the firehouse. She'd even checked some hotels in the vicinity. The hotels had offered her more information than anyone at the firehouse had last night.

The lieutenant who'd answered the door had been short with her and hadn't let her inside the building. A lot of firefighters didn't like reporters. Her brother included lately.

And now every one of his hotshot team members.

A few of his local crew didn't dislike her, though. In fact, there was one of them who liked her a little too much. So she waited in the parking lot for him to leave after his night shift ended.

The minute he exited the firehouse, she pushed open the driver's door of her small SUV and stepped out. "Tom!" she called out to him.

A grin crossed his face. He was cute and young and eager to impress her. A little too eager for Brittney. But at the moment, she was counting on that eagerness.

"Hey, beautiful Brittney," he said.

She tried not to grimace at the compliment he'd given her so many times that it irritated instead of charmed her now. *Come up with something a little more original.* And something that wasn't just about her looks. She was sick of being judged for those and deemed capable of handling only the fluff instead of the hard stuff, like the smart, savvy reporter she was.

So smart that she smiled back at Tom. "Hey, handsome," she said.

He chuckled. "What do you want, Brittney?"

"My brother," she replied. "I can't find him anywhere." Her voice cracked a little with the concern gripping her. She was worried. Very worried. And frustrated as hell that he wouldn't return her calls. And his response to her text hadn't reassured her at all. I'm okay. Back off.

"He didn't tell you?" Tom asked.

Which meant he knew where Trent was, so some of that pressure inside Brittney eased. "He's not returning my calls," she admitted. "I know that with the fire and all he must be busy…" She trailed off to see if his crew member would fill in the blanks.

Tom snorted. "I'll say he's been busy. A lot busier than any of us knew."

The comment left Brittney with more questions than answers. Was he talking about the fire? The body found in the house? The shots fired? Or something else? He could have even been talking about her exposé on the hotshot team, but that had really only exposed one member who'd been living his life as a dead man. He'd almost become a dead man because of Brittney's exposé, and her brother could have been killed as well.

Just as he could have been last night if he'd been home when the fire started. Had he been?

She didn't even know, and they'd once been pretty close. So close that she could have been in his house last night. She stayed there a lot when she was working a story in the city and didn't want to drive to her mom's place in the burbs.

Could she be the reason his house had been burned down? That someone else had died? Was she the one someone really wanted to hurt, because of the story she'd done? Guilt gripped her for a moment, and she sucked in a breath.

"You okay?" Tom asked with genuine concern.

She shook her head. "I need to know what the hell is going on." And if it was because of her. She'd had that strange sensation lately of being watched, but maybe that was just because she'd made the national news with her scoop on the Canterbury heir, so she was more recognizable.

Tom stepped closer, his arms open as if he was about to give her a hug. Was it that bad?

Someone had died in Trent's house. Of course it was that bad.

But she held up a hand to ward off the man. "I'm fine," she said. "I'm just worried about my brother."

Tom's face drew into a tight grimace. "Me, too," he admitted, his voice gruff. "He and his girlfriend could have been killed last night."

"Girlfriend?" She hadn't even known that Trent had started dating again. "And wasn't someone killed in the fire?" A female.

"Not in the fire," Tom said. "Here, last night, in the parking lot. The lieu said he saw from the kitchen window—"

he gestured toward the second story "—someone nearly ran them down in the parking lot." He shuddered.

She gasped as a sharp pain jabbed her heart. "Nearly? What happened?"

Tom shrugged. "I didn't see it. But the lieu heard the engine rev and tires squealing. That's why he looked out the window. They got out of the way just in time, and they insisted they were okay."

So the fire hadn't been about Brittney, but she wasn't relieved. She was even more concerned that it was about her brother, and maybe his new girlfriend. While she hadn't met many of his past girlfriends, usually because he didn't date them long, she always knew when he was dating.

She didn't know anything about what had been happening with her brother lately. She knew why: her damn exposé on his best friend and his hotshot team. And what if something happened to him and he never forgave her? What if something already had happened to him and that was why he hadn't returned her calls? Anyone could have sent her that text telling her to back off. Even his killer…

Chapter 8

"Ready to call her?" Heather asked as she held out his phone to him. That picture Brittney had taken and sent last night stared up at him from the screen. His house, or what was left of it, with plumes of smoke rising from the blackened structure.

The house didn't mean anything to him. He hadn't even spent that much time there. It was the woman who concerned him. Who was she?

He doubted that Brittney would know.

"She'll ask more questions than she'll be able to answer," he warned her. "And are you sure you want her to know about you? About whatever we're claiming we are?"

Her lips curved into a smile. "Can't even say the words? *Boyfriend and girlfriend? In a relationship?*" She grimaced after she said them. "Those words are hard for me to spit out, too."

He found himself smiling but was curious. "Why?" he asked. "Why is it hard for you?"

She wriggled her dark blond brows. "What are we talking about now?"

He chuckled. "I thought you didn't want to play with fire," he reminded her. But the way she looked at him across the table in her breakfast nook had his body hardening again, just as she'd teased.

"I'll leave that to the firefighters," she said.

"Calling Brittney will be playing with fire," he said. "She might do a story, especially if she senses a scandal, like the detective investigating a murder being involved with one of the suspects."

"You're not a suspect. Your alibi checked out, and you're in danger. So you're in police protection."

"I thought Sammy was my bodyguard," he said, his gaze moving to the cat sleeping on the pad on the window seat in the nook.

She glanced over at her cat and smiled at him with affection. "He's exhausted from pulling the overnight shift."

Trent touched the small scratches on his chest. "I think I needed protection from him." He grinned at her. "Too bad you chickened out last night."

Her green eyes widened, and her mouth dropped open with shock. "You think I chickened out? I'm brave," she insisted. "I'm not stupid. And last night…that would have been stupid."

He couldn't argue with her. Really. "Yeah, but it would have been fun."

Instead of agreeing, she narrowed her eyes as if skeptical of his claim.

He arched a brow. "Want me to prove it?"

"Wow…" She shook her head. "You are really trying to stall me talking to your sister."

He sighed and admitted, "I'm trying to stall *me* talking to my sister."

"Are you really just worried about her doing a story on all of this?" she asked. "Or are you still mad at her over that one she did on the Canterbury heir?"

"My best friend," he said.

Heather glanced down at his list. "What name is he going under now? In fact, most of the numbers you gave me have local exchanges, but your hotshot crew wouldn't…" She looked back up at him, her eyes narrowed with suspicion. "You didn't put any of them on your list? None of them have the key code for your place? Not even your *best* friend?"

God, she was smart.

"Nobody's around the Detroit area," he pointed out.

"So? They never visit? You've never given any of them your key code and the offer to stay if they are in the area?" she asked.

He felt like a suspect again.

A call coming in on her cell momentarily suspended Heather's interrogation of Trent. One of his local crew had returned her voice mail.

"I haven't stayed at Trent's for a while," Jerome Whittaker insisted.

Heather wasn't sure if she believed him. "Why not?" she asked.

"What? What do you mean?"

"He gave you the key code, so you've used his place in the past, so why not recently?" she asked. "I looked up your address. You don't live far from the firehouse. Why wouldn't you just stay there?"

"Snoring. I'm a light sleeper, and some of the crew snore."

"So get earplugs or go back to your own house. As I said, you don't live that far—"

"My wife and I were having problems," he confessed. "But we got back on track. I don't need to stay there anymore."

"And you didn't give that key code out to anyone else?" she asked.

"No. Everybody I know already had it."

"Your wife?"

His words sputtered incoherently into the phone until he cleared his voice and asked, "Why would I give it to her?"

"Why wouldn't you? If she had to find you and you were asleep—"

"I— She didn't know I was staying there," he said.

"I need to speak to her," Heather said. She needed to confirm that she wasn't the woman whose body had been found in the fire.

"Uh—I— Why? I just told you she doesn't know that I ever used Trent's place."

Heather glanced across the table at Trent, who was silently studying his coffee mug. Then she focused on his friend again. "Apparently, you don't want her to know. Why not? What exactly did you use his house for?"

"I—I told you," he said. "We were going through a rough patch. But everything's fine now."

Maybe because his wife was dead. Heather's detective mind always went with the worst-case scenario. "I need to talk to her and confirm that she's alive—"

"Alive? What the hell are you talking about?"

"The body found in Trent's house has not been identified. I need to talk to your wife. But I'll do that in person." She disconnected the call as Jerome was sputtering in protest again.

"My turn for the interrogation now?" Trent asked.

"What the hell was your house? A brothel?" she asked.

He shrugged. "I really thought my crew was just using it to crash because Lieutenant Stokes snores really loudly."

"You didn't know some of them might be using it to cheat on their wives?" she asked. She glanced around her house. With all the changes her dad had made, it was so damn cute with its white cabinets, light quartz countertops and sun-drenched breakfast nook. She couldn't imagine letting anyone use it but her dad. And she even sometimes worried about him, but that was just because of his eating junk food and drinking beer.

"No wonder the neighbors thought it was a drug house, what with everyone coming and going like they were," she commented. "And I think there are more people that you haven't even included on this list who were using it, like your hotshot team."

"None of them could have beat me down here after our return to Northern Lakes," he said.

"You stopped at the outlet mall and to eat," she said, reminding him, and herself, of his alibi. "They could have driven straight through."

He sighed, and his broad shoulders drooped slightly. "I'll put them on the list. But can we follow up with everyone else here first?"

She nodded. "I will. I think it's more likely someone local. Like Jerome Whittaker or the Barry dude…"

He clenched his jaw, his expression grim.

It clearly bothered him that his house had been used as it had. That his coworkers might have taken advantage of his kind offer to cheat on their spouses.

"I believe you that you didn't know," she said.

He let out another sigh and the tension eased from his face. "I really didn't. I know relationships are hard for hotshots, with being gone so much, but I didn't realize what was going on with the local crew."

"Could one of your hotshots have been using the place for the same reason?"

He chuckled. "No." But then the amusement left his face and his topaz eyes returned to that grim expression. "But one of them was hurt by infidelity like that. We lost him earlier this year to a horrific *accident*," he said, with his emphasis on *accident* implying it really wasn't.

"I take it that it wasn't actually an accident," she surmised. "I remember your sister's report referring to a string of bad luck or sabotage befalling your hotshot team."

His jaw clenched again.

"That's what you've been reluctant to talk about?" she asked.

"My hotshot team has been through a lot over the past year," he said. "I don't want to put them through anything else, especially if this has nothing to do with them."

She sighed. "I want to clear this case quickly. So I don't want to close any avenue of investigation yet. But I will put off contacting any of them for a bit."

"Until after the Christmas party?" he asked, his eyes looking hopeful. "It's just a week away."

"I hope we close the case before then," she admitted. She wasn't sure how long she could last just pretending to be his girlfriend when she was so damn attracted to him. If she ran into him in the kitchen again in the middle of the night, she wasn't sure she would be able to resist temptation.

Hell, in broad daylight now, her skin tingled with awareness, and her pulse beat faster than normal. Maybe that was from the lack of sleep and all the caffeine she'd drunk that morning.

But...

She suspected it was just him.

She jumped up from the table then to grab another cup, not that she needed it with as jittery as she already was. Trent must have wanted a refill as well, because he got up from the table, too, and joined her in the kitchen. That small galley kitchen with not much space between the fresh white cabinets. It was enough for Heather when she was alone, and she was usually alone.

But not now...

Trent's big body crowded into the space with hers, brushing against her. They were fully dressed now; he'd done up his shirt and the button on his jeans before joining her in the kitchen. But she was still affected by his nearness. So much so that she closed her eyes and imagined how he'd looked last night and this morning, lying in the guest-room bed when she would have preferred that he spent the night in hers.

"Thank you," Trent said, his deep voice low with sincerity.

She opened her eyes and stared up into his handsome, oh-so-serious face. "For what?"

He lifted his hand and gestured around him. "For giving me a place to stay and for protection. But most especially for understanding about my hotshot team and my sister."

She smiled. "I can tell that they mean a lot to you." And she hoped like hell that it hadn't been one of his team in the house. He'd said there were a couple of women on the team, but he'd claimed they were the wrong build to match that body in the morgue.

He wasn't a coroner, though.

And she was probably remiss in not investigating the hotshot angle right now as well as his local crew. She'd focus first on the locals, and if she didn't find the perp, she'd go with him to his hotshot holiday party.

"Thank you," he said again, and he reached out and slid his fingertips along her jawline. "You are very understanding as well as…"

She sucked in a breath as his eyes dilated. "As well as what?" she asked. He'd complimented her last night, but that had been last night…in the heat of the moment.

After their near-death experience.

This was daylight. And reality. The night before just seemed like a dream now.

"You're understanding as well as smart and beautiful…" As he trailed off, he drew in a shaky breath. Then he released it in a sigh and added, "And so damn sexy…"

In a baggy sweater and old, loose jeans? She'd purposely dressed this morning so that he wouldn't see her physical reaction to him like he had last night in that thin T-shirt.

But while he couldn't see it, she could feel it. The heat spreading through her, the tightening of her nipples, the pull deep inside her. She wanted him so damn badly.

"This is dangerous," she murmured.

"Yes," he agreed, but he stepped a little closer so that his body touched hers.

She could feel his heart beating, as hard and fast as hers. "Stupid even," she said but found herself reaching up, sliding her arms around his neck. She cupped the back of his head and pulled it down toward hers.

"Really stupid," he agreed.

She smiled, but then she brushed her mouth across his. And that fire ignited, not just inside her but between them.

He kissed her back, his mouth moving over hers. His lips were both hard and soft as he parted hers and deepened the kiss. His tongue slid inside her mouth, and she met it with hers.

Like last night, his hands gripped her hips, but instead of just hanging on, like he had last night, he lifted her until her butt settled onto the countertop. He'd probably done it so he didn't have to lean down so far since he was so tall.

She was glad he'd done it, because her legs had been threatening to fold beneath her as desire overwhelmed her. Shook her. She couldn't remember ever feeling such heat and passion. She nipped his bottom lip lightly with her teeth.

He groaned. Then he nipped her back before sliding his lips across her cheek and down her neck.

Her pulse leaped beneath his mouth. She moaned as the desire intensified, pulling at her core. She wrapped her legs around his hips, dragging him closer. Through his jeans, she could feel the hard ridge of the evidence of his desire for her. She moaned again with the need that gripped her.

"Heather…" he murmured.

Maybe it was a question. Maybe he was asking how

far he could go as his hands tugged at the bottom of her sweater. Was he thinking about lifting it?

Her breasts swelled as her heart pounded even harder with anticipation. She wanted his hands on her body.

"Heather." His voice was a rough whisper, and his body had tensed.

Then she heard the noise, too. This time it wasn't Sammy making it. He was still on the window seat in the breakfast nook but awake now. His little furry body as tense as Trent's against hers.

It wasn't footsteps, but a rattling noise as if someone was trying to open the door. Trying to get in…

Her dad had the code; he would have already unlocked it if it was him. No. This was someone else. Someone she'd not given access to her home. Someone she didn't want to have access to her home, like the person who'd set Trent's on fire and had tried to run them down.

What was he going to try now? And would Heather have time to retrieve her weapon from her bedroom before he got inside?

Usually after a wildfire assignment, like the one the Huron Hotshot team had just been on, Ethan Sommerly would have returned to his job as a forest ranger and the seclusion of his post in the middle of the Upper Peninsula of Michigan. But since his real identity, as Jonathan Michael Canterbury IV, had been revealed, he knew there was no place he could hide. He didn't care, though. Since the man who'd wanted him dead, his own brother-in-law, was no longer a threat, Ethan didn't want to hide anymore.

And he definitely didn't want to be alone anymore. He reached across the bed then. The sheets were cool;

Tammy had gotten up a while ago to open her salon. It was just downstairs. If he listened, he could probably hear the whir of the hair dryers and the faint rumble of voices. He tilted his head, but the rumble he heard was his cell phone vibrating against the tabletop next to the bed.

He groaned and reached for it. When he saw the name Brittney Townsend lighting up the screen, he groaned again. Trent had given her his number a few weeks ago, but he couldn't be mad at his best friend over that. Brittney had witnessed Tammy's abduction and called to inform him. While she'd helped save Tammy's life, she'd also been the one who'd put it in danger when she'd revealed his true identity, so he swiped to ignore her call.

Tammy was safe now. So he had no reason to talk to the reporter anymore, especially when she was probably going to ask him again to do a follow-up interview with her. While he wasn't going to hide anymore, he had no intention of doing any interviews with any reporter, but most especially not her.

Was Trent talking to her yet? He'd been so pissed at her. Maybe that was why she was calling.

He wasn't going to get in the middle of family drama; he'd already gone through enough of his own. That drama exhausted him even more than fighting the wildfire. Or maybe how he and Tammy had celebrated his return yesterday had exhausted him. How they'd celebrated all night long…

His body hardened just thinking about it, about her. She was so amazing. He was the luckiest man alive that she'd fallen as deeply in love with him as he had with her. He grinned over the irony of that, over the man who'd once thought himself cursed with the Canterbury family's notorious bad luck now relishing his good fortune.

The steps creaked slightly under her weight, and he could hear her voice as she ascended the stairwell from her salon. "He's probably still asleep," she was saying. Was she bringing up someone with her?

Only one set of footsteps was coming down the hall toward her bedroom, though, and it was the distinctive click of Tammy's high heels. But he heard another voice now. "I think he's probably just ignoring my call."

Brittney Townsend was smart. She was also too damn persistent. Of course she had Tammy's cell number; they had become friends when she'd been up here tearing his world apart. But it had come back together now, better than it had ever been before. As Jonathan Michael Canterbury IV and even as Ethan Sommerly.

He wasn't keeping any more secrets from people he cared about, like Brittney's brother and the rest of his team. And he was happy. Begrudgingly, he had to admit he probably owed some of that to Brittney and her damn persistence.

"Thank *you* for taking my call." Brittney's voice wafted out of the speaker of Tammy's cell. She'd stepped just inside the doorway, her phone held out.

Tammy looked like a model with her streaked hair and stylish clothes, clothes she'd bought from her best friend Courtney Beaumont's new boutique. The black leather skirt and lacy blouse had his body hardening all over again with desire for her.

Then Brittney continued. "I wouldn't have bothered him, but I'm really worried about Trent. His house burned down last night, and a body was found in it—"

"What?" Ethan exclaimed, swinging his legs over the bed as he reached for Tammy's phone. "What the hell happened?"

"I don't really know," Brittney said. "Sometime last night there was first a report of shots fired at Trent's house and then a fire started and—"

"Is he okay? Did he get out?" Ethan asked, his heart pounding hard and fast with fear. How the hell could they do what they did, battle monster wildfires, and lose their own homes to a fire?

But was his home all that Trent had lost?

"You said a body was found inside…" His voice cracked with emotion. Not Trent. He was one of the best damn firefighters Ethan had met since becoming a hotshot. Trent would have gotten out. He'd had to…

"It was a female."

"I didn't think Trent was even dating."

"I didn't think so either," Brittney said. "But one of his local crew told me that after the fire, Trent and his girlfriend nearly got run down in the firehouse parking lot."

Ethan's breath shuddered out with relief. "So he's alive."

But Brittney didn't confirm his statement.

"Isn't he?" he prodded her.

"I haven't talked to him. He left me a voice mail after the fire and sent some texts. I think he wanted to make sure that body wasn't mine."

"Of course he did," Ethan said. "He loves you."

The reporter snorted. "Sure. That's why he's torturing me with no contact."

"Or he knows he's in danger and he's protecting you," Ethan said. Maybe that was why Ethan hadn't heard from him yet either. But why, while they'd been out West, hadn't Trent mentioned he had a girlfriend? What the hell was going on?

A sniffle emanated from Tammy's cell speaker, and Brittney audibly drew in a breath. "Of course. That sounds like my big brother."

And Ethan's best friend. "I haven't heard from him," he told her.

"I thought he would call you for sure, or come up there…"

Ethan sighed. "I haven't even gotten a text from him. I don't know where he is."

"Or who he's dating? Tom, from the local firehouse, thinks Trent is with her, whoever she is."

"I don't know about her either."

"Apparently, you aren't the only one of your hotshot team keeping secrets," Brittney remarked.

Ethan already knew that because he knew who else was keeping a secret, but he suspected Rory VanDam wasn't the only one. Whoever the hell had been sabotaging the equipment was also keeping a secret. Was it one of them? And had that person gone after Trent now?

"Will you let me know if you hear from him?" Brittney asked.

Ethan held his breath for a moment, knowing that he would do whatever Trent asked of him. If Trent didn't want his sister to know that he'd been in contact…

"I'll make sure that he does," Tammy said. "And please let us know if you hear from him first."

"I doubt that will happen," Brittney replied. "I just

wish I knew if he was still giving me the silent treatment or if something else happened to him."

Like maybe the person who'd tried twice to kill him had succeeded with another attempt?

Chapter 9

"Stay here," Heather whispered at Trent.

He wished he could stay exactly where he'd been, pressed up against her warm, curvy body. But she was wriggling down from the countertop; then she slipped past him.

To investigate that noise on her own.

Someone was trying to get into the house. Someone who didn't have her access code. Someone who had no right to be there. And no reason...

But for him.

He'd brought this danger to her home. God, he shouldn't have followed her back here last night. He should have kept driving. Out of Detroit...

But where?

He hadn't wanted to return to Northern Lakes either. His team had already been through enough. They couldn't lose anyone else. And neither could he.

Despite her order for him to stay in the kitchen, he stepped out of the small space between the cabinets and stumbled forward, over the soft body of the cat.

Sammy let out a yowl, hissed and streaked past him, heading toward the basement and what he probably considered safety.

"Some bodyguard you are," Trent murmured, keeping his voice low as he listened.

Floorboards creaked. Had the intruder gotten inside? Trent hadn't heard the squeak of any door hinges. But with everything as new as it was, maybe it hadn't made any sound from that initial rattling at the front door. The noise had come farther away from them than the side door.

Trent walked past the breakfast nook and was just about to duck through the archway into the living room when a hand grabbed his arm.

"I told you to stay put," Heather said, her voice shaking in a furious whisper. "Get down just in case they have a gun."

She had a tall and wide picture window in the living room, so it would have been easy to see if someone was still out front, near that door. Trent couldn't see anything but the top of the neatly trimmed bushes of the landscaping.

Then he couldn't see anything as Heather jerked him to the floor. "Stay down," she said. She was crouching herself as she slunk toward that front door with her gun drawn, the barrel pointing down at the refinished hardwood floor.

Following the line of that barrel, Trent saw what the rattling had been. The little metal mail chute toward the bottom of her arched oak door was stuck open, a bunch of mail jammed into the slot. He chuckled. "Guess we overreacted."

But Heather didn't reholster her weapon while she peered through the front window. She shook her head. "There's someone out there."

Then he felt that creepy sensation that chilled his skin and his blood. Someone was out there, watching them. He tried to get closer, tried to look out, but Heather jerked him down again.

"You're going to get your head shot off," she warned him. "Stay out of sight." She glanced toward that mail slot again, toward the envelopes jammed in it. But there was more than that; there was something inside that bundle of envelopes. A little box.

Was it an explosive device?

Was that what had started the fire at Trent's house? Something with a detonator?

He'd just been sitting around while she'd made all those calls this morning. He should have been making some of his own to the fire department arson investigation unit. He should have found out if they'd determined the cause of that fire and how it had started.

He knew it was arson. He just didn't know if someone had set a match to a trail of gasoline or if something more sophisticated had started it. Like the bomb that had blown up his best friend Ethan's truck and nearly Ethan along with Annie, the Northern Lakes firehouse dog. Annie had saved Ethan's life that day. Trent had to make sure he saved Heather's, especially since he kept putting it in danger.

He tugged on her arm now, pulling back from the front door. "We need to get the hell out of here," he said. "There could be explosives in that box."

With the things people found nowadays on the internet, it didn't even take much to blow up a person or a home.

Heather sucked in a breath, but she didn't look too shocked. She must have considered the danger. That was probably why whoever had left it was still outside somewhere watching the house, waiting until they got close enough to the door to detonate it.

And blow them up.

"We have to go out the back," she said. "With them watching the house…"

She didn't have to spell out her concern. He understood that if the person had a gun, like she was clearly worried they did, she and Trent could get shot coming out the side door. But if they stayed inside, they might get blown up. "We need to move quickly," he warned her.

He hadn't noticed any exits but for the front and side doors. The breakfast nook had that bay window with the bench built into it. To not be seen exiting from the front, they would have to go out one of the windows.

But once they'd just about crab crawled out of the living room, Heather jerked him down the hall, past the bathroom, past the guest room to that door at the end of the hall.

Her bedroom.

He'd wished she'd invited him inside last night. Or just a short while ago. Now they might never have the chance to act on all that passion between them.

Heather rushed around the bed to jerk open blackout drapes that concealed a set of French doors to a small brick patio. "We can go out here…" She glanced around. "Where's Sammy?"

"He went downstairs," Trent said, and he started back out the door. He couldn't leave her pet in the house just in case that was a bomb. He wasn't going to let another life get lost because of him.

"He'll tear you to shreds if you try to bring him outside," she warned him as she pulled him up short and moved to pass him, clearly to get the cat herself.

She wasn't just protective of threatened firefighters but stray cats as well.

"Heather…" He knew, though, that it was no use trying to stop her. So he rushed after her, following her back through the house to the basement.

All the while, his heart pounded fast and heavy with dread that the killer might detonate whatever the hell was in that box. And if he or she did while they were in the basement, the whole damn house could cave in on top of them. "This is too dangerous," he warned her. "We need to get out before that thing goes off."

The basement was clean but unfinished. The washer and dryer, a long table and the furnace and water heater were the only things on the bare concrete floor but for the rack of shelves along one wall and Sammy's covered litter box and food bowls.

Heather headed toward the shelves. First she holstered the weapon she'd strapped over her sweater. Then she shoved aside boxes until something hissed at her. "Come on, baby. We gotta get out of here. You heard the firefighter."

Maybe that was why he hissed. The cat was smart enough to know that this was all Trent's fault.

She moved another box and tried to reach for the cat, but he slipped past her, jumping at Trent. He grabbed at the light bit of fluff and fur, clutching it close. Claws snagged his flannel shirt, so sharp and frantic he could feel them scratching through the fabric. "I got him," he said. "Now let's get the hell out of here."

He ignored the pain of those digging claws as he ran up the steps after Heather and down the hall into her bedroom. He just hoped they made it outside in time. Before the house exploded.

Heather's heart pounded fast and hard like Sammy's had when she'd taken him from Trent's arms and shut him inside the detached garage. Hopefully it was far enough from the house to protect him. After locking the cat into the garage, she'd reported a possible explosive device at her house.

Dispatch had reacted swiftly to the officer-in-distress call and the bomb squad and police units rolled up quickly to the street outside her house. Next to Trent's truck. They'd remained in the backyard, as far from the house as they could get, just in case that person waited outside to shoot them if they knew they'd gotten away from the device.

She thought they wouldn't have been noticed back here, but if that had been the case, wouldn't the arsonist have detonated the bomb?

Wouldn't they have already blown up the home her dad had worked so hard to make beautiful for her? Her heart ached at the thought of the destruction of his craftsmanship and what she had deemed her solitary sanctuary.

But she wasn't solitary anymore.

Trent hung close to her as they awaited news from

the bomb squad. He was so close that he had to be able
to hear her conversation with Bob Bernard.

"You didn't have to show up," she told the other detective. With his wrinkly suit and messy salt-and-pepper
hair, he always reminded her of Columbo. "I got this under
control."

The older man snorted. "Yeah, right. You let a suspect stay with you—"

"He's not a suspect. His alibi checked out. He's a
victim, and he's here for his protection," she insisted.

Bob snorted again. "And my ex divorced me for bringing my work home with me…"

She could think of a hell of a lot of other reasons that
Bob's wife divorced him but none for her marrying the
misogynist in the first place.

"But you'll do anything to beat my clearance rate,
won't you?" Bob mused.

"Yeah, and it'll take me just a few years to do it, while
it took you twenty," she said with a smirk. He really was
a pain in the ass.

He glanced at Trent, who was obviously listening
to every word and smirked. "Whatever it takes, huh?"
Bob asked.

She resisted the urge to blush. "I'm not sleeping with
him." But she'd been tempted. Last night and just a short
while ago. No way in hell she'd ever admit that to her
snarky, sexist coworker, though.

Bob focused on Trent now. "Be careful, Miles. She
only cares about her clearance rate."

"At least one of us does," she remarked, although she
suspected Bob was stepping up his game now; that had to
be why he'd responded to the call at her house. Or maybe
he'd just wanted to see her whole world blow up. "And

really, you should leave, just in case that really is a bomb stuck in my mail slot. You don't like dangerous cases anymore, Bob," she reminded him. "Just the easy ones. Maybe there's a stolen car you can find somewhere."

He glared at her. "Back in my day, we had respect for our senior detectives."

"Respect isn't something you should just expect," she said. "It's something you should earn." That was why she was working so damn hard to surpass his clearance rate.

The smirk on his face made it clear he knew she was working this hard because of him, just to be better than him. Her stomach churned a bit. That was probably over the fear that her father's hard work and her sanctuary was going to blow up.

But as she'd already suspected, if that box had actually been a bomb, the person who'd stuck it in the slot would have detonated it long ago. Like when she and Trent had been so close to it in the living room.

So she'd traumatized Sammy and called in the bomb squad for nothing, which they confirmed as two of them stepped out the side door. They'd already taken off their helmets, carrying them under their arms.

"Not a bomb," Bob said before they could.

The older one, who was probably as misogynistic as him, responded with a shake of his head and a grimace.

"What was it?" Heather asked the other one, a female bomb squad member.

"A box of matches," the woman replied. "And there was a card wrapped around it, along with some junk mail. We left it in there for the techs to process."

Heather had called Craig, too. He didn't often do fieldwork, but she'd wanted the best at the scene, especially if there wasn't much left of the scene to inspect.

"Thanks for coming out," Heather said to both of them.

The older man didn't even acknowledge her.

"After the arson fire at my house last night," Trent said, "it would have been stupid for us to touch that thing until we knew what it was."

"Someone blew up your house?" the woman asked, her eyes wide as she stared at his handsome face.

Was he aware of the effect he had on people with his good looks? Or was he so used to their reactions that it didn't affect him anymore?

He shrugged. "We don't know what caused the fire yet," he said. "But it went up fast and is a total loss."

The male bomb squad member turned his attention to Trent now. "You're a firefighter, aren't you?"

Trent nodded. "Yes. With Firehouse 102 on Front."

"There was also a body found in his house last night," Heather told the guy, whose face flushed a little now.

"Who was it?" the woman asked Trent.

"The body hasn't been identified yet," Heather answered for him. She knew it troubled him that someone had died in his house, maybe because of him. She wasn't so sure about that, though, not with the way his crew members had used his house and, more specifically, for what they'd used it. "The fire was obviously set to delay the identification process and destroy whatever evidence might have been left at the scene. Whoever this is knows what he's doing." Maybe because he or she was also a firefighter. When she'd called Dispatch, she'd also requested someone make contact with Jerome Whittaker's wife.

The male bomb squad guy jerked his head in a quick nod of his own. "Yeah, it was smart to get the hell out of the house and have us check out that box."

Bob snorted, but his face was a little flushed, too, now. She wasn't the idiot he wanted everyone else, including himself, to believe she was. Or maybe he just wanted her to believe that, to doubt herself so she wouldn't be a better detective than he was. Because even though he was a dick, he was good at his job. He just didn't think a female could be as good. But he would find out soon this one could be even better.

Ignoring him, with the hope that he would leave, she focused on the bomb squad members instead. "Thanks for coming out and making sure it was safe."

Sammy would appreciate going back inside the house. She could hear him rattling the door of the garage behind her, just as the front door had rattled when someone had been shoving that stuff into the slot. She wanted to see what it was and make sure her house was secure and all the doors were closed before she brought Sammy back inside.

The older bomb squad guy started down the driveway with Bob, exchanging a few remarks too low for her to catch. The female bomb squad member stared longingly at Trent for a moment before turning to follow the two older men back to their vehicles parked in the street.

Heather headed toward the house, to the side door the bomb squad had left standing open. She rushed inside and up the few stairs into the kitchen. Footsteps pounded the steps behind her, and she glanced back over her shoulder, worried for a moment that Bob had returned to try to take over her case again. But it was Trent.

He didn't look any happier with her than Bob ever did. She wasn't sure why, but before she could question him, Craig called to her from where he stood under the arch doorway to her living room. "You will want to see this, Detective. I've already bagged it, but you can see the box of matches and the Christmas card through the clear plastic." He laid the items on the table next to Trent's forgotten mug. The coffee would have gone cold long ago, like he had. One minute he'd been so hot, pressed up against her in the kitchen, and now...

Heather walked up next to the tall, thin tech. "Thanks for coming out to process the scene for me, Craig."

"Anything for you, Detective," he said, his pale face flushing. Then he glanced at Trent, who stood behind her, peering over her shoulder at the evidence bags.

One contained a brick-sized box of kitchen matches that had been jammed in the slot and was half-crushed now. If it had been a bomb, it would have probably gone off when the perp shoved it inside the slot. The other contained a Christmas card with the same factory-printed message on one side about enjoying the holidays with the ones you loved. The other side had the hand-printed message:

Enjoy the little time you have left, Trent Miles, with your girlfriend. You'll both be going up in smoke soon.

She was glad Bob hadn't insisted on coming inside to check out the scene. Maybe, since it hadn't been a bomb, he'd lost interest. This note definitely would have piqued it again, just as it had obviously piqued Craig's curiosity.

He kept staring at first her and then Trent. "Are you Trent Miles?" he asked.

Trent nodded.

Heather waved a hand from the tech to the firefighter. "Craig, Trent. Trent, Craig." At the moment she couldn't remember the tech's last name. She knew it and used it when she asked for him but was so distracted right now, so curious about how quiet Trent was being.

He should have been relieved it wasn't a bomb. Instead, he seemed pissed off, while she was thrilled it wasn't a bomb and that the perp had made another move.

"My plan is working," she said with a flash of triumph.

"You're just acting like his girlfriend?" Craig asked. "Like undercover?"

Heat rushed through her as she thought of how close she'd actually come to going under the covers with Trent. And how badly part of her still wanted to...

But if she'd been paying attention instead of making out like a teenager on her kitchen counter, she might have caught whoever had put that box and card in her mail slot. She might have closed this case already.

She was lucky it hadn't been a bomb. Or she might not have another chance...

To catch the person.

Not to have sex with Trent. She knew even better now how dangerous that would have been. And maybe not just for their lives, but maybe for her heart as well. She couldn't get too attached to having him around.

But with the way he was looking at her, his topaz eyes dark with anger and that muscle twitching above his tightly clenched jaw, she had a feeling he might not stick around much longer.

Was he furious about the note? About the threat? After how close the person had gotten to them again, maybe he didn't trust her to protect him anymore.

Chapter 10

He was furious...with himself. He'd been starting to think, to hope, she might care about him. What an idiot he'd been.

Clearly, his was just another case for her to close to beat that old detective's clearance rate. She was competitive and ambitious and determined to best the other detective. It wasn't personal to her. He wasn't personal to her. It was all about her professional career, about furthering it, which reminded him of how his sister had betrayed him and his friends to further her career.

Anger churned inside his stomach that was empty except for the coffee he'd had that morning. His anger was as bitter as that coffee and as sickening. Maybe there was a trace of jealousy roiling around inside him, too. That young tech was obviously besotted with her, since he just about fawned over her like a puppy begging for attention.

She gave Craig some. A smile. Her thanks for his showing up at the scene.

"You really should install some security cameras," Craig said. "If you'd even just had a doorbell cam, you would have seen the person approaching."

She nodded. "I know. I was waiting until my dad finished some more projects around here." She glanced up as a uniformed officer popped into the open door. "Did any of my neighbors have any footage you could use?"

He shook his head. "Nothing was trained on your house. There are a few vehicles that passed, but the camera angles didn't pick up enough to determine even make and model, let alone the license plates."

"Thanks," she said, smiling at both him and the tech as she shifted them back toward that open front door. "I appreciate you responding to the call."

Craig held up the evidence bags. "I'll get back to the lab and process these for prints and trace evidence. Hopefully I'll find something."

"If there's anything to find, you will do it," she said, and the man's thin chest seemed to expand with her praise.

"Shouldn't I stay, make sure that person doesn't return?" the young officer asked.

"I doubt they've ever left," Heather replied.

The officer glanced at Trent, and his hand moved toward his belt and the gun strapped to it.

"Not him," Heather said. "He was with me when that was put in the mail slot, so I don't know who did it. Yet. But I will."

The young officer leaned closer and whispered, "My money's on you, Detective Bolton."

"People are placing bets on us?" Heather asked.

"The whole department," the officer replied.

Heather grinned. "Good. I'll make sure you don't lose your money."

"Maybe I'll double my bet," the officer replied with a grin of his own.

Her grin widened. "And while you don't have to park outside, I'd appreciate you sticking around the area. And if I head out anywhere, I'll let you know."

The officer nodded and backed out the front door, pulling it closed behind him.

Trent drew in a deep breath, trying to calm himself. If he raised his voice at all, the cop would probably rush back in with his weapon drawn. He seemed as besotted as the tech was. As Trent had been until he'd realized what a fool he was being. She was just doing her job, pursuing her goal to the extent that she'd put her own life at risk just to close a case.

He didn't know which one of them was the bigger fool. Him for thinking she might actually be interested in him or her for going to such extremes just to prove her point.

"What the hell is wrong with you?" The question was shouted, but not by him. Heather whirled away from her front window and repeated it, then added, "You're acting all pissed off. Are you disappointed that box of matches wasn't a bomb? Did you want a chance to fight a fire at my house?"

"What the hell is wrong with *you*?" He hurled the question back at her as the fury brimmed over. "You put your life at risk just to win some damn contest!"

She snorted. "I put my life at risk whether there's a contest or not. Kicking Bob Bernard's sexist ass is just a perk for being the best at my job."

"That's all you care about," he said, and a heavy weight settled onto him.

"My job?" she asked, as if she needed clarification, and maybe she did.

He explained, "Being the best at your job. That's all you care about." But she had risked her life for her cat. For the stray that had shown up at her house, kind of like he had last night. But she'd invited him.

"And that's not what you want?" she asked. "Why did you sign up to be a hotshot when you're already a firefighter? Because you wanted to be the best at what you do. Why is it okay for a man to be ambitious but not a woman?"

"I'm not saying that…" he murmured. But he couldn't say what he really meant, that it stung that all he was to her was a case to close to beat Bob Bernard's clearance rate. His pride was already wounded; if he admitted how disappointed he was that she didn't actually care about him beyond that, he would lose that damaged pride. Of course he was just a case to her; she didn't know him. And he didn't know her.

He thought he was getting to know her. She'd talked about her family. Her home. Her cat. Her life. And it had all sounded so much like his. He'd felt connected to her, like she was a kindred spirit. But she was even more focused on her career than he was on his.

"Maybe you should ask Bob Bernard what you mean," she suggested. "Because right now you sound about as sexist as he does. That it's okay for a man to focus on his career but not for a woman."

"I'm not sexist," he insisted. And he wasn't. "It's not like I think women can't do the same jobs as men."

"And just as good or better?" she interjected.

"I'm not Bob Bernard," he said. "I just don't want to be used in your competition." Like Brittney had used him and Ethan.

She stepped closer to him then, her lips curving into a slight smile. Then she reached out and ran her fingers along the row of buttons down the front of his flannel shirt. "Would you let me use you another way?"

He swallowed a groan, unwilling to utter it. To let her know how damn badly she got to him. How damn badly he wanted her. But right now, knowing that he was in over his head, he just wanted to leave. "I'm not staying here any longer," he said. "I'm getting out of here."

"Good idea," she said.

So she wasn't even going to argue with him. She definitely didn't care about him.

After Trent went down the hall, probably to the guest room, Heather headed outside to retrieve Sammy from the garage and bring him back into the house. She shivered, and it wasn't just because she hadn't grabbed a jacket on her way out. It was because of that sensation.

The one she'd had earlier. She was right when she'd told the uniformed officer that the person hadn't left. They were still out there somewhere, watching her. Watching them...

The plan was working. Even as mad as Trent was, he surely had to see that. This was the fastest way to find out who was after him and stop the person before he or she actually succeeded. She didn't want to catch the suspect just because of her damn clearance rate. She wanted to catch them because she cared about Trent a little more than she'd ever cared about another victim, a little more than she should.

This was getting personal to her, and not just because the person had nearly run her down and now had threatened her, too. It was personal because she didn't want Trent getting hurt.

But he was a fireman and a hotshot. He was going to get hurt. And as a detective, she would probably get hurt, too. It was just the nature of their jobs.

She rushed Sammy through the side door of her house, and he wriggled out of her arms before she could even climb the steps to the kitchen. With another hiss, he streaked down the basement stairs. Either to his litter box or maybe his food and water bowls.

Mostly he probably just wanted to get away from her because he was pissed she'd taken him out of the house he loved as much as she did. A pang struck her heart that she could have nearly lost it. But it was nothing compared to losing people, like that poor woman who'd died in Trent's house, or furry friends like Sammy.

"I love you, too," she called down the stairs after him. Then she started up the couple of steps into the kitchen, and as had happened too often since Trent had come to stay with her, she nearly collided with his chest. He had on a light jacket now, and his duffel bag dangled from his fingers.

"Where are you going?" she asked.

"I told you I was leaving."

"But I thought you just meant you needed to get out for a bit…" She wanted to as well, because if Trent's stalker tried for him again, she didn't want it to be at her house. She didn't want it or Sammy to be a casualty in this war the stalker had waged against the firefighter. A war that Heather was determined to win.

"I can't stay here," Trent said. "This was a mistake."

"Why?"

His jaw dropped down, his mouth opening a bit. "Like you don't know why…"

She groaned. "I hate answers like that, like my sisters always give me when I wonder why they're mad at me. I wouldn't be asking if I knew why."

"That box of matches could have been a bomb," he said.

She resisted the urge to shudder. "Yeah, that's why we called in the bomb squad," she reminded him. "But it wasn't."

"No. It was a threat about burning down your house."

She shrugged. "So? I've received threats before. And that one wasn't even addressed to me. It was addressed to you."

"Yes. That's why I need to leave."

"Because the plan is working?" she asked.

"How the hell is it working? Because we nearly got run down? Because we could have been blown up? We're still no closer to finding out who that woman who died in my house was or who the hell is sending me those crazy Christmas cards."

She bobbed her head in agreement. "I know. While we're waiting for the rest of your list to return the messages I left for them, we should get out for a bit."

He shook his head. "Not we. Just me. I'm getting out of here for good." He started forward, but she stood between him and the stairs leading down to the side door.

"Where are you going?" she asked, tipping her head back to stare up at him. He was close, but she wasn't budging. She wasn't letting him walk out of here alone and put himself in danger.

He stepped back, as if he couldn't stand being close to her, and his broad shoulders slumped a little.

"You have no idea," she surmised. "You know wherever else you stay, you'll be putting the people with you in danger. At the firehouse here and probably even the one in Northern Lakes, and with your family—"

"No. I can't be around them."

She still wanted to call his sister and stepmom, but with as upset as he was right now, she knew not to push. Or he would be even more determined to leave. "You can't be around anyone who doesn't carry a gun and know how to handle a threat like whoever is after you," she said. "You need to stick close to me."

"So that you get killed, too?" he asked, his voice gruff with frustration.

Sticking close to him was dangerous, but for a different reason than he was probably thinking. Heather wanted to leave because she knew if they stayed alone inside her house for the rest of this Saturday, she was going to give in to this attraction. And suspecting now, with his reaction to her career competition, that he probably was a little more sexist than he would admit, she didn't want to get any closer to him than necessary.

"I won't get killed," she said. "I'll call Officer Howard and have him stick close to us in case we need backup." She hoped she would need it, that the perp would act again. She might even have Officer Howard set up a little bit of a trap with her...

Trent narrowed those topaz eyes of his and studied her. "Where are you wanting to go?" he asked.

"You need things," she reminded him, pointing at his duffel bag. "You're going to need more than you have in that bag."

"I'm used to traveling light," he said. "I don't need much."

"Then we'll shop for me," she said. "I need some things. I have to buy a gift for the precinct toy drive, and I should probably get a tree before my sisters show up with one like they did last year. It was so damn big that it scratched the ceiling and the walls up and my dad had to patch and repaint." He hadn't minded, though, because it had given him a reason to get out of his house.

"So you want to go Christmas shopping right now?" he asked, his forehead furrowed with confusion. "I thought…" He sighed. "That's not what you're really up to. You want this nut to try for us again."

She shrugged. "The more we can lure this perp out to do something, the more opportunities we have to catch him or her and end this." And it would be faster than waiting for Craig to process that note and box and for him to get through all the security footage around the firehouse.

"Close this case, you mean," he said, his voice gruff with bitterness.

"Isn't that what you want, too?" she asked. "To find out who's threatening and trying to kill you? We need to catch this person before the holidays, so you can spend it with your family and friends without risking their lives."

He released a ragged sigh now. "Damn it. You're right."

Clearly that didn't make him any happier than it ever made Bob Bernard. But Trent had to know the only way he could protect the people he cared about was for her to catch whoever was threatening them. She just had to make damn sure that this person didn't manage to carry out their threats before they were caught. She wasn't worried about her clearance rate right now. She was worried about her life and Trent's.

The bomb squad had left. The crime tech van had, too. Even the last police car had driven away. This was a great opportunity to make another move.

Another threat.

To let Trent Miles and the good detective know that their time was running out. There was no way in hell they were living until Christmas.

They'd be lucky if they lived until Sunday.

But it was fun, too, drawing it out a bit. Scaring them…

Letting them know just how close death was. But it wasn't going to come on their terms. It was coming on *his*.

He was the one in charge now. Not the detective and damn well not the hotshot firefighter. They were going to regret messing up his life…when he ended theirs.

Maybe he would wait until evening. Or maybe…

He leaned forward, peering into his side mirror that he'd been using to watch her house. Two figures emerged from the side of the house, walking down the driveway toward Trent's truck. He opened the passenger door and helped her inside like they were really boyfriend and girlfriend.

He wasn't sure if that was real. Either way, he didn't care. They both deserved to die.

While Trent walked around the front of the truck to the driver's side, the detective peered around as if looking for him. As if she knew he was there…

He was far enough away that nobody could see him. Not even them. And even if they did, they wouldn't recognize him. He was wearing a disguise. He hadn't been certain that the detective didn't have security around her house, so he'd donned a long white beard, glasses and a Santa hat and suit. Nobody was going to recognize him…until it was too late. Until they were dead…

Chapter 11

Trent wanted to stay angry, but he couldn't. Heather hadn't done anything wrong. She wanted to close a case and, whatever her motivation, it was her job, and she was professional. He was the one who'd wanted it to be personal.

And to him, it was. That was the other reason he couldn't stay mad. She was just too much fun. He was following her directions to a place just north of the city, to a little town square area with competing Christmas tree lots and stores full of holiday decorations.

"I want to find the lot with the saddest, straggliest Christmas trees available," she said. "I should have grabbed one last year that someone threw out after Christmas so that all the needles had fallen off and it had already dried out. That would totally disgust my sisters." She emitted an evil-sounding chuckle.

He laughed. "You're bad."

"Yup." She was totally unrepentant. "They think I am. That I can't take care of my own house."

He could have pointed out that her dad seemed to do it, but he didn't want her pissed off at him like she was with her sisters.

"They are Martha Stewart wannabes who think they are domestic goddesses. I'll show them."

"With a straggly dead tree from last year?" he asked. "Aren't you just going to prove them right?"

She snorted. "I'm showing them that I don't care."

"Seems like a lot of effort to prove that," he remarked with irony. "Kind of like your competition with Bob Bernard. You must care what he thinks or you wouldn't be working so hard to beat him."

"I'm showing him that I belong," she said. "That a woman can do a job just as well as or better than a man."

"But why do you care what he thinks?" he persisted. "For that matter, why do you care what your sisters think?"

She sighed. "I don't know. My two sisters are older than me and have always bossed me around and disapproved of me. I should be like you with your sister and not care what they think. But I haven't gotten there yet."

"I'm not there yet either," he admitted with a heavy sigh of his own. His chest ached over not talking to Brittney. "My sister was just the opposite of yours. She always looked up to me, worshipped me. I could do no wrong in her eyes."

"Your silent treatment is probably killing her, then," she said.

He groaned. "I know. Once we've brought your Charlie Brown Christmas tree back to your house, we can call her." As he'd said before, the two of them would hit it off immediately. They were both driven and ambitious and determined, no matter how much danger they were in or how many people they pissed off. Even him…

Maybe that was why Brittney's betrayal was so hard for him to get over, because she must no longer look up to and idolize him or she wouldn't have gone after his hotshot team just to further her career.

He would have to keep reminding himself that was all he was to Heather, another case to close so she could further her career.

"We could call her now," Heather suggested.

But he shook his head. "No." He needed to focus on driving per her directions and stay aware of the vehicles on the road around him. Last night his stalker must have followed him back to her place. And he'd thought he'd been careful then. No. If he'd been careful, he wouldn't have gone back to her place.

"He's back there," she said as she glanced out the passenger's window at the mirror.

Trent tightened his hands around the steering wheel and glanced into the rearview mirror. There were a lot of vehicles behind him. "Which one?" he asked.

"I don't know," she said. "I just *know* he's back there."

Trent didn't have to ask how because he knew, too. The short hairs on the nape of his neck rose, along with goose bumps on his skin. He wore a jacket over his flannel shirt, but it was light. More for the weather out West than Michigan this time of year. But his winter clothes had burned in his house. She'd already told the young officer where they were headed, just after she'd told Trent. So he was probably back there somewhere, too, but Trent was still uneasy.

"I have my gun," she said, as if she sensed his uneasiness. She wore her puffy jacket and red scarf again, so he wouldn't have been able to tell if she hadn't told him. But he'd already suspected. While she talked about her family and joked, Heather was still very aware of the danger.

"Are you sure we should go out in public and risk someone else getting hurt like that woman…?"

"That's another reason I picked the place. It's not super congested. We'll be able to spot someone stalking us, and with the backup I already have in place, hopefully we can grab him before anyone gets hurt."

"So this isn't just about pissing off your sisters by finding some ugly tree?"

"Oh, I still want the ugliest tree I can find," she assured him.

He turned onto the street where the buildings were farther apart with fewer people walking around. The decorations that hung from streetlamps and storefronts were worn and a little sad looking, like the tree she wanted. "Maybe we can find you an ugly wreath to match," he suggested.

She clapped her hands together. "That would be perfect. They will be able to see it without even going in the house."

He easily found an open parking spot, a parallel one in front of a dated department store. He would have had to circle the block or find a parking garage with a hefty hourly rate in the more popular area of the city. "Maybe I need to shop here more often," he remarked.

"I do most of my shopping online," she said. "But when I have to get something right away, I can usually find it here." She reached for her door handle before he could open his. While he hurried to catch up with her, she came around the front of the truck before he could. And she'd unzipped her jacket, her gloved hand moving inside it, close to her weapon.

"Do you see him?" he asked. He could feel him, that cold sensation rushing over him, making him shiver.

"Him?" she asked.

He shrugged. "Her. I don't know who it is." But he wished like hell he did, and that he knew the identity of the woman who'd died. He wanted this over, but when it was over...

He would have no reason to see the detective again. No reason but the little sizzle of attraction he felt for her. Hell, it was more than a sizzle. It had threatened to become a wildfire in her kitchen that morning, and it probably would have consumed him if they hadn't heard that noise.

"I don't see anyone out of the ordinary yet," she said as she reached for his hand, wrapping her gloved one around his.

Even through the leather, he felt a little jolt of awareness, of desire. She tugged him toward the department store. "You need a winter jacket and some gloves, or you're going to freeze when we're tree and wreath shopping."

He let her tug him into the store, mostly because they would probably be safer in it. And he would be warmer. He hadn't expected to find anything he would actually like, but the store had quite a variety of well-made clothing. He found a leather jacket, with a thick sheepskin lining, and gloves. He even picked up a couple of pairs of jeans and some long-sleeved shirts.

Heather urged him to try everything on for her, as if they were some reverse version of *Pretty Woman* with him in the role of prostitute, and then she started humming stripper music under her breath.

He glared at her even as his lips twitched with the urge to grin, and a laugh bubbled up the back of his throat. His hotshot team treated each other like this, with often very inappropriate humor. She'd fit in well with all of them. A hell of a lot better than his sister had.

But Brittney hadn't been worried about fitting in; she was only concerned with getting the story to launch her career. Heather, if she wound up accompanying him to his hotshot holiday party, was only worried about clearing a case. She probably wouldn't appreciate how cool his team was, and how much he cared about them, despite all the trouble the team had been having. Maybe because of it. In the short time since he'd met her, he and Heather had already been through a lot. Maybe that was why he was so bothered that she didn't care more about him, like he was beginning to care about her.

"Let me pay for this stuff and we can go find your Charlie Brown Christmas tree," he said. "We might have to look in some dumpsters, though."

"I'm up for a dumpster dive if you are," she said with a challenging smile. "I actually planned a little foray into an alley."

Uncertain if she was kidding or plotting, he shook his head. "I'm not going to wind up smelling like garbage just to prove a point. But if you want to…" He shrugged. "That's up to you. You'll just have to ride in the bed of my pickup instead of the cab on the way back to your place. I guess then we don't have to worry about your sad Christmas tree blowing out. You can hang on to it."

He wasn't really worried about her dumpster diving. He was worried about her putting herself in danger just to prove to Bob Bernard that she was a better detective than he was. He didn't want her getting hurt. The thought of that had his stomach churning with dread. It was the only thing inside him now. He headed toward the cash register to pay for his new clothes. Maybe he could convince Heather to eat before tree shopping or dumpster diving, whatever she planned to do.

Hell, what she really planned to do was catch a killer. That was the whole reason they were here, to lure the killer out to try for them again. Despite the warmth of the store, Trent shivered with dread.

Because he suspected her plan was going to work.

But would they survive it?

Trent walked away before Heather could determine if he was joking around or if he thought she was actually serious about getting her tree out of a dumpster. Maybe he was right that she took things a little too far with her sisters. But they were so fun to mess with...

And Bob Bernard. He deserved to be slapped down for being such a sexist idiot. No. She wasn't wrong, and she hated how Trent made her doubt herself.

This was why she didn't have the time or energy for relationships, for actually caring about another person's opinion of her and her actions. Trent had said that she cared too much about what Bernard and her sisters thought, but his opinion bothered her the most right now.

It was good that this relationship was just pretend and temporary. She had to catch whoever was after him as soon as possible so that she didn't start caring any more than she already did about him.

While he stood in line at the register, she could see him in the reflection of the window that she stared out.

She could keep an eye on him even while she watched the street. She could feel someone watching her. It wasn't Trent. She could hear the rumble of his deep voice as he responded to the women in line who were trying to flirt with him. He was so damn good-looking that everyone stared at him.

But who was staring at her right now?

Who was out there watching her, waiting for her to step outside?

She saw holiday shoppers. Mostly older couples who'd figured out this was a great area to shop for affordability and convenience without the chaos of the big malls and the shopping areas that were popular because they'd paid for publicity, like the ones Trent's sister promoted in her news stories. Heather had to get him to call Brittney Townsend; she suspected the reporter was already working the case, too, trying to find out what had happened at her brother's house. Just as she'd tried to find out what had been going on with his hotshot team.

Whatever was going on with them, Trent didn't seem to want to talk about it, and he didn't want to bother them at all if he could help it.

Maybe they could help if whoever had left the pretty holiday cards with those handwritten threatening notes tried again to carry out those threats. Hopefully their shopping trip had drawn him or her out, and Officer Howard was in place for the next phase of the plan. She could have called him to confirm, but that risked scaring off the assailant, if Howard was already in place.

She peered out the window. The afternoon was slipping away, casting shadows all around. A few mothers dragged kids along behind them, away from a Santa ringing a bell. There were more than a few Santa Clauses out there, a couple on each side of the street. Maybe it was a Santa shift change. The door opened and the scent of roasted almonds with cinnamon and nutmeg drifted in on the breeze. Her stomach growled, reminding her that she hadn't eaten.

So much had happened. With Trent...

With this maniac after him, threatening both of them. Maybe it was the cool breeze that had come in through the open door, or maybe it was that stare she could feel on her, but she shivered.

"Where are you?" she whispered with frustration.

"Right here," a deep voice rumbled close to her ear.

She jumped, startled that Trent had sneaked up on her. Some bodyguard she was proving to be for him. Good thing she'd brought in Officer Howard as backup. Maybe that was who she felt watching her. But then she didn't think she would feel so cold, especially in a warm store with her heavy coat on. She'd even zipped it up a bit so that no one would see her holster or the badge she'd tucked inside, underneath her scarf.

She wanted it on in case she needed to draw her weapon, in case she had to defend herself from the person determined to hurt Trent.

She couldn't imagine why someone would, especially when he smiled and leaned closer to her, skimming his lips across her cheek. "Hey, sweetheart, thanks for helping me pick out some new things."

Heat rushed through her from the touch of his mouth, from the closeness of his body and the desire for him that leaped to life again inside her. He was just acting; she was sure of it. Did he think the person was inside the store with them?

She glanced around and noticed a couple of the women

who'd been in line with him hovering near them. Their eyes were narrowed, their gazes running up and down her as if determining if she was worthy of him. Heather smiled and linked her arms around his neck. "You're very welcome, honey," she purred back at him.

"You ready to eat now?" he asked. "These nice ladies heard my stomach growling in line and gave me some recommendations for the restaurants in the area."

From the way they glared at Heather, clearly they had wanted to be the ones sharing a meal with him.

"I'm sorry we got so caught up in each other today that we forgot to eat," she said.

One of the women gasped. The other emitted a little sigh and offered Heather a faint smile, full of envy. Heather, resisting the urge to smirk and gloat, returned her smile. "Thanks for the recommendations," she said. "We are starving." Wrapping her hand around Trent's, she tugged him toward the door. Once they were on the street and out of earshot of the women, she said, "I'm supposed to be protecting you from serious threats. Not random women."

He chuckled. "I'm not above taking advantage of this situation." He glanced over his shoulder and whispered, "They're still there." Then he leaned down and brushed his mouth across Heather's.

Her pulse quickened, and her heart lurched as it began to beat frantically. Before she could kiss him back, he lifted his head. She blinked, trying to clear the passion from her gaze. She had to focus. Not on Trent but on their surroundings. She doubted the women were a threat.

But a threat was out there.

"I really am hungry," he said, and his topaz eyes glowed in the fading light.

Was he talking about food?

"Me, too," she said. She wasn't talking just about food, but she could certainly eat. "Where are these places?"

"There's an Italian restaurant on the next street," he said.

They were close because she could smell the seasonings: garlic, oregano, basil and rosemary. Her stomach growled.

"There's also a vegan—"

"Italian," she interjected. "Lasagna or pizza sounds good, or maybe both of them." She was just about salivating. "We can cut through this alley." She pointed to the one behind him, the one where Officer Howard was supposed to be waiting for them. If the assailant had followed them, certainly he wouldn't resist going after them in an alley. She hoped he resisted, though, so that they could eat.

He nodded. "And maybe we can find your Christmas tree in one of the dumpsters."

She shrugged. "I am sure I can find a straggly one on the lot."

The bag he carried bumped against her.

"Do you want to put that in the truck?"

He must have had them take off the tags because he wore the leather jacket. The gloves were shoved in one of the pockets. "No, it's fine. I can carry it."

"You just don't want to go back in case those women are waiting to pounce on you," she teased.

He shuddered. "You're right. Thanks for saving me from them."

The alley was flanked by tall buildings that cast deep

shadows around them. The farther they got from the street, the darker it got. And the colder. Goose bumps lifted on Heather's skin. But she wasn't sure if that was from the cold or from the sudden sense of foreboding that struck her.

Had Officer Howard made it into the alley like they'd planned?

She jerked the zipper down on her jacket, but before she could draw her weapon, someone in a blur of red velvet and white fur jumped out of the shadows. Then there was a flash of metal as Santa Claus swung something at them.

Heather had only a second to step in front of Trent before it hit her. Hard. And Santa Claus knocked her out cold.

The holidays were hell. Brittney hated this time of year because she got assigned the worst assignments. She spent most of her time outside waiting for snow to fall so they could get the perfect holiday shot of the big flakes floating down on her as decorations twinkled around her and she blathered on about some great sale and new gift idea and Santa sightings at the mall.

That shot would be coming up next. Right now she was stuck inside the mall outside a chain bookstore, covering some author's holiday book signing. Had the station forgotten about her scoop? That she was the one who found the Canterbury heir? Maybe if she'd gotten him to do that follow-up interview with her...

But she'd totally forgotten to even ask that morning. She just wanted to find Trent. To talk to him. To make sure he was all right.

And find out what the hell was going on, as she'd asked in her text with the picture of his burned house.

Not for a story but because she loved him and didn't want to lose him. But she worried it was already too late. That she'd already lost her big brother.

Chapter 12

Everything happened so damn fast. One minute they were laughing and joking about her saving him from those women. And then she saved him again, from the blow that knocked her out. Was that all it had done? He wanted to check on her, wanted to protect her like she'd protected him.

But he didn't have a gun. He didn't have the pipe that the Santa had swung at her either. All he had was the bag that he whipped at the Santa, smacking him across his bearded face and dark glasses.

When the guy was blinded, Trent grabbed for the pipe, trying to tug it away from him. But Santa was bigger than Trent and damn strong. So strong that he managed to hold on to the pipe with one hand and swing his fist into Trent's face with the other.

The blow hit his jaw and pain radiated throughout

his skull. But he dropped the bag, grabbed the pipe with both hands and jerked it from Santa's gloved grasp. The guy swung his gloved fist again, hitting Trent hard, so hard that dark spots fluttered across his vision, threatening to blind him. Threatening to knock him just as unconscious as Heather was.

Unless she wasn't just unconscious.

Fury filled him that this person had hurt her because of him. Trent swung the pipe at Santa, striking his shoulder. A curse rang out, the beard muffling it, so Trent didn't recognize the voice. Maybe he didn't recognize it because he was about to lose consciousness. To make sure the man left, he swung the pipe again. It swished through the air so fast and hard that it hit the asphalt before he could stop it, the contact jarring his arms and hurting his shoulders.

He had to lift it, had to use it to stop Santa. To protect himself and Heather, if it wasn't already too late. He lifted it, tightened his grip and swung again.

"Hey! Stop! Police!" a voice shouted. Then footsteps pounded against the asphalt.

Trent dropped the pipe, worried that he was going to get shot, that the officer was talking to him. The young man stopped next to him, but his gun was pointed toward the other end of the alley.

"You okay, Mr. Miles?"

Trent nodded, and his head swam again for a bit. "Heather—"

"I'm fine!" she said. "Go! Go after him!" She was sitting up now, leaning against the dumpster, and her gun was in her hand.

The officer hesitated. "I'll call for—"

"Go!" she yelled, and she sounded fine. Strong.

But Trent had seen how hard she'd been struck and how hard she'd fallen. He dropped to his knees beside her. "You need an ambulance," he said, and he reached out to touch her cheek where blood trailed down from her hair.

The gun she held turned toward him. Couldn't she see him? Was she not totally aware of what was going on?

She was conscious now, but with the blow she'd taken, she could have bleeding on the brain. She could still die, and with the way she was pointing that gun at him, so could he.

Heather had no idea how long she was out. It felt like hours but must have been just seconds because Trent had still been grappling with Santa over the pipe when she'd regained consciousness. But he'd taken a couple of fist blows to his head. She'd managed to unholster her weapon and draw it, but when she'd tried to aim it at the violent Santa Claus, she hadn't been able to focus.

With the two men fighting, she'd worried that she might shoot Trent instead. So Santa had gotten away, and she was pointing her gun at Trent. The safety was still on, but she jerked the barrel away from him and reholstered her weapon. "Sorry..." she murmured.

She'd screwed up so badly.

Again. She'd been so close to the perp, but due to being distracted over Trent, she hadn't reacted fast enough. She hadn't caught him, and once again, they both could have died. Where the hell had Officer Howard been? Where was he now?

"Are you okay?" she asked Trent, and she reached out, sliding her fingers along his jaw that was beginning to swell. He was a big guy, but the Santa Claus who had attacked them had been even bigger. And the young officer had gone after him alone. She needed to check on him, too.

"I'm fine," Trent said. "You're the one who needs an ambulance."

She needed to get up, to provide backup for her fellow officer. She grabbed at Trent's shoulders, using them to pull herself up. He rose with her, his hands on her waist, holding her steady. Probably holding her up, because her legs felt shaky and weak. Her head felt light, too, and black spots danced in front of her vision. She blinked to clear her eyes and drew in a deep breath. "I have to go after them."

Officer Howard hadn't been where she'd wanted him to be for her plan, but she didn't want him running off after the assailant, putting himself in danger.

"You can't help him when you need help yourself," Trent pointed out.

She shook her head, and pain reverberated through her skull. The blow hadn't hit her directly, probably because it had been meant for Trent, so when she'd stepped in front of him, it had glanced off the side of her head. "I'm fine."

"You lost consciousness," he said, his deep voice gruff with emotion. "For a second—"

"Yeah, just for a second," she interjected.

"I thought you were dead," he said. "You went down so fast…"

Her hip ached a bit, and now she knew why. She'd hit the asphalt hard. Or maybe it was aching from the night before, when they'd jumped out of the way of that speeding vehicle and had hit the ground.

"You need an MRI," he said.

"I need to make sure that officer is okay," she insisted, that her botched plan hadn't gotten him hurt, too.

Trent pointed toward the end of the alley where the officer who had run after Santa had returned. "He looks fine. Better than you."

She touched her face, feeling the blood on her cheek. It was drying. Whatever wound she had probably wouldn't need stitches. But her own injuries were the least of her concerns.

"You okay?" she asked Officer Howard.

"I'm sorry," he said. "I got stuck behind some kind of parade and didn't make it here in time to hide out in the alley." He gestured toward the end of it. "The parade is still going on out there, where I grabbed some old guy on the street and scared him half to death." He shook his head with self-disgust and frustration.

"Wrong Santa?" Trent asked.

He nodded. "There were too damn many of them running around out there for that parade. I'm so sorry I got held up. I tried calling, but it wouldn't go through."

Maybe that store had some kind of cell signal blocker; some did. Or the assailant had one.

Heather groaned, not with pain but frustration. She'd been wrong that this area wouldn't be busy, that it would be a good place to be able to spot whoever was following them. But the perp was smarter than she was; he'd been ready with that damn Santa suit.

"Are you okay?" the officer asked Heather. "Do you need an ambulance?"

"Yes," Trent answered for her. "She needs to get checked for a concussion."

"No," she said. "I'm fine. I'm mad he got away." Again.

"I'm sorry I didn't get here like we planned and that I lost him," the officer said, his voice gruff with his frustration and guilt. "He got out of the alley so fast and I didn't know which direction he went in the crowd."

He would have been closer to the perp if he hadn't wasted time checking on her. *Damn it!* She couldn't curse him aloud for doing what he'd thought was right. Hell, he was doing a better job than she was.

"You didn't do anything wrong," she assured him. She was the one who'd taken a chance she shouldn't have.

"I'm really sorry, Detective Bolton, that you got hurt." He glanced at Trent. "You, too."

He wasn't nearly as sorry as she was.

To allay his guilt, she smiled at him. "It was my plan, and it was too risky." For all of them…

She'd wanted the perp to try for them again, like he had. But once again, she hadn't been ready like she should have been. While her plan was working in flushing out the perp, she was the one who wasn't following through, who wasn't catching him like she wanted. Like she *needed* to do. Instead of protecting Trent, she was putting him in danger. She never would have forgiven herself if he had died. He hadn't wanted to go along with her plan in the first place and obviously with good reason; he kept getting hurt because of it.

She glanced at Trent then, focusing on the bright bruises on his handsome face. The one on his jaw and the other near his eye were getting darker, swelling more. He needed medical attention, too.

While she didn't need an ambulance, she would make a trip to the ER. Get that MRI, make sure her head was fine. But it hadn't been all that fine even before she'd taken the blow. She kept getting distracted, missing her chances to catch Trent's stalker. If he tried again and she missed, she and Trent might both die.

This time wasn't like the parking lot. This time he had no doubt that he'd struck them. That he'd hurt them. He'd even thought he'd killed her for a moment…until she'd come to and pointed that damn gun at him.

She could have killed him, her or that other cop who'd appeared at the end of the alley, distracting her for a second so that he could run. Fortunately, there'd been a crowd on the street, with a lot of other guys in Santa suits. So even though the uniformed cop had pursued him, he'd gotten away. This time.

But so had they.

They were both still alive. But he wasn't going to allow them to stay that way much longer. He had to end this soon. And the next time, he would make damn sure they were dead before he got away.

Chapter 13

Trent wanted to be furious with Heather for putting herself in danger. But he couldn't be angry with her when she was clearly so angry with herself.

At least that was all she was. Well, that and lightly concussed. She'd agreed to go to the ER, though, maybe more for his sake than her own. She'd seemed more concerned about his couple of bruises than what could have been a serious brain injury for her.

While they were waiting for the results of her CT scan, they'd managed to finally eat. But the hospital cafeteria food settled heavily in the bottom of his stomach, along with a sense of dread.

The guy after him wasn't giving up, not until he succeeded. And he'd seen Trent with Heather too many times for her to be safe even if Trent left her house and left her alone. The would-be killer wouldn't leave her alone.

He would know that killing her would make Trent

suffer just like he wanted. Trent wasn't even sure how he'd come to care about her so quickly and so much.

Her silence, as he drove toward her house from the hospital, unnerved him. She rarely had nothing to say, at least not since he'd met her. But then she had been focused on solving his case, on finding out who that woman was and who had killed her. So she'd been asking him a lot of questions then.

About his coworkers. About his friends. About his family.

He felt a pang of regret and concern. Brittney had left him more messages and texts. While Heather had been getting her test, he'd texted her back: I'm fine. Don't worry about me. Stay safe.

She'd quickly replied with a: Call me.

When he'd ignored it, she'd called him, but he'd declined accepting it. He couldn't talk to her now without making her worry more. And he couldn't allow her to come anywhere near him, not after what had nearly happened to Heather. Twice.

And that other woman, the woman who hadn't been as lucky. Who the hell was she? And how would they find out?

If only he hadn't let the killer get away...

But those blows had rocked him, threatening his consciousness like Heather had lost hers for those long moments when he'd wondered if she was alive or dead. He glanced across the console at her now, uneasy with her silence.

"Are you okay?" he asked.

"You heard the doctor. I'm fine," she said. "No concerns about swelling or bleeding."

She'd taken that blow for him, stepping in front of

him when the Santa had jumped from the shadows. Her first instinct had been to protect him. But that was her job; he had to remember not to take it personally.

"You've been quiet," he remarked.

She sighed and touched her temple. "Got a bit of a headache."

"I'm sorry," he said.

"You're sorry?"

"You got hurt protecting me," he said.

"Some protector I am," she replied. "I was the one who put you in danger. This was a stupid plan. And you were right to question it and me."

"It is working," he had to admit, albeit with concern.

"It's too risky," she said.

He tensed, unsure of where she was going with this. He knew where he was going, though. He turned onto her street and proceeded down it to her house. His spot was still open at the curb, and he pulled into it and reached to shut off the ignition.

But Heather gripped his hand in hers. "Don't," she said. "You're safer if you go stay at a hotel with security, and I'll send the patrol unit that followed us from the hospital with you for protection."

"And who will protect you?" he asked. "You're in just as much, if not more, danger than I am because of how damn well your plan worked."

"I'll have another officer come back here," she said. "They can take your spot at the curb."

"You have a concussion," he reminded her.

She tightened her grasp on his hand and sharply asked, "So you don't think I know what I'm talking about right now?"

"You sure don't sound like yourself," he said. "And

what I meant about the concussion was that you need someone to check on you—"

"The doctor said that wasn't a big concern," she interjected.

"Not a *big* concern," he said, repeating her phrasing. "But there could still be complications." The physician had obviously doubted it, though, or he would have tried to keep her for observation.

"I'm fine," she said.

"Really?" he questioned her. "You're giving up on closing this case? You're going to let Bob Bernard's record stand?"

She released a low growl of either anger or frustration. "I'm not giving up," she said. "I will find out who that woman was and who the hell was wearing the Santa suit in the alley."

"Do you think they could be unrelated?" he asked. "Maybe Santa just wanted to mug us?"

"He didn't try to grab my purse. Did he take your wallet?" she asked, one of her dark blond brows arched above her eyes that glowed in the light from the dashboard.

"There wasn't time," he reminded her. "It all happened so fast."

"Too damn fast," she agreed. "But I still should have been ready for it."

"You stepped in front of me," he reminded her. "You took the blow that was meant for me."

"But I let him get away…" Her voice cracked with her frustration.

"Because you were knocked out," he said.

She released his hand then and leaned back against the passenger's door. "Wow…"

"What?"

"I figured you'd be furious with me," she said. "That you'd be acting like the reason I got hurt was because I'm female and that my plan was flaky, like Bob Bernard will say once he hears about this."

"I told you I'm not sexist," he reminded her. One reason he'd been upset about her competition with the older detective was because she'd put herself in danger for it by trying to flush out the killer. The other was that he'd realized he wanted her to care more about him than that competition. "Michaela and Hank would kick my ass if I was."

"Michaela and Hank?" she asked, her brow furrowing beneath her wispy bangs. Then she flinched as if the movement had aggravated the head she'd already said was aching.

"Michaela and Hank, short for Henrietta, are on my hotshot team, and they're badasses. Like you."

"Some badass," she murmured. "I got knocked out cold."

"If you hadn't stepped in front of me, *I* would have been knocked out cold," he said. Or, with the angle at which Santa had swung that pipe, he might have been in worse shape than she was. "And you regained consciousness fast. You're probably more the reason that Santa ran away than the officer catching up to us was."

She released a shaky sigh and the tension eased from her body. He shut off the engine, and she didn't try to stop him, not even when he got out of the truck. She just got out, too, and walked up to the side door with him. Her hand was inside her jacket, probably on her gun. So she was worried.

Like he was...

Their stalker was still out there. No doubt waiting for the chance to try for them again.

Heather had fully intended to call off the plan and force Trent to leave. Ever since the close call in the alley, she'd been kicking herself that she hadn't listened to him earlier. That she hadn't let him leave when he'd wanted to.

But she couldn't know if he would be any safer away from her than he was with her. In fact, she suspected she would try harder than anyone else to keep him safe because he mattered to her. Too much, which was probably why she couldn't focus when she was around him, like she needed to.

She unlocked the side door and stepped inside first, her gun drawn, just in case the stalker had beaten them back and managed to get in and was waiting. But when she flipped on the lights, the only being she found waiting for them was Sammy, sitting on the counter. He wouldn't have been upstairs if there was someone else inside the house.

"You might need to replace your security system with a real one," Trent suggested, pointing at the cat.

"I won't replace him," she said. She reached out for him, and the black cat rubbed against her hand, purring. He'd forgiven her for his trip to the garage earlier. Or he'd forgotten.

She couldn't forget everything that had happened, how many close calls they had had. And if something had happened...

She released a shaky breath of relief that it hadn't. That, except for a few additional bumps and bruises, they were fine. Medically.

Emotionally, she was a mess. Heather couldn't remember ever feeling this unsure of herself.

Big hands gripped her shoulders and turned her around. "Are you okay?" he asked.

She shook her head.

"Is it the concussion?" he asked with concern, cupping her cheek in his palm. "Do you need some ibuprofen?"

"It's not my head," she said. She was worried it might be her heart if she wasn't careful. She certainly hadn't been careful since she'd met firefighter Trent Miles. "I'm fine. I just…"

"What?" he asked.

"I just thought you'd be mad at me," she said. "Mad about what happened…"

"I'm mad at the person who came after us, not you," he said. "And you're already kicking yourself enough. I'm not going to kick you, too. Not when I'd much rather kiss you."

She wanted that, too, so damn badly. When she'd stepped out of Trent's truck, she'd seen the patrol car pulling up to a curb behind them, in front of the neighbor's house. They had protection now.

They were safe from the stalker.

She just wasn't sure if they were safe from each other. "This was just supposed to be a pretend relationship."

"Can't we pretend it's real just for one night?" he asked. "Because if I'd lost you today…" His voice, gruff with emotion, trailed off, as if he couldn't even say aloud what he was thinking.

What she'd been thinking…

They could have died a few times over the past couple of days. Life was short. So maybe it made sense to make the most of it when you could. She reached out and caught his hand in hers and tugged him until they reached her bedroom.

He stopped just inside the door, pulling his hand from hers. "Are you sure?" he asked.

She turned to study him in the soft light from the chandelier that hung over her bed. Even with the bruises and the swelling on his face, he was so damn handsome. And the attraction between them…

It was more intense than anything she'd felt before. She needed to find out what it would be like to be with him in every way.

"Yes," she replied.

"But you're hurt. Your head…"

"I'm fine," she said. Maybe the blow had knocked some sense into her. She'd been so damn worried about being professional, about closing her case, that she'd wanted to resist temptation. If something had happened to them, she would never know what might have been. How much pleasure she might have experienced.

"I am very sure." She unzipped her jacket and tossed it onto the clawed-up reading chair. Her holster and weapon she put in the drawer beside the bed, within reach, in case she needed it.

She hoped like hell she wouldn't need it. She didn't want any alarm going off or a noise at the door to stop them this time. She pulled her sweater up and over her head, then tossed it onto the chair, too.

Trent's breath audibly caught. He still stood inside the door, as if frozen or unsure. But his eyes, those seriously beautiful topaz eyes, stared intently at her.

She glanced down at the red lace bra she wore and smiled. With the way she dressed on the outside, he probably hadn't expected it. She unsnapped her jeans and dropped them, revealing the red lace panties that matched the bra.

And he grunted like she'd punched him, like Santa had.

"You okay?" she asked with a smile.

He shook his head. "No. I'm in pain."

She stepped out of her ankle boots and jeans and tugged off her socks before walking over to him. "Do you need to go back to the hospital?" she asked as she trailed a fingertip down the row of buttons on his flannel shirt.

His leather jacket was unzipped. He shrugged it off now. Then he grabbed the sides of his shirt and pulled it open, sending buttons pinging across the hardwood floor. "I am suddenly very hot," he said.

She touched his bare chest, trailing her fingertips down the rippling muscles of his stomach. She tugged at the button on his jeans, then pulled down the zipper of his fly that strained with his erection.

He sighed as she released him. But when she pushed down his boxers to stroke him, he wrapped his long fingers around her wrist. "We'll be done quickly if you touch me," he warned her. "It's been a while."

Skeptical, she arched a brow. "Really? With the way women throw themselves at you?"

"I've been busy," he said with a sigh.

"Me, too," she said. The last time had been so damn disappointing she decided not to date for a while. But she didn't think there was any way Trent was going to disappoint her.

"So you've let this…" He ran his fingers along the top of the demi cup of her lace bra. "…go to waste?"

She shook her head. "I wear this for me." With as tough as her job was, she liked a reminder of her femininity.

He rubbed his finger along the top of the cup again but touched her skin as much as the bra. Her nipple hardened against the red lace as desire gripped her. Through the bra, he touched her nipple, rubbing his thumb back and forth across it.

She arched her neck and moaned.

He leaned down, sliding his lips along her throat, as he lifted his other hand. He cupped both breasts in his palms and teased the nipples through the lace.

Her legs shook a little as her core began to throb. He was going to make her come with just that touch. A gasp slipped through her lips at the first little jolt of pleasure.

He groaned. "You are so responsive." One of his hands slipped down her body, over her stomach to ease inside her panties. He found her heat, her wetness, as he dipped a finger inside her.

"Oh…" She needed him so badly. She clutched at him, pulling his hips against her, and he stumbled forward, onto her. She fell back onto the bed. They were a tangle of arms and legs and passion. She reached up, finding his mouth with hers. She kissed him deeply, sliding her tongue through his lips, stroking it over his.

He pushed her panties down and kept stroking her with his fingers, his thumb against the most sensitive part of her body. Then he moved his head down to her breasts, nudging one cup down. He closed his lips over her nipple and gently tugged.

And she came apart, an orgasm gripping her, making her quiver and moan. But still, it wasn't enough. "I want you inside me," she said and found him through his boxers, stroking him.

But he pulled back again and stood up, disappearing for a moment as she lay limply on the bed, staring up at the chandelier. The orgasm had been good but she needed more.

Then he was back, dropping a condom packet next to her head. But he left it there as he moved down her body. He unclasped the bra and pulled it off her, then removed her panties.

He kissed her everywhere. Her lips. Her collarbone. The curve of her shoulder. The side of her breast. Her stomach. Then his lips moved over her core, his tongue flicking and teasing before slipping inside her. And he made love to her with his mouth.

She came fast and furiously, gripping the sheets, trying to hang on as the intensity of another orgasm threatened to overwhelm her again.

Then he grabbed the packet, his hand shaking, tore it open and sheathed himself. Finally he joined their bodies, his erection easing inside her.

He was so damn big that he stretched and filled her. She arched and moved her hips, taking him as deep as she could. Then she locked her arms and legs around him, meeting his thrusts. The tension built inside her again. The friction of his chest against her breasts, of his body driving deep into hers, drove her wild. And she came again, screaming his name.

Then his body tensed, and a guttural sound emerged from him as he shuddered and joined her in the madness. Or maybe it was the sanity. Because if something had happened to either of them before this, she would have missed out on the most intense pleasure she'd ever felt.

But she couldn't help but worry that, with their lives under threat, it might be followed by the most intense pain.

I'm fine. Don't worry about me. Stay safe.

If he'd sent the text to reassure Brittney, it hadn't worked. She was even more concerned. Something was definitely going on with her big brother, and he didn't want her involved. She'd thought that it was because he hadn't forgiven her for exposing his best friend's big secret. But now she suspected he was protecting her.

Shots had been fired at his house, the body, the fire and then nearly getting run down in the firehouse parking lot.

Someone was after Trent. Maybe he thought anyone close to him was in danger, too. Or maybe she just wanted to believe that so she would stop feeling so guilty about betraying him.

She'd lost his trust. No wonder he didn't want to talk to her. But Trent, being Trent, was protective, so he still cared enough to want to make sure that she stayed safe.

She was more concerned about him and this new girlfriend of his. They were the ones in danger. From whom and why?

Chapter 14

Pain pulled Trent from his sleep, making him groan and grimace. He opened his eyes, struggling to wake up fully, and stared up into that little furry face. Once again he'd awakened with Sammy on his chest, kneading him with those tiny, sharp-clawed paws. Was that who had slept with him last night?

Had he just dreamed what had happened between him and Heather? The mind-blowing sex?

Sammy jumped off him, and now Trent could see the ceiling, the antique chandelier dangling over him. He was in Heather's room, not the guest room. He hadn't dreamed what had happened. And then happened again sometime during the night.

And maybe again this morning.

Or had he dreamed that time?

His body got hard thinking about how damn good

she felt. How hot and wet and tight. How her muscles gripped him, stroking him, and her lips and hands…

He groaned with desire, with need, for her now. But when he reached out, he found only tangled sheets. He turned his head to find her side of the bed empty, just a dent in the pillow from where her head had been when it hadn't been on his chest.

The sheets were cold. How long had she been gone?

And where had she gone?

Concern gripped him nearly as much as the desire. Had something happened? Had the stalker come back and managed to get inside this time?

Wouldn't he have heard something?

But with everything they'd been through, and all they'd done to each other last night, he'd been so exhausted that he probably wouldn't have heard a gunshot.

"Heather?" he called out softly.

Something skittered across the hardwood floor near him. He jumped up and stepped on something hard. Swallowing the curse clawing up the back of his throat, he lifted his foot to find one of the buttons from his shirt stuck to it. Sammy chased another one across the floor, and Trent smiled. Then he noticed the chair held only his clothes.

Heather's were gone. Even her puffy coat. And when he opened the top drawer of the bedside table, he didn't find her weapon and holster. She'd gone somewhere and taken her gun with her. Panic squeezed his chest, making it hard to breathe.

What the hell had he slept through?

What the hell had she done?

Heather had been awake for a while but felt like she

was still in a dream. Was Trent Miles really naked in her bed? Had they done what she thought, what her slightly aching body led her to believe they had?

Had the best sex of her life? And not just once…

The man had satisfied her over and over again. He was like a damn machine. If those women from the checkout line at the department store only knew…

Or maybe they did. Maybe it had been one of them who'd donned the Santa suit and attacked her. Knowing now what she knew so intimately about Trent, Heather couldn't really blame them. But from the size of her attacker, she didn't believe it had been either of them, so she'd checked police reports in the area for any Santa Claus muggings. She'd also checked with the uniformed officer parked outside to see if she had noticed anyone hanging around the area.

Anyone big and too damn focused on her house. Because she could feel him out there, especially when she stood at the window of that patrol car. Despite her puffy jacket, she shivered with a sudden chill.

He was out there. Watching.

Waiting for her to be stupid enough to give him another chance to kill her and Trent. She was being vigilant now, her holster strapped on, her gaze swiveling around. After she spoke to the officer, who hadn't noticed anyone, she walked back to the house.

The guy was big, so he wasn't invisible. But like yesterday on the street, he had done a damn good job of blending in with his surroundings by wearing the Santa suit. It had also hidden his face so well that she had no idea what he looked like beneath that big white beard and those dark glasses. Had that been so that nobody would describe him if he got caught? Or so that nobody would recognize him?

Was he one of Trent's coworkers? Someone he might have considered a friend? Or was he just some random stalker who had seen articles about Trent and gotten obsessed? But how would he have known the code to Trent's lock? And who was that woman? Not Jerome Whittaker's wife. The young officer at the curb had followed up on that and had worked on the list as well, but of the few additional firefighters Officer Morgan had talked to, none had offered any hints about the dead woman's identity. Maybe if they discovered who she was, they could figure out who *he* was.

He had to be someone close to Trent. Someone who knew him well. Unfortunately, he also knew what he was doing. Like that Santa disguise. Somehow he'd blended into her neighborhood yesterday. Maybe he'd worn a mail uniform, which was why no one had thought it strange that he'd messed with her mail slot.

Heather stood next to Trent's truck and studied the area. It was early morning on a Sunday, so not many people were out and about yet. A woman jogged past. An older couple backed their vehicle out of their driveway, probably heading to church.

So where was he?

Was he inside one of the couple of houses on the street that were empty because their owners had gone away for the holiday? Had he broken in to use the cover of their home to spy on her and Trent?

To watch them and wait for her to give him another opportunity to attack? She wasn't going to give him the satisfaction, not unless she was damn sure she had enough backup that he would not get away again.

Not noticing anything out of the ordinary, she turned and headed back to the house. She unlocked and opened the side door, and as she did, she heard boards creaking with a weight much heavier than Sammy's.

It could have been Trent, but with as deeply as he'd been sleeping when she'd crawled out of bed, she hadn't thought he would be awake yet. Had someone sneaked inside? Maybe through a basement window or the French doors on the primary bedroom?

She shouldn't have left Trent alone, sleeping and vulnerable. But she'd needed to get out of that bed so she wouldn't reach for him again, so she wouldn't wake him up to make love like she had in the night. And earlier that morning...

After everything he'd been through, he'd deserved his rest. And she'd gotten freaked out by how much she'd needed him. She'd never felt that way before, had never wanted anyone that badly, and had certainly never felt so damn much pleasure.

As much as Trent had needed his rest, he also needed protection. If something had happened to him because she'd left...

She drew her weapon and pointed it ahead of her as she slowly ascended those couple of steps to the kitchen.

"Don't shoot," a deep voice murmured, and she turned to find Trent standing in front of her, his hands raised above his head.

"Sorry," she said as she slid her gun back into the holster. "I heard the creaking floorboards, but I thought you would still be sleeping, and I..."

"Am a little jumpy?" he finished for her with a dark brow arched in question.

"Yes, I am," she freely admitted. "Aren't you, after last night?"

"Are you referring to what happened in the alley or what came after?"

"What came after?" she asked, making her eyes wide as if she had no clue, but she couldn't suppress the smile curving her lips.

He chuckled.

"The trip to the ER? That questionable cafeteria dinner?" she asked, feigning confusion.

"Are you criticizing our first date?" he asked.

"If that's your idea of a date, no wonder you haven't been in a relationship for a while," she teased.

He grinned and stepped a little closer to her, staring down at her with desire and mischief glinting in those light brown eyes. "So what's your idea of a good first date?" he asked.

"Oh, fighting off a deranged Santa in an alley probably wouldn't be high on my list, nor would having a bomb squad make sure my house isn't going to blow up."

He sighed. "You're the one who proposed this relationship."

"Pretend relationship," she reminded him and herself. That was all it was supposed to have been.

"That didn't feel very *pretend* last night," he said, and he stepped a little closer, his body brushing up against hers.

A jolt of desire, from the heat of contact, had her stumbling backward. His big hands grasped her upper arms, steadying her. She glanced over her shoulder, realizing she might have tumbled down those couple of stairs to the side door if he hadn't caught her.

"Careful," he said, and he stepped back, bringing

her with him, farther into her small kitchen. "After last night, you shouldn't be so jumpy."

Despite acting like she didn't know, she was well aware of what he was talking about, of how many times he'd released the tension in her body, making her feel boneless and completely satiated. Until the desire gripped her again, like now.

That probably made her the most nervous, that no matter how many times they'd made love, she couldn't get enough of him. And she might start hoping this relationship wasn't just pretend.

"Well, I've had a lot of coffee already," she said.

"So you were doing what?" he asked. "Running around the block? Is that where you were when I woke up?"

She shook her head. "No. I was bringing coffee to the officer watching the house."

"As if he wasn't already in love with you," Trent said.

She laughed. "Officer Ashley Morgan? She appreciated the coffee, but I think she's married."

Trent's long body tensed and he dropped his hands from her arms. "Like the woman found dead in my house."

"Yes." A pang of guilt struck her. While she'd been trying to flush out a killer, that woman remained in the morgue. Unclaimed. "We need to find out who she was. I had the missing persons unit forward their list to the coroner, but according to him, none of the missing women matched the size and age of the body of the unidentified woman."

"So no one's reported her missing?"

She shook her head.

"So how do we find out who she was?" Trent asked, and his broad shoulders slumped as if the burden was his.

"I think one of your coworkers knows who she is," she said. "Those guys were using your house for more than sleep." Officer Morgan had just confirmed that Mrs. Whittaker suspected the same thing.

He grimaced. "I really didn't know they were using it that way. I've been gone so much with my hotshot team."

"That's why they used it that way," she said. "For privacy." But just for an affair or for a murder as well? And was that murderer worried Trent might know who he was? Was that the reason for the attempts on his life and hers?

"All of your local crew hasn't called me back yet," she said. She was most interested in the one who'd left the firehouse right before they'd nearly been run down. Whittaker, on the other hand, had an alibi: he'd been with his suspicious wife. "I really need to talk to Barry Coats."

Trent nodded. "I'll check and see if he's scheduled to be on shift right now."

"Yes, I need to talk to him in person," she said. "If he's not on shift, I'll go to his house."

"You? What about us?" he asked. "Aren't you going to stick close to me, for my protection?"

They couldn't have gotten any closer last night. While she'd experienced more pleasure than ever before, it wasn't safe—for either of them—to repeat that.

"Maybe we're safer apart," she said.

"Then you need more police officers to follow us around if we're going different places," he pointed out.

He wasn't wrong. She couldn't leave him unprotected, or herself, any more than she already had.

She sighed.

"And Barry is more likely to tell me the truth than he is you."

She wasn't so sure about that. "I'm a pretty good interviewer," she said. "I can usually manage to get the truth out of a suspect."

"Do you beat them with a rubber hose or use your charm?" he asked with a wicked grin.

Even with the bruises from the fight in the alley, he was so damn handsome. So irresistible.

"Depends on the suspect," she said. "Some of them might like the rubber hose."

He chuckled, a low, naughty chuckle full of amusement and seduction.

Her pulse quickened. She wanted him so badly. But the more they did what they had last night, the more likely she was going to want it to continue.

Forever.

With the danger they were in, not just now, but always with their careers, there was no way they could have forever.

That cop car hadn't just driven through the neighborhood a few times like it had the day before. No. It was parked right outside her house. Sometimes another patrol car drove up, stopped and both drivers rolled down their windows to talk. They also kept glancing around the area, like Bolton had earlier when she'd brought that officer a cup of coffee.

They looked right past him, not even noticing him inside the vehicle with the tinted rear windows. They'd looked at it a couple of times, but it was clear that no one sat in the driver's seat. He was in the back, staring out the windows from under the pile of blankets that had kept him warm and concealed.

But Bolton must have sensed him there or was smart enough to know he wasn't going to give up. She'd had her hand on her holster. She was scared. Trent Miles, big brave firefighter, must have been scared, too, since he hadn't left his detective girlfriend's side since the fire at his house. Even when they'd gone shopping, they'd stuck close together, so close that she'd taken the blow meant for him. Maybe it was good that she had, or she might have shot him right away. And he wouldn't have the chance to kill Trent. She was going to die, too. They both had to. Soon.

They wouldn't be able to stay inside that house forever. They had jobs; they had to work. To fight fires and investigate crimes, they had to leave that house. And when they did, they would die.

Chapter 15

Trent didn't want to go to the firehouse. And it wasn't just because he didn't want to interrogate members of his local fire crew. He wanted to stay with Heather, in her bed, like last night, enjoying each other and forgetting about everything. About the fact that they were in danger, since someone else had already died.

He felt guilty over his selfishness. But Heather could make him forget about the guilt, too, and leave him with nothing but pleasure. Intense, mind-blowing pleasure. Just as he pushed away from the counter to reach for her, her cell rang.

She pulled it from the pocket of her puffy coat and stared at the screen. "Officer Ashley..." She swiped Accept and put the phone on speaker. "Detective Bolton."

"Detective, there's someone approaching your house right now. Do you want me to stop him?"

Holding the cell in one hand, Heather drew her weapon

with the other. Then she rushed past Trent and into her living room, where that big front window looked out over the street and the man walking up to the house, dragging a Christmas tree behind him. The guy wore a Santa hat over his gray hair and a burnt-orange Carhartt jacket, not a full suit like the man from the alley.

"What the hell…" she murmured. "Thanks, Officer, for being vigilant. But I know this Santa Claus. He's my dad."

Trent gasped at the quick jab of panic in his heart. Then he rushed toward the front door, pulling it open to help the older man with the tree.

"What are you doing, Dad?" Heather asked as she followed Trent out. "I thought Mom had projects she wanted you to do for her at home."

The older man stopped and stared at Trent. Ignoring the stare, Trent picked up the tree and maneuvered it carefully through the front door. The scent of pine enveloped him as sap stuck to his hands. He wasn't a fan of real trees, and not just because of the mess, but because people so often let them dry out. And then fires started.

"I…" Her dad glanced back at her. "Your sisters were threatening to get you a tree again this year, and I didn't want them messing up the house like they did last time."

"You've done a beautiful job with all your renovations," Trent praised him.

"Uh…thanks…" Mr. Bolton glanced back at his daughter and arched a brow much the same way she did.

"Dad, this is Trent Miles. He's a…" She glanced at Trent now, her brow furrowing. Then she continued, "…friend. Trent, this is my dad, Charlie Bolton."

"Nice to meet you, sir," he said, holding the tree steady with one hand while extending his other to her father.

"You, too," Charlie said. "You're pretty strong. I could have used your help around here for some of these projects. Wonder why I haven't met you before..."

Trent smiled. Heather obviously took after her dad with the suspicious nature and blunt questions. He liked him.

"Trent is a hotshot firefighter," Heather said.

Charlie chuckled. "She razzes you like that?"

Heather laughed. "No, Dad. A hotshot firefighter is the kind that travels around, putting out wildfires. He's gone a lot."

Trent nodded. "Yes, sir, I just recently returned to the city after a call out West."

"That big one on the news? I saw that," Charlie said. "Some guys died in that."

Trent's shoulders sagged a bit. "Yes, before our team got there." He hadn't lost another friend, fortunately, but he mourned all losses of life, especially that woman who'd died in his house and he didn't even know who she was.

"Dangerous job," Charlie observed with a glance at his daughter, as if he was worried about her getting too attached to him.

Or maybe he was just worried about her, too, because of her dangerous job. One that Trent's case had made even more dangerous.

"Dad, I appreciate you dropping off the tree, but I really don't want to get you in trouble with Mom. Shouldn't you get back to her projects?"

Charlie narrowed his eyes, the same deep green as his daughter's, and stared at her. "Trying to get rid of your old man?"

"Trent and I were just on our way out," she said.

Trent had wanted to delay that, and not just because he didn't want to interrogate his coworkers. He'd wanted to be with her again, to find out what sexy underwear she was wearing today, and experience all that passion and heat. That heat spread to his face as her dad turned his narrow-eyed stare on him, almost as if he knew what had been on Trent's mind before he'd arrived. Although he hadn't caught them, Trent felt like he had.

"You drink my beer?" her dad asked.

"Dad!" Heather exclaimed. "It's eight o'clock in the morning."

"I didn't touch your beer," Trent assured him. He got drunk enough off the desire he felt for the man's daughter; he sure didn't need any alcohol, especially with some maniac trying to hurt them.

Charlie nodded. "It's fine if you do," he said. "Just make sure you leave me at least one. I'm going to need it with all the work this one's mother—" he pointed at Heather "—has me doing on our place right now."

"Then you should get back to it before she starts looking for you," Heather warned him.

"I'll put this tree in a stand, but you'll have to decorate it," Charlie said.

"I'll help you," Trent said. And he wasn't just putting off the trip to the firehouse now. He was making sure her home wouldn't accidentally burn down. It was up to the police officers watching it to make sure it didn't intentionally burn down like his house had.

Trent rushed around, collected the stand from the basement and grabbed a pitcher of water from the kitchen. When he neared the living room, he overheard father and daughter talking.

"Don't tell Mom about Trent," she said. "She'll tell Hailey and Hannah, and it'll be a whole thing…"

Charlie chuckled. "You don't want your mom and sisters to have a heads-up before they meet him at Christmas? You want to surprise them?"

"I don't want them to meet him," she said.

"So he's not invited to Christmas?" her father asked.

"Dad…I just… We're just friends."

But after what he'd heard, Trent realized he wasn't really even that to her. Despite last night, she had no intention of taking this relationship from pretend to real. She just wanted to clear another case and prove to Bob Bernard that a woman could be a better detective than a man.

Ignoring the hard jab to his heart, Trent forced a smile and joined them in the living room. Maybe her father had realized he'd overheard them, because he gave Trent a look of pity.

Trent forced a smile back at him. He didn't deserve the guy's pity. Heather hadn't done anything wrong; he was the one who hadn't stuck to the plan, who'd started to genuinely care about her. He realized that even if her plan worked and the stalker was caught before he managed to carry out his threats, Trent was still going to get hurt before all this was over.

"How do we play this?" Trent asked as they sat in his truck outside the firehouse. It was the first thing he'd said to her since leaving her place.

She smiled. "This feels like déjà vu. You asked me that the last time we sat in this parking lot."

"Yeah, then we got out and nearly got run over," he said with a slight shudder.

"Right after Barry Coats left the building," she reminded him.

He sighed. "I checked the schedule. He's here now. But I don't understand why he would try to run us down. Or send me those stupid Christmas card threats. We've always gotten along."

"Because you let him use your house," she said. "Maybe he wants to make sure you don't figure out who died in that fire and link it to him. Maybe that's all this is about, covering up a different crime."

Trent shook his head. "I don't know. It feels more personal than that. Those notes feel more personal, like someone really wants me to suffer."

"Could one of your coworkers have it out for you?" she asked. "Could they be harboring a grudge over something?"

He shook his head again. "I don't know. Some guys might think, because the captain and my dad were good friends, that I get preferential treatment. But trying to kill me because of perceived nepotism seems a little extreme."

She shrugged. "You never know what kind of grudges someone else might be holding or secrets they might be keeping," she said.

"No, you don't," he agreed.

"Are you talking about your hotshot friend? The Canterbury heir?"

Or was there something else going on with his hotshot team? In her big news report that had exposed his friend for lying about his identity, Brittney Townsend had also hinted about other accidents and danger that had threatened the lives of everyone on his team.

"Ethan isn't the only person keeping secrets," he said.

"I had no idea why my local coworkers were really crashing at my place when I was gone."

While Whittaker had pretty much admitted it, Barry Coats had ignored her messages and not returned any of her calls. She needed answers from him. She just wasn't sure if the best way to get them was as a no-nonsense detective or Trent's pretend girlfriend.

"As for how we play this," she said, "I think we carry on as we did the other night, when we nearly got run over. We were telling the truth about who I am but…"

"Lying about what you are to me," Trent finished for her.

But would they be lying now? After what had happened last night? Or was it all still just *pretend* to Trent?

She wished it was with her. But when he leaned across his truck console and brushed his mouth across hers, her pulse leaped, and her body heated up with the desire he could inspire in her just from breathing.

She wanted more than a kiss, but remembering where they were, she pulled back and touched his swollen and bruised jaw. "Someone watching?" she asked.

She'd felt like there was, ever since leaving her house. Whoever had been there had probably followed them here. Or maybe they were already here. Maybe they'd reported for their shift this morning like Trent had said Barry Coats had after a couple of days off.

"Remember how the lieutenant said he saw us from the kitchen window," he replied. "We don't know who might be up there watching."

Or out there watching?

"Especially since it's lunchtime now," he added.

The truck cab smelled like that Italian restaurant they'd intended to eat at yesterday. Like garlic, oregano and basil, with the added scents of onions and green peppers and sausage. They'd picked up a bunch of pizzas for lunch as an excuse for stopping by the firehouse. Trent had bought them as a thank-you for fighting the fire at his house.

Her stomach growled. But she wasn't sure if she was hungry for the food or for him. If her dad hadn't shown up when he had, she might have been tempted to see if last night had been as incredible as she remembered.

Maybe it was good her dad had shown up, so she didn't get used to Trent Miles sleeping in her bed. Once they figured out who'd died in his house and stopped whoever was after them, their paths would probably never cross again unless her house caught fire. With all the water he'd poured into the tree stand, he was obviously trying to ensure that didn't happen. But what if that other Santa, the one who'd attacked them in the alley, made good on his threat with the box of matches?

"If you're hungry, you're going to want to grab a piece before the guys get a hold of these boxes," Trent warned her.

The piece she wanted to grab wasn't from a pizza, but she just sucked in a breath, smiled and nodded. "Let's do this…" She made certain to get out of the truck first and scan the parking lot.

At least the daylight made it easy to see that the other vehicles in the lot were empty. Nobody was sitting in them waiting to run them down.

Was that person already inside the building?

She carried a few of the boxes while Trent carried the rest. Helping him with the delivery was her reason for dropping in on them. Maybe if they thought she was there for a personal reason rather than professional, they would talk more freely around her.

But she kind of doubted it, especially when all conversation ceased when she and Trent walked into the dining hall off the kitchen on the second floor. A little unsettled by the silent stares, she smiled and quipped, "Pizza delivery."

"We brought this by to thank you guys for helping out at my house fire the other night," Trent explained as he dropped his boxes onto the table.

"Sorry about that, man," one of the guys said. "That was a tough break."

"I just lost material stuff and the house," Trent said. "Somebody else lost their life."

The remark drew Heather's attention and her respect. He had never once complained about what he'd lost, which would have been a lot more than he'd admitted. Like pictures and mementos of his life, of the parents he'd lost so long ago. Her heart ached as she thought of everything that had gone up in flames with that woman.

"You figure out who that was yet?" The lieutenant asked the question, looking at Heather.

She shook her head. "Not yet. She doesn't match any missing person reports. We have no idea who she is."

"Well, it hasn't been that long yet. Don't you have to wait awhile before a cop will let you file a report about somebody disappearing?" one of the guys asked.

She hadn't met him yet. He looked about her and Trent's age, thirtyish, with blond hair and what looked like a spray tan. From how his uniform stretched over bulging muscles, he spent a lot of time in the gym. He was probably as big and strong as that Santa who'd gotten the jump on them in the alley. She smiled at him. "I'm Heather. Who are you?"

"Don't you mean Detective Bolton?" he shot back at her.

She knew without a doubt who he was even before Trent introduced them.

"Heather, meet Barry Coats," he said.

The guy jumped up from the bench he'd been sitting on at the long table. He tripped over it and stumbled back into the wall. "What the hell are you up to, Miles? Bringing a detective around here to interrogate us? How the hell do you think any of us could have something to do with burning your place down?"

"The first crew on the scene said the door was closed and locked. So were all the windows," the lieutenant said. "No signs of forced entry."

Heather glanced at Stokes, surprised he'd confirmed what the techs had already told her regarding the scene of the crime. "He's right," she said. "So for that person to get inside, she'd either had the key code or somebody with the key code had let her in."

"She?" Barry repeated, and some of the color drained from his face. "I thought the body was badly burned…"

"Not so badly that the coroner wasn't able to determine sex, possible age, in her early thirties, and build, probably about mine. She was also wearing a wedding ring," she said.

Despite his spray tan, Barry suddenly looked very pale. "You're acting like you think I would know, and I don't."

"You've been using Trent's place to hook up with women," she said, as if she had confirmation, when she really only had rumors and speculation. "Like a few of you have been doing." She glanced around the long table where the other guys had fallen silent as they watched and listened to the exchange between her and Barry.

They all looked a little suspicious of him. Except for one guy who looked away from both of them, probably Jerome Whittaker, who had all but admitted to using Trent's place to cheat. Now she had to get the same confession out of Barry.

"So who was in that house that night?" she asked him. "Did you let her inside?"

"I was working," he said. "I didn't get to the scene until everyone else did to fight the fire."

"Did you give her the code to let herself in?"

Now color rushed into his face, flushing it bright red. "No. I…"

"You've been using Trent's place to hook up," she insisted. "Maybe because you're married with kids."

He shook his head. "I'm divorced."

"Just," one of the other guys remarked.

She could imagine why; his wife had caught him cheating.

"The victim was married," Heather said. "We know that. She was still wearing her rings." Even after she died. "So that's why you were meeting up with her at Trent's place. And now I suspect she's missing…?"

Tears sprang into his eyes and he turned and headed into the kitchen. Before Heather could get around the long table, Trent had already followed him through the doorway into the other room.

"You're not leaving until you answer the detective's questions," Trent told him as Barry headed toward the other door to the hall.

"The detective? So she's not your girlfriend?"

"It's none of your business what she is," Trent said. "Neither of us are married. Neither of us are dead."

"Who is she?" Heather asked. "I need to know her name. I need to notify the family."

He shook his head.

"You don't care about her at all?" Heather asked. "You're going to leave her in the morgue as a Jane Doe?"

A tear trailed down his cheek now. "If that was her, her husband would report her missing, right? Once he can, once enough time has passed?"

"He might not, if he's the one who killed her," Heather pointed out.

He gasped.

"She was shot in the head, Barry," she said. "She didn't just die in that fire."

He shook his head and a few more tears rolled down his cheeks.

"You have nothing to lose by telling me the truth," she pointed out. "You're not married anymore. You have an alibi." Or so he thought, but she'd checked it out. His shift hadn't started that night until after the report of shots fired. And the fire could have been started in the basement or somewhere inside the house where it would have taken a while to burn as hot as it had. Maybe he'd set it up that way to give himself an alibi. "Unless you have something to hide, why won't you tell me her name?"

"If someone, like maybe her husband, killed her, don't you think he'll come after me next?" Barry asked, his voice cracking with fear. Despite his size and dangerous career, the man was a bit of a coward. Unless it was all an act, like those people who got so dramatic in front of the cameras.

She glanced at Trent and an idea occurred to her. "Or maybe he'd come after the guy whose house she was at."

Barry blinked away his tears then and focused on her. "I heard about someone trying to run you guys down in the parking lot."

Heard about it or did it himself?

She couldn't be sure.

"Did her husband ever see the two of you together?" she asked. "Would he know what you looked like?"

He shook his head again. "No. We were real careful. That's why we met at Trent's."

You're going to find out how it feels to lose someone close to you...

That was the message in that card, and it made sense if the guy thought he'd lost his wife to Trent.

"Barry, I need the name now, dammit!" she snapped at him.

And his eyes widened with surprise. "Missy Dobbs. And I haven't heard from her since that night. She's not texting me or calling."

Because she was in the morgue.

"Do you know where she lives?" she asked. "Her husband's name?"

"Roy," he replied. "And she lives—lived in Wyandotte." He seemed pretty sure she was the dead woman found in Trent's house. Just because he hadn't heard from her or because he'd killed her?

Not wanting him to know she had some doubts, she said, "Thanks, Barry."

He nodded, but more tears trailed down his face. "Do you think he killed her because of me?"

Well, duh...

She didn't say that aloud. "If he killed her, it was because of *him*. Something's wrong with him." Rage over his wife's betrayal. A crime of passion, it was called. After last night, she understood a little better how someone could lose their mind and sense of self in passion.

She'd lost herself for a moment. But she felt like she was coming back now. She had a solid lead to find out the identity of the victim and maybe the killer as well.

Barry rushed from the room, and she let him go. For now. But if the husband had an alibi, she would have to track Barry down again.

"I'm going to call an officer to come pick me up and drive out to Wyandotte with me," she said. Or maybe she'd take Officer Morgan, who'd followed them to the firehouse, and have another officer come to protect Trent.

"I can drive you," he said. "And they can follow us."

She shook her head. "You don't know this guy, and he doesn't know you—"

"But he might be the one who's been trying to kill us," he said.

"Exactly. It's too dangerous for you to come with me."

"I'm with you here," he said. "I was with you in that alley yesterday."

"And look what happened in that alley." She touched his swollen jaw. "You got hurt."

"So did you."

"Then maybe I'll have a couple of officers go with me out there."

"But shouldn't I go? I can explain to this guy that his wife wasn't with me. She was with my coworker."

She ran her fingertips lightly over the bruise below his eyes. "It was your place. He must think you're the guy she was sleeping with, the one he lost her to…"

Trent groaned. "Damn Barry. Damn them all. Damn me. Why do I keep trusting people that I shouldn't?"

She didn't know if he was talking about his coworkers or his sister or maybe even her, too. When he'd heard about the clearance rate competition, he'd acted as if she'd betrayed him just because she wanted to be the best at her job.

"You should go back to my place," she said. "I'll have an officer follow you."

He shook his head. "No. I can stay here."

A chill ran down her spine with a sense of foreboding. "That's not a good idea."

"It sounds like this Dobbs guy is the one behind everything."

But they only had one man's word that any of this was the truth. And she didn't trust that man. "You'd be safer at my house," she insisted.

"So would you," he said with a slight smirk.

"I have a job to do," she said.

"A clearance rate to beat," he said.

It wasn't about that anymore. It was about keeping Trent safe. But he probably wouldn't believe her if she told him. Or worse yet, he would ask why, and she'd have to admit that she was starting to care about him. Too much.

He sighed. "I do, too. I've already missed a lot of shifts here because of being gone on hotshot assignments. I should stick around, help out if something comes in."

"But it's too dangerous."

"This is my job."

"I mean you still shouldn't trust anyone, not until we know for sure who's after you."

He shrugged. "It's gotta be this Dobbs guy."

"You have to be careful until I confirm that," she insisted.

"I won't be alone with any of them, and nobody will try anything in front of the others," he said.

"Okay." There was safety in numbers. She knew that but still had such an uneasy feeling about leaving him.

At least not without a kiss. She wound her arms around his neck and tugged his head until her lips touched his.

Passion caught fire, burning hot and bright between them, making her pulse race and her skin tingle. It didn't matter that they'd had sex over and over last night. She still wanted him. No. She still needed him.

When she pulled back and stepped away, he stared down at her with bright eyes. "Be careful," he told her.

She didn't know if he was referring to her investigation of Roy Dobbs or kissing him. After last night, it was too late for caution.

She was already in danger…of falling for him.

Chapter 16

For the first time Trent understood what he put the people who cared about him through when he went off to a fire. How they worried about him…

Because he was worrying about Heather like that.

He knew that loved ones worried. Brittney had told him; so had Moe. And he'd seen too many other fire-fighters' and hotshots' marriages fail because of the danger of their jobs and how it put too much of a strain on a relationship.

He'd heard the complaints in the past from the women he'd dated. He'd also seen the rough patch a fellow hotshot's marriage had hit because his wife thought the stress of worrying about him while he was off fighting wildfires had caused her miscarriages.

He'd commiserated with them all, but he hadn't really understood until now. Until he was worrying about someone who was just doing her job. And that was all she was doing…

That was all this was between them. A crime to solve, a case to close.

"You're really dating Detective Bolton?" Tom Johnson asked, his dark eyes narrowed as he joined Trent in the kitchen.

Trent probably could have told him the truth. If Roy Dobbs was the killer, then she would be closing this case, and she would have no reason to see him ever again. But something held him back. Maybe hope.

Not that the case wouldn't close but that she might want to see him after it had. That they might…

"You really are," Tom remarked. "I thought she might have cooked up some cover to get close to us, thinking we'd talk more."

"Really?" he asked, feigning innocence and covering his surprise that Tom had so easily figured out part of her plan. The other part had been to flush out the killer.

"Yeah. None of us even knew you were seeing anyone," Tom said. "Hell, even your own sister didn't know."

He gasped. "You talked to Brittney?"

Tom grinned and wriggled his eyebrows. "Sure did. She was trying to get close to me."

Trent stiffened with defensiveness of his baby sister. Even though she'd betrayed him, she would always be family, and he would always love her.

Tom chuckled at Trent's obvious reaction. "But she was just playing me, trying to get me to spill."

"So of course you did."

"She was worried about you," Tom said. "Probably more worried when I told her about the parking lot thing and your girlfriend." He chuckled again. "I don't know what worried her more."

Trent groaned. "You told her about Heather?"

"Heather..." Tom repeated in a singsong rhythm, like a kid taunting him on the playground.

He half expected him to spell out the word *kiss*, too.

Tom shook his head. "I didn't name names. Like I said, I didn't know if you were actually together or not. But from the look on your face, I can see that you've got it bad for the lady detective."

Remembering last night and her sexy red lace underwear, Trent groaned again as his body reacted, tightening and aching with desire. "She's so damn gorgeous. And smart and brave and..."

"Damn," Tom remarked. "I never thought it would happen to you, Miles. That you'd fall so hard."

"I..." He wanted to deny it. After all, they hardly knew each other and certainly didn't have the time necessary to nurture a relationship when they were so focused on their careers. No. He hadn't fallen for her. He couldn't.

The blare of an alarm saved him from having to say any more. Not that he had any idea what to say.

"You going to suit up with us?" Tom asked hopefully.

"I'll ask the lieu," he said.

"I'm right here," Ken Stokes said, appearing in the doorway behind Tom, as if he'd been standing there listening to their conversation. Tom hurried past him to get ready for the call. "And yeah, I can use you, especially since Barry took off."

Trent tensed. "Barry took off? When?"

"Right after your *girlfriend* interrogated him," the lieutenant said. Clearly, he wasn't as convinced as Tom that their act was real.

"I should call her," he murmured, mostly to himself. He felt compelled to warn her for some reason.

But warn her about what? Barry had probably just been upset his married girlfriend might have been murdered because of him, and he'd needed some time off, maybe to rethink his life choices.

Just like Trent was tempted to rethink his.

"You in or out?" Stokes asked, his voice sharp. "We gotta go!"

Trent bobbed his head and started after the lieutenant. Heather would be fine. She had her gun, and she was going with other officers.

But he couldn't help but wonder and worry if Barry had said what he had to set her up, to ambush her. And she'd been worried about Trent, that he shouldn't trust his crew. As he suited up and joined them, they all looked at him with suspicion and resentment.

Because of Heather?

Because she'd questioned them?

What were they so worried about her finding out? And how far would they go to cover it up?

He'd figured he was safe, safety in numbers, but what if the numbers were against him?

The house was in Wyandotte, just as Barry Coats had told her. And the husband's name was Roy Dobbs, and on the deed search, the wife was listed as Melissa. But Heather could see Melissa being shortened to Missy.

She could also see the rest of it.

If the man had followed his wife to her secret meetings with her affair partner, he might have done what Heather had and looked up the owner's name in an online property search. Then, furious that he was losing his wife, he'd left that threatening card for Trent.

But why at the firehouse?

Why not at the house where he'd followed his wife? Maybe he hadn't wanted her to see it? To recognize her husband's handwriting, to be warned that he knew where she was going and who she was meeting. But Roy hadn't really known. He'd just made the assumption it was Trent because Barry had been using Trent's house for his meetings with Missy.

It all made sense.

Maybe a little too conveniently, which was why Heather was suspicious. She didn't trust Barry Coats. The guy had no qualms about cheating and lying, so she had no reason to trust him. She wasn't sure she should have left Trent at the firehouse. She'd requested an officer to stick close to him, but Officer Howard couldn't follow Trent into a burning building. Hopefully they wouldn't get any calls while she was here.

The officer driving her to the suspected victim's house pulled into the driveway of the address Heather had found for Roy and Melissa Dobbs. No other vehicles were present, and the garage door was closed.

"Doesn't look like anyone's home," Officer Ashley Morgan murmured as she looked at the house. The blinds were closed.

"I'm going to check," Heather said.

"I'm going up to the door with you," Ashley said, and she reached for her door handle with one hand and her weapon with the other.

Heather smiled at the officer, seeing a lot of herself in the earnest and determined young woman. "Good," she said. After her loss of judgment with Trent, she didn't entirely trust herself right now.

Or maybe that was her niggling concern that she shouldn't have trusted Barry Coats.

She opened the passenger's door and stepped out onto the driveway. As she glanced at the house, she noticed the blinds opening. Someone was inside, watching them. She reached for her weapon, too.

But then the door opened and a woman stepped onto the small front stoop. "Hello, Officers," she said. She was in her thirties, about Heather's height and build, and looked very similar to the driver's license picture Heather had pulled up of the woman.

"Missy?"

"Melinda," the woman said.

"I thought it was Melissa," Heather said.

She shook her head. "No. My sister and I look very much alike. But she's a few years younger than I am."

As she stepped closer, Heather could see more lines on this woman's face than had been in her sister's driver's license photo. And beneath Melinda's blue eyes were dark circles.

"Are you here to take the missing person report?" Melinda asked.

"How long has your sister been missing?" Heather asked.

"She and I went Black Friday shopping together, and she was going to stay in the city for dinner and a movie with an old friend from college. I left her and came back home." She gestured with a finger to another house down the street. "I live there."

"But you're here?" Heather asked.

"I'm checking with Roy to see if he's heard from

her," Melinda said. "Or if the police finally agreed to take a report." Bright color appeared in her cheeks. "I'm sorry, but it's not like Missy to not at least shoot me a text. And she hasn't even opened any of mine."

"Her husband is home?" Heather asked.

Melinda nodded and tensed. "I know what you're probably thinking, but Roy adores my sister. He wouldn't do anything to her. And he has no idea where she is either." She stepped back. "I'll go get him."

Heather shook her head. "Not yet. I have a few more questions for you about your sister and who she was really meeting in the city."

Melinda's face flushed again; clearly, she knew about her sister's affair. Since Missy's sister knew, maybe her husband did as well. Melinda pulled the door of the house closed behind her and joined Heather and Ashley on the driveway. She must not have been in the house long, because she was still wearing her jacket. "Roy doesn't know."

"Are you sure?" she asked.

She bobbed her head in a quick nod. "Missy was really good at keeping secrets."

"From everyone but you," Heather guessed.

"We're sisters," she said. "We share everything."

Heather shook her head again. "Not all sisters do." She didn't want hers to know about Trent because they would definitely scare him away. Not that she expected him to stick around once this case was closed. He was very busy with his career, just as she was with hers.

And she needed to focus on that career now. "But your sister told you," she continued. "So what did you know about who she was seeing? Have you met him?"

"No, she wouldn't share him with me," Melinda said,

and she glanced down the street, probably at her house.
She wore a wedding ring, too. Was she worried that her
husband might overhear her?

"What do you know about him?" Heather asked again.

Melinda smiled. "That he's a hunky fireman."

"Do you know his name?" she asked.

"Trent. Trent Miles."

Heather sucked in a breath, feeling like she'd been
punched. Had Trent lied to her? Had he been seeing
the dead woman?

"You okay?" Ashley asked in a whisper.

Heather nodded. "Yes. Did she show you a picture
of him? Or describe him?"

"Big," she said. "Really big. With a tan…"

That could have described either of them, Trent with
his natural skin or Barry with his spray tan.

"And blond," Melinda continued. "Like Chris Hemsworth."

Heather released a slight breath of relief. Not that
she would have described Barry as looking like Chris
Hemsworth, but *he* probably thought he looked like the
movie star.

"That's not Trent," Ashley whispered, as if reassuring Heather.

Had she taken her act too far that the uniformed police officers believed it? After last night, she had to
admit she had certainly done more than protect a crime
victim.

Trent was the victim. Of the attempts on his life
and of another betrayal by someone he'd trusted. Barry
hadn't just used his house; he'd used his identity as well.

"What do you mean?" Melinda asked. "That's not

Trent?" Despite the officer's whisper, she'd heard her. "He lied about his name?"

"The man who admitted to having a relationship with your sister is not really named Trent Miles," Heather said.

"So you've talked to him? You know where she is, then?"

Heather had a horrible feeling that she did.

"Has he told you? Have you seen her? Is she okay?" Melinda asked, her voice rising with a trace of hysteria. "Where the hell is she?"

Missy's sister must have finally figured out why Heather was there. And it wasn't just to take a missing person report.

"Hey, you didn't tell me the police were here," a man said as he stepped out of the house and joined them on the driveway. He was big, like Barry Coats, with pale skin and thinning hair, despite probably being in his thirties.

Ashley reached for her weapon again. Heather's hand was inside her coat, resting on the handle of her Glock.

"Roy Dobbs?" Heather asked.

He nodded.

"I'm Detective Bolton. Would you consent to letting Officer Morgan search your person?"

"What?" he asked.

"Just to make sure you have no weapons on you," she clarified. If this was the man who'd attacked her and Trent in the alley, she wasn't about to let him ambush her again.

He shook his head. "I—I don't have any weapons on me."

"You don't own a gun?" She knew damn well that he did. She had pulled up his permit for the weapon. The coroner was still working on determining the caliber of the gun that had killed the woman, since the bullet had passed through her skull and hadn't been recovered.

"I—I do have one, but I'm not carrying it on me," Roy said.

"What's going on?" Melinda asked. "Why aren't you answering me about my sister? Do you think Roy killed her? Is she dead?" Her voice cracked as a sob erupted out of her, followed by a keening howl, and she dropped onto the driveway on her knees.

"Melinda!" Roy said. He grabbed her arm and tried to get her up as he gazed around, as if worried the neighbors were watching. "Can we go inside?" he asked in a whisper, concerned they were listening, too.

"After you consent to a search," Heather persisted.

He nodded and held out his arms. Officer Morgan frisked him quickly but thoroughly. She stepped away from him and nodded at Heather.

"Okay, we can go inside," she agreed and followed the man and his sister-in-law into the modest ranch house. Roy had his arm around Melinda, half carrying her as she continued to weep.

"Calm down," he told her. "We don't know anything yet."

"They know stuff," Melinda said, and she pulled away from Roy now. Her blue eyes narrowed and she stared at him. "Did you know? Missy didn't think so but…"

He lifted his hands. "Know what? What the hell are you talking about?"

"Her affair," Heather said, and she watched his face carefully.

He sucked in a breath as if she'd punched him. He might have already known and it just still hurt. Or he might have had no idea.

"I thought you were here to take the missing person report," he said, and he lifted his hand to run it over his thin hair. His fingers were shaking.

"They know something," Melinda reminded him, her voice nearly a shriek now. "They must have found her."

"You did?" he asked. "Is she okay? It's not like her to not reply to text messages."

"We don't know if it's her," Heather admitted. "We need to get something with her DNA on it."

Melinda screamed again and started to fall. But when her brother-in-law reached for her, she jerked away from him and stumbled back into Officer Morgan. Ashley caught her and held her up as she sobbed.

"I—I—" Roy stammered and rubbed his hand over his head again.

"I could use her toothbrush or a hairbrush," Heather explained.

"We can't see her?" Roy asked.

He might have been able to handle it, but there was no way her sister would, from the way she was wailing. Maybe she'd already had some inclination Missy was dead.

If Melinda thought that just because Missy hadn't answered her texts, then Heather's sisters would have often thought she was dead. And that was definitely the case with Trent, who kept ignoring his sister's messages.

"Her toothbrush is in here," Roy said, as he started out of the living room, down a short hall.

Heather followed him, her hand on her weapon while the young officer was trying to untangle herself from Melinda, who clung to her now as she kept crying.

"Is she dead?" he asked.

"We have found a body that could be hers," Heather admitted. "We need DNA to confirm."

He sucked in another breath. "That's…" His voice trailed off, emotion choking him. But he betrayed nothing but those nerves as he pushed open a door at the end of the hall.

The bedroom was dark, all the blinds shut like in the rest of the house. Clothes were scattered around the floor and even at the foot of the bed.

"Missy's a little messy," he said.

Some of the clothes were his, so he obviously wasn't any neater. Maybe realizing that, he stooped to pick up some jeans. "The toothbrush is in there." He pointed toward the open door to a small bathroom. "The pink one."

Heather pulled an evidence bag from her pocket and used it to take the brush out of the holder. Then she sealed it inside. "I would also like to see your gun, Mr. Dobbs."

"I have a permit."

"I need to see your gun," she repeated. She would be able to determine if it had been fired recently just by examining it. When she stepped out of the bathroom, with the bagged toothbrush, Roy Dobbs stood in front of her, pointing the barrel of the gun she wanted directly at her.

Tom had texted her, just as he'd promised, when he'd heard from Trent. He's here. At the firehouse.

But by the time she got there, they were all gone. Not just Trent. His truck was actually in the lot now, but the big rigs were gone.

They'd been sent out on a call.

To a fire.

Her pulse quickened with the trepidation she always

felt when her brother was fighting a fire. Every time there was the possibility he could get hurt or worse. Like those other hotshots who had died after they'd responded to the recent wildfire out West before Trent and his team had arrived at it.

Trent had lost one of his team members recently, too. And some other ones had nearly died as well. His job was dangerous no matter what.

But now…

After someone had burned down his house with a body inside…

After someone had tried to run him down in this very parking lot…

He was in a lot more danger than he'd ever been in. And once again Brittney worried that she might never see her brother again.

At least not alive…

Chapter 17

If looks could kill…

Trent wouldn't have survived even before they got to the fire as he rode in the back of the rig with his crew. "What the hell, guys?" he asked. "I brought you pizza and you're all looking at me like I tried to poison you. What? You're all on diets I didn't know about?"

"You brought us pizza and a detective who's already been treating us like suspects over what the hell happened at *your* house," Gordy Stutz replied, as if he was speaking for all of them.

And maybe he was.

Tom wasn't glaring at him quite as hard as the others. He almost smirked instead, like he knew something Trent didn't. Hell, they'd all known something he didn't.

"Anybody who had access to my house probably is a suspect," Trent said. "Somebody was killed there, and not because of the fire. And somebody's been trying to

kill me. If anyone has a reason to be pissed off, it's me!"
And he was, anger surging through him. He'd been hurt
and confused since the fire, but the only person he had
actually gotten angry with had been Heather.

For just doing her job and having a little fun competing with the chauvinistic detective.

Trent needed to be pissed at the people who had really
betrayed him. She hadn't. She hadn't done anything but...

Make him start falling for her. That was on him, just
like she'd been once last night. He closed his eyes for a
moment, grappling with the heat of that memory. When
he opened them, they were pulling up to the fire.

A run-down apartment building was ablaze, burning
so fast and hot that he could feel the heat the minute he
stepped out of the rig. "Is everyone out?" he asked the
lieutenant, who was yelling orders at the crew.

"You need to check, Miles. Place is mostly empty,
but a few die-hard tenants have remained, despite the
bad conditions."

This reminded him of another fire last year. Another run-down apartment building that was supposed
to be mostly empty. He'd checked that one, too, but
he'd missed someone on his first time through. When
neighbors told him the apartment he'd thought was de-
serted was occupied, he'd gone back, but not in time
to save her.

A pang of guilt struck him, and a moment's panic,
too. He had to make damn sure he didn't miss anyone
this time. He nodded at the lieutenant and headed toward the fire. He adjusted his helmet, putting on the
mask with the oxygen. With as hot as this fire was, he
would need it.

This place reminded him of the other building, full

of trash and falling down from neglect. Almost as if the fire was putting it out of its misery. He found an older couple, huddling together in one unit, and helped them out through the smoke.

Then he went back inside, making sure to check every apartment. In the one farthest from the fire he saw someone. The person wore a mask and a helmet, too, but through the smoke, it wasn't clear if it was the same as Trent's, the same crew. Other departments had responded to the call.

Trent gestured at the guy, trying to get him to indicate if he'd checked the place. But the guy didn't gesture back. Instead, he swung something that he'd been holding behind him. Like the pipe the Santa had swung in the alley.

This time Heather wasn't there to jump in front of him. Trent stumbled back, trying to duck, but it hit him. Hard, so hard that it knocked off his helmet, sending it skittering across the floor.

The next blow struck him in the legs, knocking them from underneath him, and he dropped to the ground next to his helmet.

Then the pipe swung toward him again…

The way the gun was pointed at her, the barrel directed at her heart, she didn't have time to draw her weapon. She didn't even dare draw a breath.

But he hadn't pulled the trigger yet. His eyes were glazed over, almost in a trance of some sort, or just so damn tired he didn't know what was going on. Like his sister-in-law, he had dark circles beneath his eyes.

Heather could relate; she was tired, too. Maybe that

was why she'd momentarily turned her back on the guy. But after he'd been searched…

Still, she'd known there was a weapon in the house. She should have secured that first before the damn toothbrush.

"Roy, you don't want to pull that trigger," she said, as if she knew. But she really had no idea what the man was capable of doing, especially if he'd killed his own wife.

Roy glanced at the gun as if he wasn't aware that he was holding it, pointing it, but even then he didn't lower it. The barrel was still aimed directly at her.

Officer Morgan noticed that when she stepped into the room, her eyes going wide. She pulled her own weapon, but Heather gave a slight shake of her head, silently telling the officer to stand down.

For the moment.

She didn't want the guy shot if he truly was so out of it he didn't know what he was doing. She hoped giving him the benefit of the doubt didn't wind up costing her…her life.

"Roy, I got the toothbrush," she said, holding the bag out. "We'll see if the DNA matches. And thank you for getting the gun."

"I…I had it out at the range the other day," he murmured. "I took it out on Black Friday when Missy and her sister were shopping."

So it had been recently fired. Heather wouldn't even have to examine it, but she was going to damn well take it. She took a step closer to him. As she did, Officer Morgan stepped farther into the room.

Then Melinda rushed up behind her. "What the hell are you doing, Roy?"

He moved then, swinging the barrel toward the door,

at the young officer and his sister-in-law. Heather rushed forward, locking her hand around his wrist as she threw her weight against him, knocking him to the ground.

Ashley rushed forward, helping her secure the weapon. "I've got it." Then she unhooked her cuffs from her belt and snapped them around his wrists while Heather held him down. "I got him."

"The safety was on," Roy said. "I wasn't going to shoot."

"Don't ever point a weapon at anyone," Heather admonished him. "But especially not a cop."

"You're lucky I didn't shoot you." Ashley added her admonishment.

"I wasn't going to shoot," he murmured again and began to cry like his sister-in-law, but his sobs were quiet little gasps of breath as tears rolled down his face.

Ashley looked at her. "We're bringing him in?"

She nodded. "He pointed this gun at both of us." And she needed time to determine if his wife was who had been found in Trent's house. Though, she was pretty damn sure it was Missy lying in the morgue. "We're confiscating the weapon and arresting him for threatening us."

"I wouldn't shoot you…" he cried. "I wouldn't…"

"What about Missy?" she asked. "Did you follow your wife to where she was going to meet her lover? Did you shoot her and then set fire to that house?"

Melinda shrieked again. Then she rushed forward and tried to kick him as he lay on the bedroom floor on top of the clothes that were strewn across the carpet. Ashley held her back.

"I didn't do it," Roy said. He was talking to Melinda, though, not her. "I wouldn't hurt Missy. I would never hurt Missy."

Not like she'd hurt him.

If he'd known about the affair...

He'd acted like he hadn't known, but Heather couldn't be certain that wasn't all he was doing: acting. Maybe he'd even intended to shoot her but had known that Officer Morgan would have taken him out.

Was he the one who'd attacked her and Trent in the alley? Who'd tried to run them down? Who'd put that box of matches in the mail slot?

She intended to question him until she got the truth out of him. About everything...

She was tempted to tell him the truth, too, that Trent wasn't his wife's affair partner. But as much as she wanted to take the target off Trent, she couldn't reveal too much to a suspect. She couldn't give him anything he could use in his defense. Fortunately, he hadn't asked for a lawyer yet. But once Ashley read him his rights, he might.

"Let's bring him out to the car and Mirandize him," she said.

He'd seemed reluctant to let his sister-in-law make a scene in front of his neighbors, so he probably wouldn't make one himself. The faster they got him out of the house, the less chance he had of resisting. Even though the guy was handcuffed, he was big. She and Ashley had to both help him up from the floor.

The hallway was too narrow for them to walk beside him, so Ashley walked behind them as Heather steered him away from the bedroom, toward the exit. But before they could get to the front door, a call came through the radio on Officer Morgan's collar.

"Officer, please have Detective Bolton contact Dispatch."

Ashley touched a button on the radio speaker. "She's with me now."

"Have her contact Dispatch."

So whatever they wanted to talk to her about, they didn't want to do it over the radio.

Heather's pulse, which had already been fast after staring down a gun barrel, quickened even more. She helped Ashley get Roy Dobbs secured in the back seat of her patrol car before she pulled out her cell and called Dispatch.

"This is Detective Bolton."

"Hold one moment, please." The line went silent for a long moment.

"Detective?" a male voice asked.

"Yes."

"This is Officer Howard."

The one she'd assigned to stay at the firehouse, to watch Trent and make sure nothing happened to him. And she knew, even before she asked, that something had happened.

"There was a fire," he said. "I followed the rig to it, but I couldn't go inside the apartment complex."

But Trent had. He'd suited up and gone in with the crew he already knew he couldn't trust. She silently cursed. "What happened?"

"He got some people out and went back in, but he didn't come out again—"

"He got trapped in the fire?" Pain gripped her heart, squeezing it tightly. Was he going to wind up like Missy Dobbs had?

Burned beyond recognition?

Tears stung her eyes, so she closed them and prayed.

"I made them go back inside, and they found him."

"Is he alive?" she asked, her heart pounding so furiously with hope now. They'd gotten him out.

He couldn't be dead. Not Trent.

"He's at the hospital now. I don't know his condition."

"Which one?" Heather asked, hoping it was close, that she could get to him.

The officer told her the name, but then sputtered a bit as he tried to tell her something else.

"What is it, Howard?" she asked.

"I don't know…" he murmured. "The lieutenant tried to act like it was an accident. But I don't think it was."

Neither did she.

But if someone had attacked Trent in that fire, it hadn't been Roy Dobbs. She and Officer Morgan and his sister-in-law could alibi him.

So was there someone else out there? Someone else who wanted Trent dead and had maybe succeeded?

After talking to Brittney Townsend the other morning, Ethan had sent a few texts to Trent.

What the hell is going on?

Are you all right?

All he'd gotten in response was a thumbs-up message each time. What the hell did that mean? Was he trying to assure Ethan that everything was fine?

Ethan couldn't believe that, not after Trent had lost his house in an arson fire. And a body had been found inside it.

Thankfully not his.

This time.

But someone was after him.

Someone nearly running him down in the firehouse parking lot hadn't been an accident. None of it had been. His best friend was in danger, and too damn proud and stubborn to ask for help.

So Ethan had asked. He sat now in the office at the firehouse in Northern Lakes, in one of the too-small chairs in front of his boss's desk. Braden Zimmer had made some calls for Ethan, and he'd told him he had news.

Ethan stared across the desk at the hotshot superintendent's grim expression. And he knew it wasn't good news.

Chapter 18

Trent had managed to avoid that last blow. He'd rolled out of the way of the pipe and scrambled to his feet. Ignoring the pain in his legs, he'd run from that apartment unit, and his attacker, back into the smoke-filled hallway. To escape the pipe-wielding maniac, he'd had to leave his helmet and the oxygen behind. With the smoke blinding and choking him, he'd lost his way and eventually his consciousness, falling to the floor in some back hallway.

He could have lost his life, too.

Or had he?

He struggled to open his eyes, and as he did, they burned and watered, like his throat and lungs burned. He definitely wasn't dead, unless he'd gone to hell. But a mask covered his face, pumping more oxygen into him. He blinked against the bright lights and listened to the beeps and the voices. He had made it to the hospital.

He wasn't dead yet…despite someone's efforts to kill him. Who the hell had been in that building?

He'd been wearing a helmet, too. Was he a firefighter? One of Trent's crew?

Heather had been right that he'd needed to be careful. She hadn't trusted any of his coworkers, and apparently neither should he have. He should have gone back to her house and decorated her tree. He could show her sisters that she could damn well be Martha Stewart if she wanted. Or at least he could help her fake it. Just thinking of her made him smile beneath the mask.

"There he is," a deep voice murmured. "Back among the living."

With his eyes still burning, his vision wasn't clear. He could see the uniform. The hat. And he tensed with fear. Had the guy come to finish him off? He tightened his hands into fists. He wasn't going out without a fight. He was mad now, like he'd realized while in the rig that he should have been.

This firehouse crew wasn't like his hotshots. He could trust his hotshot team. Couldn't he?

Or was one of them the saboteur?

He was being more than sabotaged now. Someone was trying to kill him.

"Trent? You okay?"

And he recognized the voice. Manny.

He blinked again and could focus on his boss. His dad's friend. Surely he could trust the fire captain. He tried to move the oxygen mask aside to speak, but Manny caught his wrist.

"Leave that on for now," he said. "You need to get your oxygen levels up."

"They're getting there," a woman in scrubs said as

she leaned over the bed. "We need to take you for an MRI, make sure you don't have any internal injuries."

He ached all over from that damn pipe, and not just from today, but from the day before in the alley.

She glanced at the captain. "You have just a few minutes before we take him up," she said. "And then you need to report back to the waiting room that he's stable and doing well. There's about to be a riot out there."

"My men?" Manny asked, his voice hard with disapproval.

She chuckled. "Two women, actually."

Two women?

Heather? Brittney? It had to be; Moe was still on her cruise.

Trent smiled.

"Sounds about right," Manny said. "Women are always fighting to get close to this guy."

"One said she's his sister," the nurse said. "And the other is a detective."

Brittney and Heather.

"Two minutes," she told Manny, and she ducked behind the curtain that was surrounding the bed Trent was lying on.

"Glad you're improving," Manny said. "I told your hotshot superintendent that you would be fine." But from his tone, it was clear he hadn't been as confident of that as he'd led Braden to believe.

Neither had Trent, but the pain in his throat and lungs was easing now and his eyes were clear.

"He and the team were about to descend on Detroit like they were putting out a wildfire, so I had to convince them everything was under control." Manny stepped closer and lowered his voice. "But it isn't, is it?

What the hell is going on, Trent? This all started with that damn Christmas card."

You're going to find out what it feels like to lose someone close to you. Soon.

That hadn't been the only one. He'd gotten one at Heather's house, too. Threatening her.

Something niggled at him, something about that apartment fire today. It was so eerily similar to that fire last year. But there had been so many fires over the years, so many casualties, and none of the survivors had the code to his door lock. So, like Heather, he'd suspected it had to be someone closer to him.

"What the hell happened, Trent?" Manny asked. "You lost your helmet and the oxygen, and I know you're too damn good for that to have happened by accident."

Manny's hand had slipped away from his wrist, so Trent tugged his mask down. "Good that you know that."

"Of course I know that."

"I need to talk to…" A cough overtook him, choking off his breath for a moment.

"You need your oxygen back on," Manny said, and he tried to pull the mask back up.

"I need to talk to Heather…"

Manny's forehead creased. "Heather? I thought your sister's name is Brittney."

"The detective," Trent said.

"Well, I'll be damned. You really are seeing her."

He would say he wanted to talk to Heather about the case, but he realized that wasn't the only reason he needed to see her.

He could have died.

And he just *needed* to see her.

"That cop that was at the fire," Manny said, "the

one who insisted the lieutenant send people back in to find you, he said something about the detective having a close call. That someone pulled a gun on her..."

While he'd been attacked, Heather had been threatened? Just like Manny, he wondered what the hell was going on.

"I need to see her!" Now more than ever.

"She's fine," Manny assured him. "She knocked the guy down and got his gun."

Trent sucked in a sharp breath, and his lungs expelled it in another hard cough.

Manny slipped the oxygen mask back up. "She's fine," he said again.

Of course she was. She was damn tough.

"I'll go get her," Manny offered. But when he reached for the curtain, the nurse was already pulling it aside.

She'd returned with an orderly. "Time to take you for the MRI," she said.

He tried to protest, but another cough racked him. And he knew he would have to wait to see Heather. To make sure that she was all right...

Because even though she'd taken care of whoever had pulled that gun on her, Trent knew another threat was out there, the guy who'd nearly killed him. He couldn't help but worry that he might be out in the waiting room with Heather and Brittney.

And if he still wanted Trent to feel the pain of losing someone close to him, he could take one of them. Because if Trent lost either of those women, he would be in a hell of a lot of pain.

Heather didn't feel any safer in this hospital waiting room than she had staring down the barrel of a gun.

His local firehouse crew had gathered around, acting all concerned now. But she didn't trust any of them.

If Officer Howard hadn't been there, would they have left Trent in the fire to burn up like Missy Dobbs's body had? Had one of them done that?

She'd arrested the woman's husband, but with charges related to pointing his gun at her. She intended to hold him until she had confirmation of whether or not his wife was in the morgue. But maybe he hadn't killed Missy. Maybe he hadn't even known about her affair. Because if he was her killer, who had gone after Trent again? And why?

It had to be one of them. She glared at them like they'd glared at her and Trent earlier. She was tempted to have them all locked up like she'd locked up Roy Dobbs. If Trent wasn't okay, she would damn well do it.

The only one she could probably trust in this room, besides Officer Howard, was Brittney Townsend. But then she reminded herself that Trent didn't even trust his sister. Not after her betrayal...

And she glared at her, too, her frustration bubbling over. She started toward the information desk again, determined this time to get some damn information. Every time she and Brittney had gone up before, the man at the desk had claimed they were awaiting tests.

Tests for what?

How badly had he been hurt?

And why had she separated from him?

She knew how much danger he was in, how determined someone was to hurt him. But she'd left him. Tears stung her eyes, but she furiously blinked them back. She would not cry. She would not show any sign of pain or weakness in front of these people, suspecting that one of them had probably hurt Trent, had wanted him to suffer.

She was the one suffering now, her heart aching as she awaited news. News that seemed like it was never going to come. Damn it.

Damn them!

"Hey, Detective Bolton—"

She jumped and whirled toward Trent's sister, who held up her hands. "I'm sorry," Brittney said. "Guess you're on edge, too. I overheard the officer saying that you had a gun pulled on you earlier today." She smiled. "I'm unarmed."

"Somehow I'm not reassured," Heather replied. But she was amused. She was also aware that Brittney's smile was as strained as the one Heather gave her. "Since you're on edge, too."

Brittney turned her eyes, the same unique topaz as Trent's, on the information desk. "They won't tell us anything. And it's so damn frustrating."

It was frightening. Not knowing how Trent was…

If he would be okay…

Heather could see that same fear in Brittney, as tears glistened in her eyes. But she blinked, fighting them back, just as Heather was determined to do. Maybe Brittney didn't trust these guys any more than Heather did.

Obviously the reporter had good instincts or she wouldn't have found the scoop she had in Northern Lakes. She wouldn't have found a dead man living under another identity. Jonathan Canterbury hadn't died in a plane crash like everyone had believed he had five years ago. But the man whose identity he'd assumed, a hotshot firefighter named Ethan Sommerly, had.

"You guys have been seeing each other for a while, haven't you?" Brittney asked, and she was intently studying Heather's face, probably seeing that same fear and concern she was feeling over Trent.

"Why do you think that?" She and Trent had not bothered coming up with much of a cover story. Their ruse of a relationship had been to flush out the killer, to make him try for her instead of Brittney or someone else close to him. It had worked because the killer had believed it, so she couldn't tell the truth and risk him overhearing if he was one of the firefighters sitting in the waiting room.

"He's been acting weird for a while," Brittney said, "but maybe that's just because of everything happening with his hotshot team."

"I think he's acting weird with you because he's mad at you for doing that story on his best friend and his hotshot team," Heather said.

Brittney narrowed her eyes. "You two are close for you to know that. Then you must also know he was acting weird before that, which was why I went to Northern Lakes in the first place. I knew something was going on with his hotshot team and I wanted to find out what, especially when so many of them were getting hurt or worse."

She'd mentioned all that in her story, but the focus had been on the big scoop, on Jonathan Canterbury. What else was going on in Northern Lakes? And had it followed Trent back to Detroit? Her head began to pound as she considered that there could be more suspects, and she already had too many. Roy Dobbs. Barry Coats. Maybe any other of his coworkers who had something to hide...

"What I didn't realize," Brittney continued with a heavy sigh, "was that he was in danger here, too."

"He's a firefighter," Heather said. "He's always in danger on the job."

"I'm not talking about what happened today, and you know it," the reporter said. "I'm talking about what happened at his house. The fire. The dead body. I have sources everywhere, even in your department, Detective. I know the body found in Trent's house had a gunshot wound to the head, and that the fire was deliberately set."

"I can't comment on an ongoing investigation," Heather said, which was her standard reply for reporters.

Brittney snorted derisively. "You shouldn't even be working this investigation, since you're intimately involved with what must be one of the suspects."

"Trent was gone on a call out West." Although technically he had returned. "His alibi checked out. He is definitely not a suspect." But if they had been involved before the fire, she wouldn't have taken the investigation. Brittney wasn't wrong. Because the reporter was so damn smart, Heather wanted to distract her, so she questioned her like a suspect. "What about your alibi, Miss Townsend?"

Brittney laughed. "You think I burned down my brother's house after murdering someone in it? That's ridiculous."

"Besides your mother, you're the only female he knows who had the key code to his house."

Brittney's eyes narrowed with real suspicion now. "You didn't?"

Damn. She was too smart. Distracting her probably wasn't going to work. But the guys were watching them and obviously listening to them, too. So she had to continue the charade. Only it wasn't really a charade anymore.

Heather smiled. "Trent and I meet at my place." Then she glanced around the waiting room at the blatantly eavesdropping firefighters. "Unlike his house, which seemed to have a revolving door on it with people coming and going all the time and using it for all sorts of things, my cat is the only other one around my house."

And her dad and her sisters. But until she knew for certain who was threatening her and Trent, she would make sure they stayed away. Just like she had to somehow get Brittney to stay away.

"I hate to interrupt," an older man said as he walked up to them. He hadn't been at the firehouse earlier today when she and Trent had brought the pizzas, but she remembered him from the scene of the fire. He was the one who'd given him the cards. "But Trent is back from his MRI now and would like to talk to you."

"Me?" Brittney asked, her voice bright with hope.

He shook his head. "No. The detective."

Heather's heart warmed. Then she reminded herself that he probably just wanted to tell her about what had happened. Maybe he'd seen who'd attacked him.

She was torn between hoping that was the case, so this could be over, and fear that if he had seen his attacker, the man would be even more determined to kill him than he already was.

* * *

Apparently Trent Miles had survived. Again. He and that detective were like cats with nine lives. But eventually their luck and their lives were going to run out.

And he was going to make damn sure that happened, just as he'd promised in those cards, soon. Very soon.

Chapter 19

Thanks to his gear, Trent didn't have a concussion or any broken bones. While he had inhaled too much smoke, his oxygen levels had come up and the MRI showed no lung damage, so the doctor thought he would be fine. Still, she was going to send him home with some oxygen.

Not that Trent had a home anymore. But he had Heather's place, that cozy little bungalow with the cat who stood guard over him while he slept. And her...

And all the passion that burned between them, nearly as hot as that fire had. She was so beautiful. Such an incredible lover.

He'd just pulled on his jeans when she ducked around the curtain and stepped inside his cubicle. "What are you doing?" she asked as she rushed up to him. But she stopped just short of reaching for him, and he wished she hadn't. "You shouldn't be trying to leave."

He wanted to close his arms around her, to hold her close. But it was just them in the cubicle. No audience to play up their *fake* relationship. They'd had no audience last night, and that hadn't stopped them from getting as close as two people could get.

Closer than Trent had ever felt to anyone else. With the rest of his world spinning out of control, he just wanted to grab her and hang on.

"Trent? Are you okay?" she asked.

Realizing he was probably staring at her stupidly, he nodded. "I'm fine. No brain damage."

She smacked his chest lightly with her open palm. "You must have some to be trying to leave AMA."

"I'm not leaving against medical advice," he said. "I'm fine." He picked up the portable oxygen pack. "Just getting sent home with this in case I need it." Thinking of what they'd done the night before, the intensity of the passion and the pleasure, he grinned. "I probably needed this more last night."

She smiled, and her beautiful green eyes sparkled. "You're bad…"

"That's not what you said last night."

"I don't remember either of us doing a lot of talking," she acknowledged.

He grinned as his pulse quickened.

"I thought you just wanted to talk to me now," she said. "That's what that older man told me."

"Older man? Captain Rodriguez. Manny," he said. He'd told him he wanted to tell her something. But first he wanted her to talk. "Are you okay?"

Her forehead creased beneath her wispy bangs. "Yeah. I'm kicking myself for not guarding you myself. I knew there was nobody in that firehouse you could trust—"

"Manny," he said. "I trust him. He and my dad served together. He's a good man."

"One of the few there."

"I hope you include me in that number," he said. That she didn't think he would have knowingly let his house be used the way some of his coworkers had used it. "I asked if you were okay because of what happened. Officer Howard told Manny someone pulled a gun on you."

She shrugged. "He pulled a gun, and it was pointed at me. I'm not sure he intended to threaten me with it."

"But you tackled him anyway," he said with awe. She was so damn tough.

She shrugged. "He was pointing the gun at Officer Morgan and his sister-in-law when I tackled him, but the safety was on. It wasn't as if I jumped in front of a bullet."

"Like you jumped in front of a pipe for me in the alley," he said. "I could have used you in that building."

"What happened?" she asked.

He glanced around the small cubicle area, not certain who could be standing behind the curtain or lying in one of those other beds. "Let's just say it was a lot like the alley."

She gasped and reached out now, lightly stroking his still-swollen jaw. "So I should have Craig looking for another pipe?"

He nodded.

"Was it Santa Claus again?"

"No…" He heaved in a deep breath that had him coughing and sputtering for a moment.

She stepped back and glanced around. "Do you need help? Should I call the doctor?"

He cleared his throat and shook his head. "No. They already signed me out, and they probably need this spot." The ER at this hospital was always busy. He'd brought people here himself. Coworkers. Fire victims.

And he thought again of that victim from a year ago. And the fire that was so similar he'd felt a flash of déjà vu. He needed to tell her about that, too.

"Then let's get you out of here," she said. She helped him finish dressing in the long-sleeved shirt and leather jacket that Manny must have brought him from his locker at the firehouse.

The patient exit from the ER emptied into the waiting room, and as Trent stepped through the doors, everyone jumped up. His coworkers cheered, and his sister rushed forward and hugged him tightly.

"Oh, thank God! Thank God you're all right," she murmured, and when she pulled back, tears shimmered in her eyes.

He wanted to hug her back, but he kept his arms at his sides. After the apartment fire, he didn't trust any of his coworkers. If one of them wanted him to feel the pain of losing someone close to him, they might go after Brittney.

But the one who was actually the closest to him was Heather. She'd insisted on setting herself up as bait to lure out the killer. Unfortunately, it was working too damn well.

"Are you all right?" Brittney asked.

He nodded. "Yeah, I'm fine."

"Come back to Mom's with me," she said. "You can stay there, and I'll take care of you."

"He's coming home with me," Heather said, and she slid her arm around his waist. "I'll take care of him."

Brittney glanced at the detective, then looked back up at him. "Are you ever going to forgive me?" she asked, and her voice cracked with pain.

He relived those long moments he'd been so scared that burned body was hers. He leaned down and whispered, "I'm doing this because I forgive you, because I love you." Then he straightened up and raised his voice. "Leave me alone! What you did is unforgivable. I don't want anything to do with you anymore!"

"You're an ass," Brittney shot back at him. And he didn't know if she was just playing along or if that was how she really felt.

He didn't talk to any of the crew. Yelling at his sister had strained his already sore throat and drained what was left of his energy. But he did stop to tell Manny, "Thanks for bringing my clothes."

"Your truck is in the lot, too," Manny said. "The keys and the parking voucher, with the location of it, are in your coat pocket. I figured you wouldn't be staying even if the doctor didn't release you. But just because she did, don't think you're coming back to work anytime soon."

"I don't want to," Trent admitted. And he raised his voice so that the other guys standing around could hear him. "I don't want to work with people who don't have my back."

"Are you quitting?" Manny asked.

Trent shook his head. "Not yet." He wanted some time to think about it, some time for Heather to nail whoever was coming after them.

"Good," Manny said, and now he gazed around him. "Give me some time to clean house. I know there have been some issues. Some guys who want the glory of calling themselves a firefighter more than they want to do the job."

There was a bigger issue than that, but Trent suspected Manny knew that, too. He squeezed the guy's shoulder, then headed out of the waiting room with Heather. Once they were in the elevator that brought them down to the parking garage, he asked, "So how are you going to take care of me?"

She winked at him. "You'll see…"

When they stepped out of the elevator into the dimly lit parking structure, she showed him how. She drew her weapon and stayed between him and the shadows. Maybe she sensed what he did, that deep chill of a cold gaze staring at them.

But how? Had someone slipped out of the waiting room and beat them down here?

He'd been so angry with his crew that he hadn't paid much attention to who had been in the waiting room and who hadn't. Had Barry been there? Or was he here, somewhere, waiting to jump out at them in another disguise with another makeshift weapon?

With her gun drawn, and her gaze scanning those shadows, Heather was ready for him or whoever the hell else might be after them.

"You're acting more like a bodyguard than a detective," he said.

"I've done my share of protection detail," she said. "And I won't be caught off guard again."

Was she talking about the alley or earlier today when Roy Dobbs had pointed that gun at her?

Heather had vowed, back at the parking garage, not to get caught off guard again. By whoever was after them and by her own damn feelings…

But the minute they stepped inside her house, desire overwhelmed her. He could have died. *She* could have died. And all she could think of was celebrating that they were alive with each other.

Her pulse was racing, and she was very aware of her breathing, like she was panting for air. Like he must have been panting when he'd lost his helmet and his oxygen.

On the drive home, he'd told her about what had happened and his eerie sense of déjà vu over the fire reminding him of a previous one involving a fatality.

This time he was almost the fatality. She'd made some calls from the truck and discovered that the same company owned both run-down apartment buildings.

Arson for insurance money? The cause of the prior fire had been arson, but no one had been charged with it. But why would the owner or the arsonist be out for revenge against just one of the firefighters? Maybe the victim's family had been. Heather was waiting for more information about her. The name had sounded a little familiar to her, which was weird because the fire hadn't been her case.

"Hmm…" she murmured.

"What's wrong?" Trent asked, and she realized she hadn't spoken since they'd walked into the house.

Maybe because she hadn't trusted herself. Or maybe he'd noticed her erratic breathing. He was breathing heavily, too, but then he had every reason.

"I'm fine," she said, but she had to swallow hard to force down the lie. She wasn't fine. She was still unsettled by how close she'd come to losing him. But he wasn't even really hers to lose. "You should go lie down and get some rest." That would give her some space, so she could get her emotions—her desire—under control.

He walked out of the kitchen but stopped at the arch

to the living room. She followed him, glancing into the room at the dark tree.

She sighed. "It looks kind of sad," she said.

"The tree's not the only one," Trent murmured.

"What's wrong? Are you upset about Brittney?"

"Worried about her," he said. "I think she understands now why I'm being such a hard-ass."

"Is it the guys, then? Knowing you can't trust any of your local crew?"

He snorted. "No. That pisses me off."

"Then what's bothering you?"

"You are," he said. "I don't know what room you want me to go to. Back to the guest room or…"

"My room," she said.

"Yeah, I don't know which one to go to," he said.

"My room," she repeated with certainty. She could have lost him or lost her own life today.

He tensed and stared down at her, his eyes gleaming with the same desire that was coursing through her body. "You mean that…"

"At the hospital I said I would take care of you," she reminded him. She reached for his hand, to lead him down the hall like she had the night before. But instead, he reached for her, winding one arm under her legs and the other around her back, and lifted her up against his chest. "Trent!" she protested. "You're hurt!"

"I'm hurting," he agreed. "For you. I need you so damn bad!"

Her heart seemed to swell and warm with his admission. *He's just talking about sex.* That had to be what he meant, all he meant. People with careers like they had didn't have time for anything else.

They really didn't have time for this either, not with

someone trying to kill them. But she didn't protest again when he carried her down the hall and through her bedroom door.

He lowered her to the mattress and followed her down. He was breathing hard, maybe from the exertion, maybe from the smoke inhalation. But that didn't stop him from covering her mouth with his, from kissing her passionately.

Heather wrapped her arms around his neck and kissed him back, teasing his lips with the tip of her tongue. He chuckled and deepened the kiss.

She needed him just as badly as he'd said he needed her. So she pulled at his clothes and hers, haphazardly tossing everything onto the floor except for her holster that she put on the table beside the bed. She was going to be careful with their lives even as she risked her heart.

"I wondered all day what you were wearing beneath your clothes," he said, tracing his fingertip along the top of her green lace bra. "Red yesterday. Green today. I should have known."

"Keeping it festive," she said, her breath catching when his finger dipped inside the bra and stroked her skin.

"The green matches your eyes," he said. "Your beautiful eyes…"

She laughed. "You're the one with the beautiful eyes. Such a light brown." Except now, with his pupils dilated with passion, they were nearly all black.

Then she couldn't see his eyes as he lowered his head and ran his lips along the curve of her neck and lower. He moved his hand beneath her back and unclasped her bra. Then his soft hair brushed over her skin, his lips across her nipple. She arched and moaned, wanting more, needing more…

She reached for him, closing her hand around the length of him, stroking up and down.

He groaned and the cords in his neck stood out as he struggled for control. She arched up, kissing his neck, beneath his bruised jaw.

"Heather…" His voice was gruff, his throat probably raw from the smoke. "Heather…"

Knowing what he'd been through, how he could have died, she pushed him onto his back and made love to him with her mouth. Or she tried.

But he wouldn't give in, wouldn't lie back and take the pleasure. His hands moved all over her, down her back, over her naked breasts and then between her legs.

The tension built inside her, then broke, and she cried his name. Then he lifted her and eased inside her. Last night she'd told him about her IUD and that he didn't need to wear a condom since it had been so long for both of them.

"I thought of this…" he murmured. "Of your heat and your wetness and how you moved on top of me…"

She chuckled. "Sure, make me do all the work…"

He chuckled and kissed her, sliding his tongue inside her mouth like he slid in and out of her body, arching his hips, driving deep. His hands cupped her breasts, flicking over her nipples.

That tension built again, so hard and fast that she thought she might break. And then she did…as she came again.

Then he bucked his hips and tensed as if in pain. Or maybe, like for her, the pleasure was so intense that it was almost painful. A groan tore from his throat as he shuddered with his release.

She leaned forward, settling onto his chest, which heaved as he panted for breath. Then he coughed. "I'll get your oxygen," she said, with a flash of guilt that he probably shouldn't have exerted himself like this.

"I'm fine," he said, his voice raspy. "Stay here. I just want to hold you."

That was what she wanted, also, to feel safe and happy and loved. But he couldn't love her yet, if ever; it was just the intensity of their situation. The danger. The rush of adrenaline. Once the killer was caught, they wouldn't have that anymore, and she probably wouldn't have him.

But if they didn't catch the killer and he kept trying to kill them over and over again, eventually he was going to succeed. Then Heather wouldn't have Trent or her own life anymore.

Brittney should have felt better. Her brother had whispered that he had forgiven her. Then he'd stepped back and shouted at her that he never would.

The situation he was in had to be very dangerous, not just for him, but for whoever was close to him. So were he and Detective Bolton really a thing? Or were they just carrying off some ruse to fool whoever was after Trent? She could ask, but she knew they wouldn't tell her anything. For her protection and maybe for theirs as well.

But she wasn't in danger. Was she?

She had had a strange feeling lately like someone was watching her. She had it now as she walked from her vehicle back into the television station. But since her big scoop, she was getting recognized more. People knew who she was and sometimes they approached her, sometimes they just stared. Like everyone had in the waiting room earlier when Trent had shouted at her.

He hadn't been any happier with any of them, though. Did he think one of his crew could be responsible for what was happening with him?

She'd stuck around the waiting room for a while, listening, talking to them, trying to find out what the hell was going on. But nobody had been willing to say any more than they already had, not even Tom.

Because they wanted to protect Trent or themselves?

Chapter 20

A faint buzzing noise pulled Trent from his sleep and Heather from his arms. But he reached out, wanting to hang on to her, wanting to keep her close and safe.

He opened his eyes to see her clearly in the glow of the screen of the cell phone she held. "Detective Bolton…" she murmured softly.

Her long hair was mussed and tangled around her face. Whatever makeup she'd worn, if she ever wore any, was gone, leaving her looking fresh-faced and young. But such intelligence and resolve shone in those green eyes.

"Yes, thank you for rushing the results for me," she said. "I think this is the fastest I've ever had DNA results returned." A smile curved her lips. "You have money bet on me, too?" She chuckled softly. "Any idea if the gun I turned in to evidence could have been the murder weapon?" She expelled a soft breath. "You need the slug and then could declare it a definite match? Okay, I'll go over the scene again. Thanks." The light went off as she ended the call, plunging her bedroom back into darkness.

He waited for her to settle back against him, her head on his chest like she'd been moments ago. But instead she pulled away from him, and cool air rushed over him as the covers lifted up. "Where are you going?" he asked.

"Back to your house," she said.

"My bed won't be as comfortable as yours," he said jokingly, but there was really nothing funny about her going there.

She chuckled, though. "I'm hoping to find something around your bed," she said.

"The bullet that killed that woman? It was Missy Dobbs, Barry Coats's married lover?"

"Yes, it was. The coroner confirmed the DNA from her toothbrush matched the DNA he managed to get off the body."

He expelled a ragged sigh of relief. At least now they knew who she was; she wasn't just a Jane Doe anymore.

"I'm sorry the call woke you up," she said. "You need your rest."

"So do you," he said. But he flipped on the lights and got out of bed, too. "I don't suppose you'll just send the techs back out on their own?"

"I'll have Craig meet me," she said.

"It's late," he pointed out. "And dangerous." Not that that would stop her.

"So was going into a burning building with people you can't trust," she said. "I trust my people."

"Your people worship you," he said. "And they all

have money on you beating Detective Bernard's clearance rate."

She laughed. "That's a great incentive for them not to kill me."

"I really don't know for sure that it was someone I work with who attacked me in the fire," he said. "Anybody could have gotten a helmet like that online."

"True," she agreed. "But someone attacked you in that building. And I had Roy Dobbs in custody."

"So he's probably not the one who killed his wife and threatened us." It would have been so much better if it had been. Then they would be safe and Trent would be able to trust his coworkers again.

Her teeth nibbled at her bottom lip that looked a little swollen already. "I don't know. He had some story about going to the shooting range on Black Friday,"

"You don't think he did?" Trent asked.

"I don't know what to think anymore." She was staring at him now, her teeth sinking into her lip once more.

"Are you talking about Roy Dobbs or me?"

She smiled. "I don't know…except that if we have a chance to close at least one case, we need to do that as soon as possible. If you don't want to stay here comfy with Sammy, you can come along."

He'd expected more of a fight from her, but maybe she'd realized that it was probably safer, at least for him, if they stuck together.

Heather had wanted to keep Trent close to keep him safe. But she hadn't thought about how he might feel to see his house reduced to blackened joists and ashes. The ashes blew around on the cold breeze, looking like snowflakes in the first light of dawn.

With so many new leads to follow and a suspect in custody to interrogate, she hadn't meant to fall asleep after they'd made love. But she'd been so exhausted and so damn comfortable in his arms. Maybe leaving Roy Dobbs in a cell while they confirmed if the body belonged to his wife was a good thing and would make it easier for Heather to crack him if he'd killed his wife.

She wouldn't know until she found the bullet that had passed through Missy Dobbs's skull. "We need to go inside and start looking," she said as she looked up and down the street, checking out the vehicles parked along it and looking for Craig's crime scene van. She was also trying to determine if someone else was out there other than the uniformed officer who had followed them there. The police cruiser was parked at the curb right behind Trent's truck, Officer Popma leaning against the side of it.

Morgan's and Howard's shifts had ended. But she wished one of them would have worked overtime to cover their protection duty. They'd proved themselves to her, and she trusted them. She didn't know this officer. He'd barely acknowledged her and had given Trent a dismissive glance, reminding her of that strange rivalry between police officers and firefighters.

She had enough rivalry within the detective squad. She didn't want anyone else as a rival, especially not Trent. It was bad enough that someone was after them. She wanted to beat that rival even more than she wanted to beat Bob Bernard.

"I don't want to wait for Craig much longer," she said. She only had so much time she could hold Roy before they had to arraign him. She could get him for threatening an officer, but he could argue that she'd asked for the gun and he'd just been handing it to her, albeit barrel first. And when the others had walked into the room, he hadn't realized he'd been pointing it when he'd turned toward them. Even a half-assed public defender would be able to get him bail, if not the charges thrown out. She needed more to hold him. Like a bullet from his gun, if he was the one who'd shot his wife.

Barry Coats could have done it. Maybe Missy had decided to end their fling, and he'd lost his temper over her rejection and killed her. Who the hell knew?

Without a confession or evidence, she had nothing to prove either man had killed her. Yet.

Trent switched on one of the big flashlights he'd had in his truck. She turned on the one he'd handed her. "You have to be careful in there," he said. "The fire burned hot. That and all the water used to put it out weakened the structure. You have to test every place you step before you put all your weight on it." He groaned. "Maybe I should just go in there alone."

"I'll be fine," she assured him. "And I have the evidence bags."

"You could hand me an evidence bag," he pointed out, his sexy mouth curved into a slight grin. He was so damn good-looking even with the bruises he'd gotten in the alley. He had new ones from the attack in the apartment building. But those were mostly on his legs, where the blow had knocked him to the ground.

He was lucky he'd gotten away from his attacker. But she wasn't sure he'd gotten far enough. She glanced around the area, feeling the chill again that had nothing to do with the early morning breeze scattering the ashes around.

"Craig's still not here," Trent remarked.

She hadn't been looking for Craig.

"I'll let you know when the tech gets here," the officer told her. Clearly, he had no intention of going inside the burned house with them. Officer Morgan and Officer Howard would have tried or at least offered to help search.

Maybe that was why she felt so uneasy right now; she wasn't entirely sure she could trust this guy to protect them. "Make sure you keep an eye out," she cautioned Officer Popma.

"I told you I'd let you know when the tech gets here," he said, his voice sharp with annoyance.

Now she was pissed. "I want you to keep an eye out for whoever the hell has been trying to kill me and Mr. Miles," she sharply replied.

The officer shook his head as if disgusted. "I know how to do my job."

Heather bit her bottom lip like she had earlier with Trent. But this time she did it to hold back the insult she wanted to hurl at the cop. At least he was here; he was better than nobody at all. Maybe just his presence would keep their attacker from coming at them again. She ducked under the crime scene tape and started toward the house, Trent close behind her.

He sighed. "Now you know how I felt earlier today."

"Guess he has his money on Bernard," she replied.

Trent chuckled. "If that's the case, then we might be in trouble. He might decide to take you out himself since he has to know that's the only way to stop you from winning."

Pride and pleasure warmed her, chasing away that

chill she kept feeling. While she appreciated his confidence in her, she had to remind him, "I thought you disapproved of my competition with him."

"That was my pride talking," he said.

She furrowed her forehead. "What? You think if I prove to one guy that I'm better than he is at his job that I prove it to all guys?"

"No," he said. "I wanted you to want to clear my case for *me*, not for a contest."

She sucked in a breath with sudden understanding. "Trent, of course that's why I want to clear it." Had she come across like she didn't even care about victims? "Do you think I'm not concerned about justice, just bragging rights?"

He shook his head. "I know you better now." And in his eyes that suddenly went hot, she could see the memories of just how well, how intimately, he knew her.

Flustered, she moved to start around him into the house.

But he caught her arm and held her back. "I know this house better than you do," he said. "So let me lead the way. If something can hold my weight, it'll be able to hold yours no problem."

Her body heated as she remembered how easily he'd held her earlier, when he'd carried her down the hall to her bedroom. Then after, all through the night, he'd held her against him, his heart beating strong and steady beneath her head.

She blinked, trying to clear those images, that feeling from her mind and her body. She had to focus, not just to find that bullet, but to keep them alive. She couldn't trust Officer Popma to be as vigilant as Officer Morgan and Officer Howard had been.

She drew in a deep breath, then coughed and sputtered over the smoke she'd inhaled from those swirling ashes. "How do you do this?" she muttered.

"Usually I have a helmet and oxygen on..."

When someone hadn't knocked it off.

She shone the flashlight beam through the holes in the walls that must have once been windows. She couldn't see anyone hiding inside, like that person had been hiding in the unit in the apartment building, lying in wait to attack Trent as if he'd known he was one of the firefighters who cleared the buildings, who made sure everyone got out safely.

He hadn't managed that last year. At the fire in the building owned by the same company that had lost another building just now...to another arson fire. Was Trent right? Were those fires related to what was happening to him? To all these attempts on his life and the fire that had taken his home? But he'd admitted that there had been other people he hadn't been able to save over the years, not just that person.

"Is this hard?" she asked. "To come back here?"

He moved his flashlight beam across the floor. "It's dangerous. Not hard."

"It doesn't bother you that you've lost your home? All your possessions?" she asked.

"Missy Dobbs lost her life," he said. "That bothers me a lot more than this."

She nodded. "I get that. Human life is far more important than material things, but..."

"But what?" he asked.

She shrugged. "I guess I'm a material girl," she admitted. "It would have bothered me to lose my house, my things…" Her cat. She'd been so scared when she'd thought that box of matches was a bomb.

"You care because it's all your dad's hard work," he said. "If it was just what this place had been to me, a place to sleep between jobs, then you wouldn't have cared either."

He was right. A house had been the same thing to her, until Dad had started personalizing the place. Making it so comfortable, making it her home. But the past few days it felt even more like home with Trent staying there with her.

But he wasn't staying forever. He might not even stay in Detroit. If he left his local firehouse, he might become a full-time hotshot. If there was such a thing…

"It's safe here," he said, "just stay to the left."

She hadn't even realized he'd stepped inside; she wasn't any better protection than Officer Popma.

She started after Trent, concentrating on stepping where he had. But even then the wood gave slightly beneath her, feeling spongy from the water it had absorbed. It was slippery, too, from the water having frozen in the cold, like her breath and the snowflakes that started to flit around with those wind-scattered ashes.

"The bedroom was here," he said. He grimaced in the faint light of dawn. "All the bedrooms were on this end."

"Which is probably why the other guys stopped coming here," she said. They hadn't wanted to be part of the affair. "Some of them really were just using the place as you intended, to sleep."

"Maybe Tom," he agreed, then sighed. "Or he was just coming here hoping to run into Brittney."

She glanced around, half expecting that maybe his sister had followed them. Brittney probably wasn't going to listen to her brother's warning to back off.

But when she glanced over her shoulder and through the gaping holes in the structure, she didn't even see the officer standing on the street where he'd been moments ago. "Hey!" she yelled. "Officer Popma! Officer Popma!"

Where the hell had their protection gone?

She started back across the floor. But she didn't pay enough attention to where Trent had told her it was safe to step. And the floor gave way beneath her just as shots rang out.

He squeezed the trigger and fired. He had a gun now. And not just any gun that he could have scored easily enough on the street. He had a police officer's gun, the police officer knocked out cold on the other side of his car, where Detective Bolton couldn't see him.

He couldn't see her now either. Had he hit her?

It would be the ultimate irony if this police officer's gun killed Detective Bolton. She was all about law and order, with no understanding for people who got in bad situations, people who just wanted to do the best they could.

Since she thought that only bad people made mistakes, she would learn that good people made mistakes, too. Mistakes that could cost people their lives, and she was going to pay for her mistake with her life, just like Trent Miles was going to do. He was still visible, a tall, dark shadow in the ruins of what had once been his house.

And standing there, on the other side of the vehicle, concealed in the shadows like the prone officer, he fired again and watched Trent Miles fall just like the detective had.

Chapter 21

Panic gripped Trent. He didn't know if Heather had been shot or if the floor had given way beneath her. He rushed to where she'd disappeared and fell through, too, just as more bullets shot past him.

Wood grabbed at his clothes, tearing them. Or maybe a bullet had done that, and then his knees struck concrete and debris. And a curse slipped through his lips.

"Shh…" Heather whispered out of the darkness. Her flashlight was either broken or switched off.

"Are you okay?" he whispered back.

"Yes… You?"

"Yes…" But they wouldn't be if the shooter came into the house to make sure they were dead.

He fell silent, like she had, and strained his ears to listen. Finally, tires squealed, metal crunched, and then a voice called out. "Detective Bolton?"

"Craig!" she called back. "We're in here…" She

flipped on the flashlight and shone her beam around the debris that had fallen through the floor like they had. The light reflected back from the short concrete walls.

"We're in the crawl space," Trent said.

"Is Officer Popma all right?" she called out again.

"He's down, but he's breathing!" Craig called back. "I already called it in when the van almost hit me. Are you two really all right?"

Sirens wailed in the distance, growing louder as backup and hopefully an ambulance headed toward them. They would be safe now. The shooter wouldn't risk coming back.

"I'll help you up," Trent said, reaching for Heather, but she'd moved her flashlight beam back across the floor, and something metal glinted back at them.

"There it is!" she exclaimed. "The bullet..." She pulled out one of those bags and collected the evidence, no doubt to give to Craig.

Craig extended his hand through the hole in the floor, helping them up from the crawl space. Once they were safely out of the precarious structure, he also gave them a description of the shooter's vehicle. A commercial van with dark tinted windows. He hadn't been able to see the plate, though. And he hadn't gotten a look at the driver.

It had been a few days since they were at Trent's house and the van hadn't been found yet. Trent glanced in his rearview mirror to see if it was following them now as they headed up the highway toward Northern Lakes, just a few hours north of Detroit. They could have driven up the day of the Christmas party and made it in time, but they'd decided to drive up the night before.

Maybe a change of scenery would bring them some

clarification. Trent tried for some now. "So the bullet that you found in the crawl space, that was the one that killed Missy Dobbs?"

Craig had confirmed it the day before, but Trent still didn't understand everything. Fires made much more sense to him than people.

"And it was from Roy's gun," she said.

"Did he confess?"

She'd spent some time over the past few days inter-rogating the man. She sighed. "He just cries."

"Do you think he did it?"

"He admitted he had his gun that day," she reminded him. "If he'd said that it had disappeared, then I might have believed that someone else had used it."

"But Roy was locked up when someone shot at us," he said. "And he wasn't the one who attacked me in the apartment complex."

She sighed again. "I know."

"So what does this mean, Detective?"

"That there could be more than one person after you," she suggested.

He groaned at the thought.

"Maybe Roy followed his wife to your house, killed her and set it on fire, but he didn't send you those cards. Maybe he didn't even know it was your house."

"So the two things are totally unrelated? Missy Dobbs didn't die because of me? Because her husband thought she was cheating with me?"

She groaned now. "I forgot to tell you that part of it."

"Part of what?"

"Barry used your name. According to Missy's sister, Melinda, she thought Missy was having an affair with Trent Miles. Apparently, Missy thought that, too."

Trent's temper flared that Barry had used him that way, betrayed him that way. Even if the man hadn't attacked him and Heather, Trent would never trust Barry Coats again. "Thanks to my coworker, Roy might have also thought his wife was having an affair with Trent Miles."

"But he couldn't have gone after you in that apartment fire or that morning at your house."

"So someone else has it out for me?" He always tried to do the right thing, like his dad had, like Manny, and his hotshot team. At least most of his hotshot team...

"I checked out that company this week, the one that owned both those apartment complexes," she said. "There were complaints against them. Even a lawsuit filed over that fire at the first complex. Wrongful death."

Trent grimaced. "The place was a mess. A definite fire hazard and health hazard. I hope they lost that lawsuit."

"They won," she said. "They used the fire department as the reason the woman died, that they should have gotten her out in time."

He groaned, his stomach churning with the guilt he always felt over that. "She'd already been overcome with smoke and had collapsed beside her bed. With the ceiling tiles that had fallen on her, I missed her the first time. When neighbors asked about her, I went back in, but I was too late. If only I'd found her earlier..."

Heather reached across the console and squeezed his arm. "Don't torture yourself this way, Trent. You did what you could, what anyone else on your team would have done."

He released a shaky sigh. "I don't know about that."

"Your team nearly missed you in that apartment

fire," she reminded him. "But that might not have been an accident."

"My hotshot team would have found her. They're really good firefighters," he said. "The best I've ever worked with, all of them."

"You really love them," she said.

"Yeah…"

She squeezed his arm again. "What is it? What's going on with them?"

"I wish I knew," he said. "Someone has been messing with some of the equipment. Some hotshots have gotten hurt and it could have been worse. Way worse."

"I know one guy died—"

"That was a murder. His wife did it."

"Like Roy probably killed his wife," she said.

"There were other things that other people were responsible for. Then there are incidents for which everyone denied responsibility," he said.

"Doesn't mean they didn't do it," she said. "Just like Roy Dobbs. He might be saying he didn't do it, but that doesn't mean he's telling the truth."

"But you don't know," he said.

"I think he's lying, but if I'm wrong and he is telling the truth, then Barry is probably the one responsible for her death and the attempts on our lives," she said.

"Why?"

"He stole your identity," she said. "There's something not right with the guy."

"If Missy's husband found out she had a lover, he wanted the guy to think it was me, not him," he pointed out.

"Yeah, and there's that…"

"Barry will have a reason to come after me now," Trent said. "Manny told me that he fired him."

"He's trying to get you to come back," she said. "Will you? Or will you become a full-time hotshot?"

He glanced across at her, wondering about her tone and the sudden tightness of her face. She seemed worried about his answer. As if she didn't want him to leave Detroit…

She looked away from him, gazing out the window at the pine trees on either side of the road. "It is pretty…"

Even though they were just a few hours farther north, it had snowed more up here, the pine boughs covered and glittering with white, the road coated with it. His truck was four-wheel drive, so the tires gripped, despite the snow. But he also drove slower, making sure to keep the truck under control.

He noticed the vehicle behind them was coming up fast, too fast for conditions. When it slammed into his back bumper, he realized it was a commercial van, like the one that Craig had seen at his house, the one the shooter had driven away in after stealing Officer Popma's gun.

Their attacker had followed them from Detroit all the way to Northern Lakes. They were just outside the village limits now, coming up on a sharp curve around one of the many inland lakes in the area.

But the van struck them again, on the curve, and the truck spun out of control, off the road, toward the snow-covered surface of the lake that couldn't be fully frozen yet, not enough to hold the weight of the truck. They were going to crash through it into the icy water.

The impact knocked the breath from Heather's lungs, the seat belt squeezing her chest, rubbing against her throat, nearly strangling her. She had to fight against it, had to fight to breathe.

What the hell had happened? Where were they?

She couldn't see anything. Even the dashboard lights had gone dark. She couldn't see Trent. But she thrashed her arms out across the console, trying to feel him.

She only felt the sudden jolt of icy water. And she realized what had happened: the truck had gone into a lake, had gone through the ice…

And if she didn't find a way to get the seat belt loose, she would go down as deep as the lake was. And even if she could get out, she would freeze before she could swim to the surface.

And Trent…

Where the hell was Trent?

Would he die with her? Or was he already dead from the crash?

"They should have been here by now," Ethan said. He sat in the corner booth in the Filling Station bar, studying the door on the other side of the scarred wood floor with peanut shells strewn across its surface. Trent should have come through that door before now. "Where the hell is he?"

"You don't know something happened," Rory Van-Dam said, but he didn't sound all that convinced himself. He was the one sitting closest to Ethan in the booth that overflowed with hotshots and their significant others.

Tammy sat on the other end of the booth, next to her friends, the dark-haired twins Serena and Courtney Beaumont. But she caught his gaze across the table and offered him a reassuring smile. Despite her efforts to ease his concerns about his best friend, Ethan couldn't stop worrying.

"I told you what his sister said," Ethan reminded Rory. While he was as bonded to the man as a brother, he and Rory looked different. Ethan had dark hair and a beard, that was neatly trimmed now, while Rory had a blond buzz cut and a cleanly shaven face.

Rory grimaced at the mention of the reporter. She'd exposed Ethan's secret about the plane crash that had ended his life as Jonathan Canterbury IV and rebirthed him as Ethan Sommerly. But he wasn't the only one who'd been in that crash and was keeping a secret about it.

"You can't trust that reporter," Rory said.

She wasn't the only one they couldn't trust, and they weren't the only ones with secrets. Someone else was keeping a secret, harboring an agenda or a grudge that had compelled him or her to sabotage their equipment, to cause those accidents that could have been so much worse, that could have taken lives, like Dirk Brown's wife had taken his.

"She's probably up to something, trying to get you to talk to her," Rory said with suspicion.

"Braden talked to Trent's captain at the firehouse in Detroit," Ethan said. "Even more stuff happened than Brittney told me." He didn't know if she knew; she hadn't called him again after that first call.

And Trent had only sent him text messages. Those stupid thumbs-up emoji things and then three hours ago: On our way now.

"They should have been here by now," he insisted.

"Maybe his girlfriend made him stop at the outlet mall or something," Carl Kozak, sitting on the other side of Ethan, suggested. He was the oldest of the hotshots. Maybe that was why he shaved his head, to hide his gray hair. But he was probably in as good or better shape than a lot of them. Except Trent.

A former Marine like their team member and local paramedic, Owen James, and like his dad, Trent was fit and muscular. He was strong. Whoever was trying to kill him wasn't going to find it an easy job.

The door opened, and Ethan expelled a breath of relief. But it wasn't Trent who walked in. It was Braden, and he was running. "A truck went in Half Moon Lake!" he shouted.

And Ethan knew why Trent hadn't made it to the bar yet. It was his truck that had gone through the ice, his truck sinking deep in the icy water.

He jumped up and ran out with his crew, but no matter how fast they got to the lake, it was probably going to be too late. Trent would have already frozen to death.

Chapter 22

"You forget how to drive on snow like all the other people from downstate?" Ethan asked, jabbing his elbow into Trent's side as he joined him near the pool table in the back room of the Filling Station. The bar had closed for their Christmas party.

In response to the physical and verbal jab, Trent glared at his friend. "Downstate?" He snorted. "Like you're from Northern Lakes."

"People say *downstate* in other states, too," Ethan said. And they probably did where he was really from, out East. "And at least I know how to drive on snow."

"I do, too," Trent said. "As long as nobody's trying to drive me off the road."

"Really?" Trick McRooney asked. "When we showed up, we didn't see any sign of another vehicle, just your truck blowing bubbles as it sank to the bottom." The red-haired firefighter had joined their team when Dirk died, and everybody had resented him for taking the place of their dead friend and because they'd figured he only got the job because he was the superintendent's brother-in-law.

Braden hadn't hired him because he was his brother-in-law but so that Trick could give him an unbiased opinion on the team and figure out who the saboteur was. But Trick had fallen hard for Hank, so he was no longer unbiased or resented.

Trent looked at him now. "Yeah, you guys took your sweet time showing up at the scene. Had to finish your beers first?" he teased.

"Had to finish a game of pool," Owen James said. "You know how long Kozak takes to sink the eight ball. He's gotta study every angle."

"Damn good thing I got myself and Heather out before the truck went under..." He would never forget those long moments he'd had to hack through her seat belt with his knife, that he'd had to break her window to get them both out. As it was, they probably would have frozen to death if they hadn't gone in the shallow side of the lake and managed to get onto some ice that had held their weight.

But their clothes had been so wet, freezing to their bodies when Owen had shown up in his paramedic rig along with the rest of the crew in a fire truck. They'd spent the night in the hospital, getting warmed up, making sure they didn't succumb to frostbite. His face was chafed, and hers, too.

She stood across the room talking to Braden's wife, Sam McRooney-Zimmer. Heather was a lot like Sam, who was an arson investigator. They were both beautiful women dominating a male-dominated field.

Heather's face looked only flushed and not frozen like his still felt. Although when she met his gaze across the room, heat rushed through him again. He didn't even realize he'd crossed the peanut-strewn floor of the Filling Station until he suddenly stood beside her. He'd just been drawn across the room toward her, and his arm was around her waist, pulling her close against him.

Ethan, Owen and Trick had followed him. "So you've just gone undercover as his girlfriend, right, just to protect his weak ass," Ethan teased. "You couldn't actually be interested in him."

"Ignore him," Trent said of his best friend. "He's just jealous. When Braden got rid of his rule against hotshots dating, Ethan thought I was going to ask him out. It was a whole awkward thing…"

Heather laughed so hard tears sparkled in her eyes. She got them. Got their sometimes very politically incorrect camaraderie. And for some reason, he was so relieved, since he wanted her to like his friends. His real friends.

He wanted his relationship with Heather to be real and not just what Ethan had correctly joked about her being, his undercover girlfriend.

"Look at him, though," Trick said. "He's such a homely guy. No woman could really want to go out with him."

Hank walked up and wrapped her arm around Trick's broad shoulders. "Yup, he's about as ugly as you are," she told her fiancé. A diamond on her ring finger reflected the twinkling Christmas lights Charlie Tillerman had strung around the bar he owned.

"Hey, I'm way better looking," Trick insisted. "I don't have those bruises all over my face."

"Did you have to beat him up to get him to behave?" Hank asked Heather.

Heather shook her head. "No, Santa is the one who kicked his ass. Guess he was on the naughty list."

Everybody laughed, accepting her easily into their circle. She fit with her wicked sense of humor and sarcasm and wit.

"That makes sense," Ethan said. "Is that why you burned your house down, Trent? So Santa wouldn't come down your fireplace to finish the job?"

"I think he did it so he could move into my place," Heather said.

They all knew he hadn't burned down his place and that someone had run them off the road. And everyone in town was on the lookout for that commercial van with the dark windows. But this was the way they handled stress and fear, mercilessly teasing each other.

Heather had instinctively understood that, just as she understood his bond with these people. She leaned against his side, her arm winding around his waist.

"Now, that makes sense," Ethan said.

"Yeah, smarter than blowing up your beard or your truck," Trent teased. Neither of those explosions had been Ethan's fault or accidents. His brother-in-law had been trying to eliminate the heir to the Canterbury fortune.

Tammy walked up to join Ethan, who wound both arms around her. "I don't know," he said. "If I hadn't blown off that beard, I wouldn't have had a reason to come to this one's salon."

"You looked like a Sasquatch before you burned off your beard and hair," Trent said. "That was a reason to go to her salon."

"And he's pretty much never left," Tammy said. "So be careful, Heather. Trent might never leave either." She winked.

Heather laughed, but it sounded a little uneasy now. Maybe she was worried about him never leaving.

Tammy wasn't worried about Ethan staying. She snuggled into him just like he snuggled against her. Ethan was happier than Trent could ever remember seeing him. Too bad all the hotshots weren't. Rory was hiding in the shadows of the bar for some reason. And Michaela kept ducking in and out of the bathroom as if she was sick or hiding from someone. And Trent...

He couldn't get over how close he'd come to dying. Again. How close he'd come to losing Heather. Again.

He tightened his arm around her. "You guys all need to stop trying to scare her off," he said.

"If you driving her into the lake hasn't scared her off, I don't think anything will," Owen said with a chuckle.

If only that were true...

She had been scared in the truck, panicking as she'd fought the seat belt. And when they'd gotten onto the ice, she'd clung to him for more than warmth.

He let out a shaky breath as he remembered it all. And his friends moved closer. "Stay up here," Ethan said. "We've got your back. We'll make sure nobody kicks your ass but us."

Now tears stung Trent's eyes, but he blinked furiously. "It would take all of you together to take me," he joked back.

"Or just Santa Claus," Owen quipped.

Heather laughed. But she eased away from him.

With everyone else crowding around, he couldn't snake her back against his side. Then suddenly she was just gone, disappearing into the crowd in the bar. No matter where he looked, he didn't see her.

Where the hell had she gone?

Trent should stay here in Northern Lakes with his hotshot team. As much as they teased him, they loved him even more. As Ethan Sommerly or Jonathan Canterbury had said, they all had his back. They would keep him safer than she had.

He was the one who'd saved her the night before, getting her out of that truck and out of the icy water. She would have died for certain if he hadn't been there. If he hadn't cut her loose and stopped her from sinking to the bottom of the lake, where she would have drowned and froze.

She shivered now as she stepped out of the bar and the cold air and snow hit her in the face. She just needed a minute. A minute to catch her breath. A minute to stop acting like she and Trent were more than they were.

That they were in love like so many of those other couples in the room. She was losing him, just as she'd nearly lost her life in that lake.

She was losing him because how could he go back to the firehouse where he couldn't trust the rest of the crew to get him out of a burning apartment? But these guys and women…

Every one of them would have jumped into that freezing lake for him, would have given up their lives to save his. Or died with him…

That was a team. No. That was a family.

An even closer family than his biological one, than her biological one. He would be safer here with them than he would be in Detroit.

But the killer was here. Even though everyone had been looking for that van and hadn't found it, she didn't believe like they did that he'd left town. That he'd run them off the road and driven away, back to Detroit.

He was here. Somewhere…

Then she shivered, and not just from the cold or the falling snowflakes. She shivered because she sensed that stare on her, that stare she'd felt so often at her house and at Trent's that early morning.

Then she saw him as he stepped out of the shadows and pointed a gun at her, the gun he'd taken off Officer Popma. She narrowed her eyes, studying his face more than that gun pointed at her. He was so big, tall and muscular. But with his rosy cheeks and freckled face and red hair, he looked like a kid. A kid she'd arrested for robbing a gas station. Over a year ago…

"Were you after me this whole time?" she asked. Had this had nothing to do with Trent at all?

Had she put Trent in more danger when she'd brought him home with her than if she'd just let him go to a hotel? She'd screwed up so damn badly.

But she could make it up to Trent right now, if she could get the kid away from the bar, away from Trent and his friends. She didn't want them to hear the gunshot and rush out and get shot as well.

She didn't want anyone else getting hurt because of her, but most especially not Trent.

Billy hadn't bothered with a disguise this time. He didn't care if she saw him now. He didn't care if anyone saw him. This was the day. The year anniversary of when he'd lost his grandmother. The only person who'd ever loved him.

He couldn't let them live a year longer than she had. He couldn't let them live a minute longer.

"We need to get out of here before someone sees you, Billy," she said.

She had recognized him, just like he'd feared she would. But he'd also had his doubts that she would even remember him. How the hell many people had she arrested over the years, over the year since she'd arrested him?

He wasn't the only one in juvie who'd wanted to get revenge on her, who'd wanted to kill her. He really wanted to kill her. But not just her...

"You were supposed to die so many times," he murmured with frustration. When the truck had gone into the lake, he'd been so sure that it was over. That they were dead. He'd driven off but not far.

They'd survived too many times for him to trust that they were really dead this time. So he'd hung around the hospital and watched, and sure enough, an ambulance had raced up to the ER, lights flashing. And they'd been in the back. They'd even walked themselves into the ER.

They'd survived again.

"Come on, Billy," she said. "Where's your van? Take me wherever you want to take me, wherever you want to go to kill me."

He snorted. "Like you're going to go without a fight."

"I will," she promised. "You don't have to hurt anyone else like you hurt that officer and Trent. You don't have to hurt anyone else. Just me."

Now he laughed. "You think this is just about you? God, you're full of yourself, Detective Bolton. This isn't just about you. I wanted to kill Trent Miles even more than I wanted to kill you. He was the one who didn't get her out. Who let her die. I almost forgot about you until I saw you with him on the news, standing outside his burning house."

"Did you set his house on fire and kill that woman?" she asked.

He snorted. "I wouldn't have sent his card to the firehouse if I knew where he lived. Hell, if I knew where he lived, he would have been dead a long time ago." But he couldn't be sure about that. Was it Bolton who'd kept Miles alive or just plain dumb luck?

Dumb luck might have been what had had him watching the news that night. He never watched the damn news.

"When I saw you with him, it all made so much sense. If you hadn't put me in juvie, I would have been there that night. I would have done what he was too stupid to do. I would have saved my grandma. I wouldn't have let her die like Trent Miles did. Some hero he is."

"What?" she asked, as if she didn't know. "Your grandma died?"

Tears rushed to his eyes, but he blinked them away and focused on her, on pointing that gun directly at her heart. "And now you're both going to die, just like Grandma did."

This time he could not fail. He had to do this for her. She was the only one who'd ever been there for him, who had ever cared about him. And he had to repay her for her love with his loyalty and with Detective Bolton's and Trent Miles's lives.

Chapter 23

Charlie had let him know Heather had stepped outside. "She probably just needs some air," he'd said. "You
guys can be a lot." But he hadn't looked at the guys then.
He'd glanced across the bar to where Michaela leaned
against the wall outside the restroom.

Trent felt a flicker of concern for Michaela. Maybe
she was sick. But he had a sick feeling of his own, a
sick feeling that something was wrong with Heather.
So he hadn't rushed out the door after her. Instead, he'd
just pushed it open a little, and he'd heard the voices.

He'd heard every word Billy and Heather said.

And he'd realized what she was trying to do. She
was trying to protect him at the risk of her own life. No.
At the certainty of her death. Billy was determined to
kill her. But he was even more determined to kill him.
Probably so determined that he might charge into the
bar with the gun drawn.

And innocent people, his friends, might get hurt as well. Maybe if he could distract Billy, Heather could get her gun…if she was even wearing it beneath her sweater.

"We need to get Trent Miles out here now," Billy said, his voice getting louder as if he was moving closer to the door.

"You can't go in there," she said. "Someone will try to stop you."

"Then I'll shoot them, too."

Just like Trent had feared. He pushed the door fully open and stepped out, his hands raised above his head. "I'm here, Billy," he said.

While Billy whirled toward him, he expected Heather to pull her gun. But instead she moved closer to them, stepping between them like she was his damn bodyguard. "Billy, your grandma wouldn't want you to do this," she said.

Billy glared at her, waving his gun at her. "Don't you dare talk about my grandma! You didn't know her!"

"The hell I didn't," she shot back at him, her voice sharp. "I didn't know she died." Her voice cracked a little. "But I knew her. Your grandma was fierce. I talked to her a lot over your arrest for robbing that gas station."

"She probably yelled at you," Billy said. "She always protected me."

Heather shook her head. "She couldn't anymore. She told me that you got into a bad crowd and you stopped listening to her. She didn't know what to do. And when I offered to reduce the charges, she told me she would kick my ass if I did that. That I was her last chance to get you on the straight and narrow again. She wanted you to go to jail, Billy."

"You liar!" he shouted. "You liar!"

"You didn't ignore her? Stay out past your curfew? Stop going to school?"

He cursed now, and tears started to roll down his face.

"She wanted her sweet boy back, she told me," Heather said. "She wanted her Billy Boy back, and so she asked me to put you in juvie so that you would never commit another crime. So that you'd get your life back."

"And she died…"

Heather started crying now, tears trailing down her face. "I'm sorry. I didn't know that was her. The lawsuit you filed used different names for both of you than what was in my case files."

"Grandma always called herself by her maiden name, but she was legally still married to my grandpa, who took off a while ago. And sometimes I used her name and sometimes I used that married one," Billy explained.

That must have been why Heather hadn't made the connection when she'd looked up that prior apartment building fire.

"She was such a beautiful person," Heather said. "I'm so sorry for your loss."

"That was his fault!" Billy shouted, and he swung the gun toward Trent now. "He didn't get her out. He failed her!"

"No, Billy, that was an accident. He couldn't see her because of all the trash in that building—"

"But the owner's lawyer said it was his fault."

"The owner didn't want to pay you," she said. "He didn't want to lose any money. That's why he didn't take care of those buildings."

"I took care of that one for him," Billy said. "I burned

it down, and Miles was supposed to burn up in it, just like he let Grandma burn."

Trent felt like crying now. "I am so sorry, Billy. I didn't see her. I didn't know she was in there, and when I went back and found her..." His voice trembled as tears threatened. "She was already gone."

"How come she didn't get another chance, like you both do?" he asked, his voice cracking. "Why won't either of you die?"

"Because of your grandma," Heather said. "Because she wanted you to be her good Billy Boy again. She didn't want you to be a thief, and she certainly wouldn't want you to be a killer, Billy."

A sob broke out of the kid, and his big body began to shake. "I just want her with me again."

"Killing us won't bring her back," Heather said. Then she actually laughed. "Although, from what I remember of her, she probably would come back to kick your ass for trying to hurt us, for trying to hurt anyone."

Billy's wide shoulders shook, but he wasn't crying now. He laughed with Heather. "She would. She really would kick my ass." Then the sobs overtook him again. "I'm so sorry. I screwed up. I screwed up so bad."

"No," Heather said as she took the gun easily from the kid's grasp. Then she closed her arms around him, holding him while he cried. "We'll fix this, Billy. You didn't kill anyone. We'll figure this out. We'll get you some help, like Grandma did."

"She was the only one who helped me."

"Not anymore," Heather said. "Not anymore..."

Standing there, watching her hug and console and reassure the kid who'd tried again and again to kill them, Trent lost something, too. He lost his heart. To Heather...

* * *

Trent hadn't returned with her and Billy to Detroit. He'd stayed up in Northern Lakes with his hotshot team. He was probably furious with her, furious with the way she intended to deal with Billy.

She didn't want to put him in prison. Or even back in juvie, if she could have. He was old enough to be tried as an adult. She didn't want him prosecuted, though. She intended to get him real help, psychological help. Because his grandma had been right. He was capable of being her Billy Boy again. If only Heather hadn't gotten so damn caught up in her competition with Bernard, she would have followed up with him after his release, would have remembered his damn name and alias. Maybe she would have checked up on his grandma, too. This was her fault that Billy had spiraled, more so than it had ever been Trent's.

Trent's friends and his sister probably realized that they had been right, that she and he weren't really involved. Since the case was closed, they didn't even have to pretend they were.

So he hadn't come back. Over a week had passed since she'd seen him last. She'd spent most of that in the office, finishing up her paperwork, clearing those cases. Missy's murder. The arson at Trent's. She'd finally gotten Roy to confess to both. And Billy...

Billy had done so many things. He'd attacked them in the alley. While hanging around the firehouse, he'd stolen some gear and had attacked Trent in the apartment fire. He'd shot at them at Trent's house and struck their truck by the lake. He'd admitted to all of them on the condition that he be treated at a psychological facility. So Heather had cleared a lot of cases.

And everybody who'd bet on her had won a lot of money. Even Bob Bernard. He'd grinned and shaken her hand when he'd congratulated her. "My money was always on you, Bolton. You are a damn good detective. Better than I ever was."

She had his respect. Apparently she'd had it all along. But the victory wasn't as sweet as she'd thought it would be. Hopefully the cookies that Bob and his grandson had baked for her would be sweet.

She turned her vehicle onto her street, lifting her foot from the accelerator, dreading going home to that empty house again. Well, empty but for Sammy. But he was snubbing her, sleeping in the guest room instead of with her.

She hated sleeping alone now.

But it wasn't Sammy she missed in her bed. It was Trent. Hell, she just missed Trent everywhere. And she dreaded going to that dark, quiet house. Maybe she should have taken up some of the people on their offers to buy her drinks to celebrate her victory. But she hadn't felt much like celebrating.

She just wanted to go home, but she wasn't sure she was pulling into the right driveway, because the house wasn't dark. The front window was aglow with multicolored, twinkling lights. Her sisters must have gotten the new code out of Dad and decorated her damn tree.

She'd kind of liked it standing there, bare and stark and dark, looking as empty and lonely as she'd felt. It didn't look like that anymore. It looked bright and happy.

She was going to take all the codes out now so that not even Dad could get in. But at the moment, she just wanted to get in and tear down that tree. Maybe she'd torch it in the backyard. Maybe she would start such a big fire that the hotshot crew would get called in…

Sighing at her own drama, she climbed the stairs to the kitchen, dropped the tin of Christmas cookies on the counter and rushed into the living room. But when she started toward the tree, she hit something and fell, sprawling onto a long, hard body.

"You can't let this tree dry out," Trent admonished her as he scooted out from under it with an empty pitcher.

"I was just thinking about burning it up," she said, her heart pounding fast and hard at his presence.

"Why?" he asked, staring up at it. "Don't you like how I decorated it?"

"You decorated it?"

"Yeah. Think your sisters will approve?"

"I don't give a damn what my sisters think," she said. But she could imagine, and she had to laugh and admit, "They won't think you're any Martha Stewart either."

"Only Martha Stewart is," he said.

"True."

"So did you win your bet?" he asked.

"I didn't place a bet," she admitted. "But Bob Bernard did."

"How'd he feel losing his money?"

"He didn't," she said.

"But with all the cases you closed…"

She smiled. "He bet on me."

"Wow…"

"Yeah." She'd been so wrong about him. Who else had she been wrong about? Trent? Was he not mad at her for how she'd dealt with Billy?

"So why were you going to burn up the tree?" he asked.

"To get a certain hotshot to come home," she admitted.

"Home?" he asked, his eyes twinkling like the lights on the tree. He leaned closer and brushed his mouth across hers.

"Yes," she said. "You can stay here, if you're going to stay in Detroit."

"I am," he said. "For now..."

"Just for the holidays?" she asked. Of course, he would probably want to spend those with his sister, now that he knew he wouldn't be putting her in danger anymore. But if he stayed with Heather, at least she would have a hotshot hero for the holidays.

"Until I get called up for a wildfire or a hotshot meeting, or you get sick of me," he said. "How long can you handle me staying with you, Heather?"

She wrapped her arms around his neck and leaned closer, moving her lips over his before she pulled back and asked, "How about forever?"

He grinned. "Sounds good to me."

"You look good to me," she said. "Like the perfect present under my Christmas tree." And just like all her presents, Heather couldn't wait until Christmas to unwrap him. She undressed him as he undressed her, and they made love under that tree.

A long while later, boneless with pleasure, panting for breath, they lay staring up at the tree. "Merry Christmas to me," she murmured with satisfaction.

"Merry Christmas to me," Trent repeated, and he leaned over to kiss her again. "This is real, right? No more pretend?"

"Who was pretending?" she asked with a smile. "But if you wanted this to be real, where have you been?"

Her smile slid away. "I thought you were mad at me for not being harder on Billy."

"That was the minute I knew without a doubt that I love you and it wasn't just because you kept saving my ass."

"You kept saving mine, too," she said. "You are definitely my hotshot hero. I could have died in that lake."

He shuddered against her. "I came too close to losing you too many times."

"So why did you stay away?" She tensed. "Did something happen in Northern Lakes? More sabotage?"

He shrugged. "I don't know. Maybe it was an accident."

"I can investigate—"

He kissed her. "Still working on that clearance rate?"

"Still working on keeping you safe, and I don't want anything to happen to your friends either," she said.

"That's another reason I love you," he said. "You fit right in with my family."

"My family will love you, too," she assured him.

"What about you?"

She realized she hadn't said the words yet. "I love you, Trent Miles. I wouldn't want you here forever if I didn't know that I will love you forever. And, despite our dangerous jobs, we will have forever."

"We will," he agreed. "We'll also make time for each other. Make each other a priority."

"Yes…" Nobody else was slipping through the cracks of her busy life like she'd let Billy and his grandmother slip. She would make certain of that.

"Merry Christmas to both of us," he said and kissed her again.

Then something suddenly rustled in the branches

of the pine and the decorated tree tipped forward, falling onto them. Sammy jumped and scrambled away, claws scratching the hardwood in his haste to escape the mess he'd made.

"You okay?" Trent asked from beneath the branches and lights and bulbs that covered them. "Are you hurt? Cut anywhere?"

"No. He's why I buy shatterproof decorations. But we're going to have some fun getting off the pine sap."

"Yes, we are going to have some fun."

She knew they would, no matter what life threw at them. They would face it together with a sense of humor and a forever love.

* * * * *

Get 3 FREE REWARDS!

We'll send you 2 FREE Books plus a FREE Mystery Gift.

FREE Value Over **$20**

Both the **Harlequin Intrigue®** and **Harlequin® Romantic Suspense** series feature compelling novels filled with heart-racing action-packed romance that will keep you on the edge of your seat.

YES! Please send me 2 FREE novels from the Harlequin Intrigue or Harlequin Romantic Suspense series and my FREE gift (gift is worth about $10 retail). After receiving them, if I don't wish to receive any more books, I can return the shipping statement marked "cancel." If I don't cancel, I will receive 6 brand-new Harlequin Intrigue Larger-Print books every month and be billed just $6.49 each in the U.S. or $6.99 each in Canada, a savings of at least 13% off the cover price, or 4 brand-new Harlequin Romantic Suspense books every month and be billed just $5.49 each in the U.S. or $6.24 each in Canada, a savings of at least 12% off the cover price. It's quite a bargain! Shipping and handling is just 50¢ per book in the U.S. and $1.25 per book in Canada.* I understand that accepting the 2 free books and gift places me under no obligation to buy anything. I can always return a shipment and cancel at any time by calling the number below. The free books and gift are mine to keep no matter what I decide.

Choose one: ☐ **Harlequin Intrigue Larger-Print** (199/399 BPA GRMX) ☐ **Harlequin Romantic Suspense** (240/340 BPA GRMX) ☐ **Or Try Both!** (199/399 & 240/340 BPA GRQD)

Name (please print)

Address   Apt. #

City   State/Province   Zip/Postal Code

Email: Please check this box ☐ if you would like to receive newsletters and promotional emails from Harlequin Enterprises ULC and its affiliates. You can unsubscribe anytime.

Mail to the Harlequin Reader Service:
IN U.S.A.: P.O. Box 1341, Buffalo, NY 14240-8531
IN CANADA: P.O. Box 603, Fort Erie, Ontario L2A 5X3

Want to try 2 free books from another series! Call 1-800-873-8635 or visit www.ReaderService.com.

*Terms and prices subject to change without notice. Prices do not include sales taxes, which will be charged (if applicable) based on your state or country of residence. Canadian residents will be charged applicable taxes. Offer not valid in Quebec. This offer is limited to one order per household. Books received may not be as shown. Not valid for current subscribers to the Harlequin Intrigue or Harlequin Romantic Suspense series. All orders subject to approval. Credit or debit balances in a customer's account(s) may be offset by any other outstanding balance owed by or to the customer. Please allow 4 to 6 weeks for delivery. Offer available while quantities last.

Your Privacy—Your information is being collected by Harlequin Enterprises ULC, operating as Harlequin Reader Service. For a complete summary of the information we collect, how we use this information and to whom it is disclosed, please visit our privacy notice located at corporate.harlequin.com/privacy-notice. From time to time we may also exchange your personal information with reputable third parties. If you wish to opt out of this sharing of your personal information, please visit readerservice.com/consumerchoice or call 1-800-873-8635. **Notice to California Residents**—Under California law, you have specific rights to control and access your data. For more information on these rights and how to exercise them, visit corporate.harlequin.com/california-privacy.

HIHRS23

HARLEQUIN
PLUS

Try the best multimedia
subscription service for romance
readers like you!

Read, Watch and Play.

Experience the easiest way to get
the romance content you crave.

Start your **FREE TRIAL** at
<u>www.harlequinplus.com/freetrial</u>.